SPECIAL ASSIGNMENT

Hometown Heroes: Book 3

J L CROSSWHITE

Blessings!
Jennifer

Tandem Services Press
SOUTHERN CALIFORNIA

Praise for J L Crosswhite

"This is a very suspenseful story and I'm looking forward to the next book in this series."—Ginny, Amazon reviewer

"I was impressed with the suspense in this book as well as the romance. Great storyline. Morality issues were great. An overall great read."—Kindle customer

"Absolutely loved it. Fast paced and kept me guessing concerning the outcome. I highly recommend it to all who like a good mystery or suspense."—Linda Reville

"Very well written, with interwoven stories and well developed characters"—Mary L. Sarrault

Other books by JL Crosswhite

Hometown Heroes series

Promise Me, prequel novella

Protective Custody, book 1

Flash Point, book 2

Special Assignment, book 3

In the Shadow series

Off the Map, book 1

Out of Range, book 2

Over Her Head, book 3

The Route Home series, writing as Jennifer Crosswhite

Be Mine, prequel novella

Coming Home, book 1

The Road Home, book 2

Finally Home, book 3

Contemporary romance, writing as Jennifer Crosswhite

The Inn at Cherry Blossom Lane

Eat the Elephant: How to Write (and Finish!) Your Book One Bite at a Time, writing as Jen Crosswhite

Devotional, writing as Jennifer Crosswhite

Worthy to Write: Blank pages tying your stomach in knots? 30 prayers to tackle that fear!

© 2019 by JL Crosswhite

Published by Tandem Services Press

Post Office Box 220

Yucaipa, California

www.TandemServicesInk.com

Ebook ISBN 978-0-9995357-7-6

Print ISBN 978-0-9995357-6-9

Library of Congress Control Number: 2019904745

Scripture quotations are from the New International Version. THE HOLY BIBLE, NEW INTERNATIONAL VERSION®, NIV® Copyright © 1973, 1978, 1984, 2011 by Biblica, Inc.® Used by permission. All rights reserved worldwide.

This book is a work of fiction. Names, characters, places, and incidents are either products of the author's imagination or used fictitiously. Any similarity to actual people, organizations, and/ or events is purely coincidental.

Cover photo credit: Lightstock and JL Crosswhite

To my favorite pilot, my dad, David Crosswhite. I couldn't have written this one without you. Actually, I couldn't have done a lot of things without you.

Because of the Lord's great love we are not consumed, for his compassions never fail. They are new every morning; great is your faithfulness.—Lamentations 3:22-23

Prologue

Orange County, California, 1995

The announcer's voice came over the loudspeakers at the El Toro Marine Air Station saying that the Blue Angels, the finale for the airshow, would be taking to the skies shortly. The sun was hot, but the breeze coming off the ocean cooled Scott Blake as he hustled across the concrete airfield with his friends Joe Romero and Kyle Taylor. They had seen all the static displays of the planes, many of which he had hanging as models in his room. He'd taken pictures of his favorite ones with the camera he got for his birthday. But he had only enough film for thirty-six photos, so he had to be careful.

Dad had brought them and then staked out a good spot at the center of the runway to watch the airshow, and there he'd sat all day. At eleven, Scott and his friends were old enough to run around and see everything by themselves. They even had their own money for snacks. Scott hadn't been sure Dad would even bring them to the airshow. After Scott's older brother, Christopher, had died, Dad hadn't been in the mood to do much of anything. But he knew how much seeing the Blue Angels meant to Scott. He'd hadn't even had to beg too much.

It had been a full day so far, one of the best ever. Kyle was even checking out the weapons the marines carried. He wanted to be a cop when he grew up. A parachutist had kicked off the show by descending from the sky with an American flag flying from his heels while the National Anthem played. Everyone had clapped as he landed on the infield.

Scott couldn't believe they were going to close this base in a couple of years. His whole life had been lived out to the sound of the planes landing and taking off on maneuvers. There was even a sign on the Carl's Jr. drive-thru that warned people not to place an order when the jets were overhead. They were loud, but it was cool.

He glanced at Dad who was staring off into space. Was he thinking about Christopher? He'd have been finishing his final year in college now, playing football on a scholarship somewhere. Scott's chest hollowed out like it did whenever he thought about his brother. He'd make his parents proud, just like Christopher would have done.

The roar of an F/A-18 shrieked above them. Those were the coolest planes. He nudged Joe and Kyle. "That's what I'm going to fly. You just watch."

The announcer switched over to the Blue Angels' emcee, and the show began. Scott wiped his hands on his shorts. This was it!

The planes split the sky with their tight formations and acrobatic moves in a mesmerizing routine. Unbelievable! He couldn't tear his eyes away. The planes came so close to the ground that he could see the pilots' helmets. What would it be like to be one of them? Feeling the positive and negative G's as they made those tight turns and sweeping loops?

When the last Blue Angel came in for a landing, Scott let out a breath. His sno-cone had dripped all over his hand. He hadn't even noticed.

Dad stood and folded his chair. He nodded in the direction of the parked planes with their canopies popped open. "Want to go meet them?"

"Yes!" He had two pictures left on his camera roll. He dropped the sno-cone paper in a trash can and snagged a couple of napkins from a hot dog stand that was closing up.

By the time they got to the pilots standing on the other side of a waist-high plastic fence, a small crowd had already formed. The pilots were chatting with the kids, signing programs, and taking pictures. The pilot closest to them was smiling as he talked with a couple of older girls.

Scott nudged his way forward, comparing the pilot with the picture in his program. He folded it back so the pilot's picture was up and got his pen ready. "Excuse me, sir?"

But the man didn't seem to see him. He was too busy paying attention to the girls. They didn't even have a program for him to sign. Scott's stomach sank.

He turned, but a voice snagged his attention. "You interested in planes?" Another pilot stood there, grinning at Scott.

"Yes, sir. I'd like to fly an F/A-18 one day. And I've got models of just about every other plane hanging from the ceiling in my room." Scott thrust the pen and program at the pilot. "Would you sign my program?"

"I'd be honored to. What's your name, pilot?"

"Scott, sir. Scott Blake."

"Well, Scott Blake—" the pilot scribbled on Scott's program but didn't give it back to him. "Do you know how to fly this kind of airplane?" He began folding the program into a complicated paper airplane before handing it back to Scott.

"Wow, that's cool! Thanks!"

The pilot winked at him. "You can fly that kind of plane most anywhere." He gestured to the camera in Scott's hand, the one he'd nearly forgotten. "Can we get a picture together? That way when you're famous, I can say I knew you when."

"Sure!" Scott handed the camera to Kyle. "Get a picture of us." He moved to the fence and turned around.

The pilot set his hand on Scott's shoulder, and Scott held up the paper airplane and smiled.

"Say cheese!" Kyle said as he snapped the shutter.

Scott smiled then turned to the pilot. "Thanks a lot!"

The pilot stuck out his hand. "Anytime. See you in the air!"

Scott shook it and grinned.

They moved off to let someone else get closer to the fence. He glanced over at the other pilot who was still talking to the girls, ignoring the kids trying to get his attention.

When he was a pilot, he'd be like the cool one that had talked to him and not the one that just wanted all the girls' attention. Who needed girls anyway when you could fly those awesome planes?

"Dad, did you see that? We got a picture together, and he made this cool paper airplane for me."

Dad squeezed his shoulder and smiled. "I did. Looks like you had a good time."

"I did. Thanks for taking us, Dad." For a moment, all was right in their small world. Him, his friends, and even Dad seemed like he'd had a good time. He'd do whatever he could to keep that feeling.

Chapter One

Orange County, California, Present day

Melissa Ellis scrolled through the profit-and-loss statements on her computer screen. The numbers blurred. She blinked and tried to focus. The financial meeting was in thirty minutes, and she had to make sense of these numbers. The problem was, they weren't making any sense. Unease swirled in her stomach, making her regret the third cup of coffee. According to these numbers, Broadstone Technologies was hemorrhaging money. She just couldn't figure out why.

She stepped away from her standing desk and paced her office. Moving around usually helped. She'd suspected something was wrong for a while now, yet all of her digging uncovered nothing. But numbers didn't lie. Something didn't add up.

As vice president of operations, she should have her finger on the pulse of how the company was running. Her ability to sniff out problems and deliver solutions had rocketed her to her position, the youngest VP ever in the company's history. Which was saying something in an industry staffed by an old-boys network.

But this had her stymied. Maybe it was beyond her abilities.

The old imposter syndrome raised its ugly head, and she forced it back down. There was no time for an emotional crisis. She was still in charge, still had a problem to solve.

She stopped pacing in front of her credenza and picked up a framed photo of her and her two best friends, Halley and Gracelyn. They were in middle school at Camp Eureka, a science camp. In the photo, slimy Oobleck had splashed on their tie-dyed shirts. They were grinning, arms slung around each other. It had been the best summer of her life, working with the girls to solve science riddles and having fun. Not having to worry about being in charge. Sharing the load and accomplishing something as a team.

She set the photo back on the cherrywood and let out a breath. Maybe she should call Halley and Gracelyn, see if they had any ideas. She nixed the idea the second it popped in her brain. As much as she'd like to, as a defense contractor, security clearances prohibited that.

Pulling open her door, she stuck her head out. "Danielle? Do you have a minute?"

Her perky assistant peered over the top of her monitor, Bluetooth headset firmly in her ear. "Sure. What do you need?"

"I'm going to send you the P&L I'm working on, see if your fresh eyes can make sense of it. The meeting's in—" she glanced at her Apple Watch— "twenty minutes. Sorry, just do what you can. Maybe it's obvious, and I'm just missing it."

Danielle gave her a soft smile. "I'm happy to look at it. Why don't you close your eyes for a few minutes, and I'll let you know when it's time to head over?"

"Good plan." The best she'd heard all day. She stepped back in her office and closed the door. Heading over to the couch, she kicked off her heels and laid down. Maybe just a few minutes. Who knew? Maybe the solution would appear in a dream.

The caffeine coursing through her bloodstream kept her brain spinning. Maybe she needed to head to the pottery studio tonight and throw a pot. That always helped. She visualized what she might create and concentrated on breathing steadily in and out.

But all she could see were all the people who depended on her, whose jobs were in danger if she couldn't solve the company's financial crisis.

MELISSA SET HER TABLET AND PHONE ON HER DESK, blowing out a breath. The financial meeting had not gone well. In fact, Gavin Broadstone—the namesake of Broadstone Technologies and her boss and mentor—seemed to be blaming her. He was kind about it, but he made it clear that he thought the problem was in operations and she needed to solve it. She'd never seen him blame anyone without evidence. One of the things she admired about him was his fairness, waiting until the facts were in before making a judgment.

Her phone vibrated. She swiped the screen. Anything to get her mind off what just happened. A text from Heather inviting her to dinner tomorrow. Her finger hovered over the screen. She really didn't want to drive anywhere but home on a Friday night. Though dinner with friends seemed a better option than what she'd likely be doing, going over those financials again. And didn't that just show what a well-rounded life she lived. She started to reply when she got another text from Heather.

SCOTT'S COMING TOO.

OH. SHE HADN'T SEEN HIM SINCE THE FOURTH OF JULY barbecue at Kyle's. He'd been injured in a training accident—which was what they always called it—and was back home on medical leave.

What she had thought would be a relaxing time with friends

morphed into something else. She didn't feel like the vibrant, confident woman she had projected at the Fourth of July party. She didn't even think she could fake it. Her friends wouldn't mind, but Scott? She just didn't know him that well.

She really should go throw pots instead. That always eased the tension from her shoulders. The wet clay slipping through her fingers, creating something new from a formless lump. She hesitated. Then again, being alone with her thoughts hadn't been helping. Maybe being around company would. And it's not as if this was a date. There would be plenty of people to carry the conversation. In fact, Joe, Kyle, and Scott would likely tell stories the whole time.

Plus, it could possibly be the last break she'd have in a while, since their avionics system being tested by the Navy was coming back for review, and it would require all of her attention. That Navy contract would provide a needed cash infusion, saving the company, .

And Scott was a Navy pilot. He might have an idea or a new perspective. At least she could talk to him about it.

She texted Heather that she'd be there. Checking the time, she saw she had a few more hours of productive work. She popped out the door. "Danielle, did you come up with anything in your scan of those numbers?"

"No, but I didn't get to do much more than a cursory look. Want me to keep looking?"

"Yeah. The answer has to be there. I'll start looking at all of our recent projects."

"Sounds like a plan." Danielle spun back to her computer.

Melissa closed the door and went back to her desk, plopping in her chair. She started pulling up the recent projects. But her mind kept drifting to the handsome naval aviator.

An automated voice came over the speaker in her office, and the light in her ceiling strobed. "There is a fire. Please evacuate your office via the stairs on the northside of the building and gather in your assigned area on the west parking lot." The strobe in her office added to her headache. She powered down her computer, grabbed her coat, her purse—shoving her phone and tablet inside—and made sure her badge showed around her neck. She pulled her office door shut behind her, double checking that it locked.

"Danielle?"

"On it."

Danielle held the emergency evacuation sheet, and she and Melissa moved through the cubical farm, making sure everyone was headed out the door and all computers were powering down for security purposes. "Was everyone here today?'

"Dana called out, but that's it."

They'd do a head count once they got to their assigned area in the parking lot. Likely it was just a drill, but security would come around and check to make sure everyone complied. Not a great day for a drill. Then again, when was it ever?

They headed toward the stairwell, their footsteps echoing off the walls along with everyone else's. She heard sirens. Outside, a cold gust of wind made Melissa pull her coat on and wrap it around her.

The fire department's equipment and personnel added to the controlled chaos. Was Joe Romero on this call? She scanned the area briefly, but first she and Danielle had to make sure everyone on their team was accounted for. Then they had to wait for the all clear.

While their computer whiz, Jeremy Chao, kept them entertained with stories of his adventures and near-death experiences, Melissa studied the firefighters. The one who seemed to be in charge turned so she could see that his coat said ROMERO on the back. That was Joe. She didn't want to interrupt his work, but it was somehow reassuring that someone she knew was taking care of things.

Gavin Broadstone strode over. "Everyone out okay?"

"Yep." She gestured behind her. "What's going on?"

By the look on Gavin's face, this wasn't a drill. "Did you see anything in your area? Smell any smoke?"

"No. Why?"

"The alarm was manually triggered from your zone."

She frowned. "Why would someone do that? I can't imagine —" She scanned her team huddled against the wind, talking in small groups. "If someone from my team had done it, they'd have told me what they saw. It wasn't someone from my team."

"The CCTV will show us who it was." He nodded toward Joe. "Let's talk to the fire captain and see what they've discovered."

Melissa followed Gavin, and they headed toward Joe. Her mind shuffled through the information, trying to make sense of it. Joe was talking to Broadstone's head of security, Adam Martinez. Joe spotted her, and she waved.

"Hey, Melissa."

Gavin's head swiveled. "You know each other?"

"Yes. Gavin, this is Fire Captain Joe Romero. Joe, this is my boss and the president of Broadstone Technologies, Gavin Broadstone."

Joe nodded. "As I was telling your head of security here, we've been through the building. Your fire system detection control panels aren't showing any heat, and neither are our thermal imaging cameras. None of the clean fire suppression agents were triggered. We can't detect any fire."

Melissa blew out a breath. "That's a relief."

Adam turned to her. "From a fire perspective, yes. But it creates another problem for us. We don't know how the alarm got activated."

"Can't you just look at the CCTV?" Gavin asked.

Adam winced. "We took a quick look, but it seems like the cameras were out in that particular area. Additionally, the alarm can be triggered via the control system by anyone that has access to the computer. But as of right now, that doesn't seem to be what happened. We'll do a thorough examination of the whole system and figure it out."

Joe motioned with his head for Melissa to step to the side while Gavin tore into Adam. She was happy to be out of the line of fire and glad that Gavin was targeting someone besides her. Though she felt bad for Adam.

Joe lowered his voice. "We're going to wrap up here, but I think you might want to call in Kyle to take a look at things. Something's not right. And be careful."

Melissa nodded as Joe moved back to his engine, his words still echoing in her head. The missing money and now this strange situation. Could they be connected? And what could she do to find out? She pulled out her phone and scrolled for Kyle's number. At least she could bounce ideas off him, and maybe he'd tell her she was worrying for nothing.

But she doubted it.

Chapter Two

Scott Blake paced along the sand, the salt-crusted wind off the ocean helping to ease the pain behind his eyes. His month-long stay with his parents had been about three weeks too long. But his daily afternoon trips to the beach to walk along the storm-packed sand made it tolerable. Even though it was winter and the wind off the icy water was bracing, he enjoyed being at the beach he usually had to himself. There was the occasional person shore fishing or the hardy surfers in drysuits, a better option in cold water than wetsuits that still let water in. But the sand wasn't wall-to-wall bodies like it would be come spring and summer.

There were a few surfers out there today. He squinted across the water, the sun reflecting off the waves. It had been a long time since he had surfed, something that was currently prohibited by his doctor due to his head injury. The head injury that was doing its best to destroy his life. Keeping him from doing the things he loved, the things he was good at, like being a Navy pilot. And forcing him to do things he didn't want, like living with his parents.

The wind was cutting through his jacket and burning his ears. Probably time to head back. Plus, if he was gone longer than a couple of hours, his phone would blow up from Mom calling and texting, worried about him. He stared across the ocean one more time, wondering if he'd ever have the freedom to climb on a surfboard or in his beloved EA-18G Growler again, the electronic warfare version of the F/A-18 Super Hornet he longed to fly as a boy.

He studied the two guys trying to conquer the storm-swelled surf. One wasn't very good. He struggled with his board and the waves. A newbie who probably shouldn't be out in these kinds of swells. He spent more time in the water than on his board. Scott hoped the kid would give up trying before he got too tired and couldn't swim against the current.

Sure enough, the kid timed the wave wrong. It knocked him off his board, which shot toward the shore, pushed by the force of the wave, then bobbed up from the churn. Scott studied where the kid went down, straining to see a head reappear.

He counted to twenty.

He kicked off his shoes, ripped off his jacket, and ran for the water.

The moment his feet splashed into the surf the water froze his toes. He pushed it aside and kept running until the water was deep enough to dive into. Thankful he was keeping up some semblance of a daily workout due to his physical therapy, he pulled strong strokes in the water, searching for where he last saw the kid go under.

A head popped up, but the kid was stuck at the breakpoint. A wave smashed over him again. Scott pulled harder, but the distance didn't seem to get any less. He dove under the waves before they crashed against him, and he popped up the other side, scanning. There was no sign of the kid. In this water churned up with sand and storm runoff, Scott would have a hard time finding him underwater.

There. The head popped up. Another wave approached. "Duck under it!"

The kid turned toward Scott but obviously couldn't hear him

as the wave smashed against him. Scott dove under, swam hard to where he last spotted him. His hand grazed the neoprene of a drysuit, and he grabbed whatever he could as he pulled for the surface. He broke the surface just as the kid did. Scott immediately spotted another batch of swells. "We gotta dive, okay? Don't worry, I've got you." He wrapped his arm around the kid's waist and began a side crawl.

His wet jeans were leaden, and his arms like blocks of ice. The kid had blue lips. Just before the wave crested over them, they went under it. He popped them back up on the other side. "Quick breath! We're going under again." Down, under, back up.

Finally, there was a break. "Okay, we're going to swim for shore now. We might not make it in one go. We might have to stop and duck some waves, but we got to get out of here."

The kid nodded. He was clinging to Scott's arm, exhausted. He never would've made it back to shore alone. Fatigue enveloped Scott as the icy water pulled the heat from his body. *It's not cold. You're Superman. Focus.* There was a reason that was his call sign.

His foot brushed the sandy bottom, and he dragged his feet underneath him so he could stand. The wind whipping against wet clothes instantly chilled him to the bone. He and the kid stumbled to the sand where both collapsed. He took a few deep breaths. *Thank you, God.*

He turned to examine at the kid. "What's your name?"

"Derek Billings." He coughed and retched into the sand.

"I'm Scott Blake. You okay? Do we need to call 911? Maybe your parents?"

"Nah, I'm fine." He coughed and spit up more water. "At least my board made it to shore okay." He nodded toward where his surfboard lapped against the sand. "Guess I'm not quite ready to surf these waves. It just seemed like it would be a lot of fun."

"Famous last words. Most of the times I've gotten myself

into bad situations have been because something seemed like it might be a lot of fun and I didn't calculate the downside." Scott was shivering uncontrollably; his fingernails were blue. While the wind was less down here on the sand, he knew he had to get some dry clothes and get warm as soon as possible. Hypothermia was a real possibility. A mental inventory of his car came up with nothing.

He heard the jangle of the collar a moment before a furry head appeared in his line of vision. Winter. The only time dogs were allowed on the beach. A dog tongue swiped his face. He knew this dog. Shadow. He propped up on his elbows as his best friend since high school, Fire Captain Joe Romero, strode across the sand.

What was he doing here? "You're a little late for the rescue. And you have the wrong equipment." But he'd bet Joe had something warm in his car.

Joe bent over. "Did you decide to go swimming? Your mom's been worried about you."

Scott tilted his head toward Derek. "He got in a little bit over his head with those waves. I helped him out."

Joe squinted at Derek. "You okay? How's your breathing?"

"I'm fine." The kid got to his feet. "Thanks, man. I really appreciate it. You saved my life. But I'm okay. I'm going to grab my board and head home." He trudged across the sand to his board.

"You gotta get out of those wet clothes." Joe shrugged off his jacket and handed it to Scott. "I've got a thermal blanket in my car."

Scott grinned. "I knew you would." He took Joe's proffered hand and heaved himself off the beach, wrapping the jacket around him to keep the wind off his torso. His teeth chattered, and they slogged across the sand. Scott bent to pick up his shoes and jacket where he'd left them. Shadow bounded across the sand next to them.

When they reached Joe's truck, Scott stood behind the open

door, grateful for the windbreak it provided. He shucked out of his wet clothes, appreciative that there wasn't an audience, and wrapped himself in the two jackets and the thermal blanket. A fashion statement he wasn't. He climbed in the cab while Joe cranked up the heater. His fingers started to thaw.

Joe handed him a bottle of water.

Scott downed half of it. "Why are you here?"

Joe opened the extended cab door for Shadow to jump in before answering Scott's question. "Your mom called me. Guess she called Kyle, too, but I'm off today."

Scott reached in his jacket pocket for his cell phone. Half a dozen texts and phone calls from Mom asking where he was and when he'd be home. He swiped his hand across his face. "She worries too much. They both do."

Joe backed the truck out of the parking spot and headed toward the highway. "She said she hadn't heard from you and you weren't responding to her calls. When you weren't home when she expected, she called us." He glanced at Scott. "She means well."

"She's smothering me. I'm just glad only you and Kyle can track my cell phone and not her. I'd never have a moment's peace. The US government trusted me with multi-million-dollar planes. I think I can manage."

"I'm sure she feels helpless. You did have a significant head injury. You scared her pretty bad." Joe paused. "You scared all of us." He glanced at Scott. "Want something hot to drink? There's a Starbucks up here."

"Yeah, sounds good." He already had his one-cup allotment for the day. But he figured avoiding hypothermia would be better than any sleeplessness he might suffer. It was rare he slept through the night anyway. He pulled the thermal blanket tighter around him. He'd need a hot shower to really feel warm. He sent off a quick text to his mom saying he was fine.

In the drive-thru line, Joe glanced over at him again. "How's the head doing? Any vision troubles, nausea?"

"It's fine. Nothing we didn't have after a Friday night football game." So he did have some pain and was a little sick to his stomach. It was nothing. He slid his gaze out the side window, away from the probing eyes of his friend who was also a paramedic. One mother was enough. What he needed to do was to get back into his plane and get his life back to normal. Because if he wasn't Superman, who was he? It didn't bear thinking about.

Joe handed him his coffee. He blew across it before taking a sip, the hot liquid burning his mouth, but he didn't care. The warmth from the cup made his hands tingle. They rode in silence for a while. They'd been friends for so long, they didn't need words. He knew Joe saw through him about the pain, but he appreciated Joe not pushing.

"Where are we going, anyway?" Given his lack of clothing, there weren't a lot of options. But he didn't want to go to his parents. He just couldn't deal with their smothering right now.

"To my place. You can take a hot shower, borrow some clothes, take something for your headache that you don't have. I already told your mom you'd hang out with me." Joe slid a grin at him. "Your mom likes me."

And that's why they were still best friends after all these years.

"Thanks, man." Which made him think. "Hey, you have a spare room. Mind if I crash with you until the doc signs off for me to go back to duty? I'm not sure I can bear any more time at my folks' house. I love them and all, but it's too much."

"Sure. Stay as long as you want. I'm over at Sarah's most of the time anyway."

The pain behind Scott's eyes eased a bit. "Great, it'll be like I have the place to myself."

"Just buy your own food."

"And maybe, since my mom likes you so much, you can tell her?"

Joe shoved his shoulder. "Not a chance."

He chuckled. "It was worth a try. Hey, all we need is Kyle,

and we can relive that summer we put on that football camp for those kids."

Joe grinned. "That was a great summer. Staying up late thinking of drills and plays to teach those kids and then seeing their faces the next day as they caught on. It was awesome."

"Yeah, it was." After winning the football championship for their high school their junior year, a local charity had asked them to put on a football camp for underprivileged kids. The three of them stayed at Kyle's house while they figured out how to do something they'd never done before. It had been the best summer of his life.

He missed these guys. He had friends, good friends, in the Navy. But nobody knew him like these guys, and with his assignments, he didn't get to see them nearly enough. It was the only good thing to come from his head injury.

They turned into Joe's condo complex. "We can go in through the garage so you don't scare the neighbors." His single-car garage door whirred up. The garage was too small for Joe's truck, but he pulled up close so Scott could hop out.

Scott grabbed his various coverings tight and hustled out the truck and through the garage into the condo. He wandered back to Joe's room and grabbed some sweats and a fire department hoodie before hitting the shower. The hot water might have been the best thing ever, and by the time he was out of the shower and in the sweats, he thought he might have the nerve to call his mom. Maybe.

Joe was in the living room when he came out. "There's Dr Pepper in the fridge and some ibuprofen on the counter."

"Thanks." Scott helped himself.

"Sarah wants to know if you're up to dinner tonight. Kyle and Heather are going, and whoever else we can round up."

All he really wanted to do was lie down and close his eyes. But he hadn't spent as much time with Joe and Kyle as he'd like. And given that he was hoping to get back to duty soon, he'd better take advantage of the opportunities he had. He didn't know his friends' girlfriends that well, but at least around Joe and Kyle he could be himself. They wouldn't fault him if he needed to leave early.

"Yeah, I'm in. But we need to swing back by the beach and get my car."

"I'll tell Sarah to pick a place by the beach, then." He nodded to Scott's phone. "You going to call your mom? We need to get your stuff."

He nodded. He'd call his mom. And then, he needed a nap.

So much for being Superman.

Chapter Three

Scott waved to Joe and slid into his two-toned silver 1978 classic Corvette parked where he had left it at Doheney Beach. At last. Joe had taken him to get his stuff from his folks. Mom had cried when he told her he was staying with Joe, but Dad nodded in understanding. He promised to come over often for dinner. Dad had a heart condition, another thing for Mom to worry about. Maybe when they all had some distance from each other things would be on more of an even keel. After all, he hadn't lived at home in sixteen years.

He stared out over the now-dark ocean, thinking about the boy he pulled from the waves. Hopefully, he'd been no worse for the experience and learned a good lesson. But some lessons were harder to learn than others. He started the car and headed back toward the harbor, a quick jaunt that had him pulling into the parking lot behind the restaurant.

He slotted the 'vette next to a navy-blue Audi and got out. A woman was on the other side of the Audi, dark hair spilling over her face and shoulders as she bent over.

The woman's head shot up. Melissa. His heart tripped an extra beat. No one had told him she'd be here. Why was that? Or did it matter? He flashed back to the Fourth of July party at

Kyle's house where he and Melissa had flirted a bit. He had been interested and thought of calling her, but he had been leaving and she was too special for a casual date. However, her presence would make tonight more enjoyable. And a fun and relaxing evening was just what he needed.

He climbed out of his car. "Hey, what a coincidence."

She turned his direction, gaze wary, then broke into a smile. "Scott. Good to see you."

His name on her lips made his stomach tumble like those earlier waves. He came up next to her. "So who all is going to be here?" That was a dumb thing to say, but his brain was failing him.

She headed toward the restaurant. "I'm not sure. Heather might have told me, but after this week, I'm surprised I remember my own name."

They walked around to the front of the restaurant. "So, not a good day?"

She let out a sigh. "Nope." She turned to him. "Ever have a problem where you just can't figure out the answer?"

He laughed. "Yeah. More often than I'd like."

She nodded. Given she worked for a defense contractor, he knew she wouldn't be able to share much. But he could just about see the weight sitting on her shoulders.

"How's the head?" Her brow furrowed.

He used their arrival at the front doors to delay his answer. He pulled one open and held it for her.

She stopped just inside the foyer and studied him.

He shrugged, scanning for Joe or Kyle. "Good days and bad days." He met her gaze. She wasn't buying it. Well, let her think what she wanted. "I can't believe we're the first ones here. Joe should be here. He dropped me off at my car."

"There they are." She headed toward the back of the restaurant, near the doors to the patio closed for the winter.

Joe and Sarah, Kyle and Heather sat at a table with two

empty seats. Next to each other. He glanced at Melissa. Was she in on this? Was he being set up?

But her face wore that same veil of exhaustion he'd seen earlier. He grabbed a chair for her and then seated himself.

The conversation flowed with comfortable chit chat. No one brought up his injury, and Joe didn't mention Scott's swim in the ocean earlier today. He even enjoyed sitting next to Melissa, watching some of the weight ease from her shoulders. If they were being set up, she didn't seem to know it.

While the others were discussing a movie they'd seen, Melissa leaned closer to him. "If you've got some extra time, I could use your advice on something."

He turned toward her, but Joe shot out of his chair and left the table. He hurried over to another table, asking the man some questions, shaking his shoulder. Kyle was on Joe's heels. The man was unresponsive. Joe and Kyle laid the man on the ground, and then Kyle placed a call while Joe started working on the man. Looked like a medical emergency that Joe and Kyle had under control.

Scott scanned the area. The diners at the neighboring tables moved away while the others cast curious stares at the commotion. But across from the man sat a little boy of about seven with tears running down his cheeks. Maybe the man's grandson?

Scott nudged Melissa and nodded to the boy. "Let's distract him. I'll be right back." He headed to the hostess station and grabbed a stack of kids' menus. When he came back, Melissa sat next to the boy. Scott slid into the booth on the other side of him. "I'm Scott. Don't worry, he's in good hands. Those guys are my best friends. One is a firefighter paramedic. The other is a policeman. They're helpers. They always know what to do. What's your name?"

The boy tore his gaze from the man on the ground. "Jaxon. That's my grandpa. We were having dinner. We were supposed to go see a movie tonight. Is he going to be okay?"

Melissa patted Jaxon's arm. "Joe and Kyle are the best at

what they do. He's in good hands. Hey, do you know what my friend Scott here does for a living?"

The boy shook his head.

Melissa leaned in closer. "He's a Navy pilot. Have you ever been in a plane before?"

The boy shook his head again but turned to Scott with wide eyes.

"She's right. And you know what that means? I'm the best at making paper airplanes. Want to help me make one?" He slid one of the menus in front of the boy.

"I want to try too." Melissa grabbed another menu. "Okay, Mr. Pilot, show us how this works."

He folded the paper, explaining each step to Jaxon but keeping an ear attuned to Joe and Kyle. They were doing two-person CPR. Didn't seem like the restaurant had an AED, an automated external defibrillator. He hoped the fire department got here soon, but with traffic on a Friday night…

Jaxon held up his plane. "Like this?"

"Good job. Now let's make another kind so you can compare them." Scott handed out another set of menus. He met Melissa's gaze. Her eyes darted to Joe and Kyle, and she shook her head slightly.

"I have an idea." Scott gathered up his planes. "Nobody's sitting out on the patio. Let's try out our planes there. You'll really be able to see the difference. This one is meant for distance, and this one does loops."

Tears welled in Jaxon's eyes. "What about Grandpa?"

"Our friends are taking care of him. And we can see him through the patio doors."

Melissa slid from the booth and put her arm around Jaxon, whose gaze had slid back to his grandpa. "It's okay."

Scott followed and opened the patio doors. "Let's get to the end here and see how far these go." And then they needed to figure out how to call his parents now that he was calm and distracted from his grandpa's emergency.

"Jaxon, do you know your mom or dad's phone number? I can call them so they won't worry." Melissa had pulled out her phone.

As if she had read his mind.

Jaxon recited a number, and Melissa moved to the side, phone to her ear.

Scott lifted one of his planes. "Okay, get your plane that looks like this." He positioned Jaxon's fingers correctly. "Now let it go."

A brief smile lit up Jaxon's face as his plane flew across the patio into a closed umbrella. While he retrieved it, Scott glanced inside the restaurant and saw that the fire department had arrived. He turned back to Jaxon. "Look at that. Great job. Now let's try the other."

Jaxon ran back to stand next to Scott, and they let the next round of planes fly. These did loops. Jaxon sprinted to catch his from the air.

Melissa moved next to Scott and leaned in. "Jaxon's mother is coming. Grandpa is her dad. We can let her know what hospital they take him to." She shivered. "It's cold out here. There's a reason no one is out on the patio."

Another look inside the restaurant showed the paramedics loading the man onto a gurney and moving him out.

Jaxon was tossing the looping plane up in the air again.

"Hey, Jaxon." Scott squatted down as the boy came over. "The paramedics took your grandpa to the hospital to check him out. Your mom's going to be here in a few minutes to come get you. You want to go inside and get some ice cream while we wait?"

His lip trembled. "Is Grandpa okay?"

Scott squeezed Jaxon's shoulder. "They'll take good care of him at the hospital. They're really good at that there." He didn't want to lie to the kid and say that everything would be fine, because he didn't know if it would be. But he also wanted to reassure the kid. A fine line.

They headed inside back to the table. Kyle came over and pulled Scott aside. "Someone coming for the boy?"

"Yeah, his mom. Melissa called her. How'd the guy do?"

Kyle shook his head slightly. "Thanks for keeping him occupied."

"Sure." Not good news, but the boy didn't need to be further traumatized by seeing the paramedics trying to save his grandpa. Sometimes the heroics looked pretty bad themselves.

Joe stood off a ways, talking with a man that looked like the manager. The man shook his hand, and Joe headed back to the table.

Jaxon played with his airplanes at the table until the ice cream came.

Scott showed him how to modify the folds on the wings to do different stunts.

A woman hurried up to their table. "Jaxon?"

He whipped around. "Mom!" He jumped out of his chair into her arms.

Tears welled in her eyes as she wrapped her arms around him. "You okay?"

He wiggled out of her embrace. "Yeah, Scott's a Navy pilot, and he showed me how to make paper airplanes that do stunts."

She scanned the table. "Thank you for taking care of him. And my dad."

Kyle came over and gave her a low-voiced run down of what had happened and what hospital her dad was at. After a round of thanks, she and Jaxon headed out the door.

The table was silent for a moment, then Joe spoke up. "The manager said our dinner was on him. Whatever we'd like."

Nobody had much of an appetite, though they made an effort. Scott replayed the events of the evening, his mind automatically doing an after-action review. He realized Melissa had asked him something he hadn't had a chance to answer. He leaned closer, not sure if she wanted the whole table to hear. "Before all this, you said you needed my advice on something?"

She looked at him a moment, her dark-brown eyes studying him. "You were amazing with Jaxon. I probably would have just let him play games on my phone."

He shrugged. "I could never sit still as a kid. A really cool pilot showed me how to make paper airplanes once, and I've been using it as a distraction ever since." He paused. "But that wasn't what you wanted to ask me."

Now it was her turn to shrug. "Maybe you could come to my office on Monday."

Chapter Four

Melissa rubbed her eyes then swiped underneath to catch any mascara she'd smeared. She wasn't sure what she was seeing on her computer screen. It had been a stressful morning, so she might not be thinking clearly, right?

She stood. A trip to the coffeemaker would help her sort things out. She exited her office. Danielle wasn't at her desk. Melissa glanced at her watch. Lunch time. No wonder her stomach was growling.

In the break room, she shoved her mug under the coffee dispenser and plopped in a new pod. She waited for her cup to fill. Back in her office she had a small fridge that she kept stocked with fruit and cut-up veggies. Combined with a granola bar from her desk, it would stave off hunger pangs. She grabbed her coffee mug and headed back to her office. Kyle would be here any time. Hopefully she could sneak in a few bites.

She wandered through the cube farm of her department. She'd personally hired everyone here, so the fact that one of them might have pulled the fire alarm felt like a personal affront. As she passed each cube, she glanced inside as if that would give her some insight as to who the perpetrator was. Everyone was out to lunch except Jeremy Chao.

He had earbuds in and was tapping a pen on his desk to the beat of whatever music was leaking out. His back was to her, and she peered at his screen. Nothing unusual there. He was running a debugging routine on their latest avionics software. Something hadn't been quite right with it, but no one knew exactly what it was.

She knocked on his cube doorway, and he spun around, yanking his earbuds out.

"Hey. Didn't want to startle you. You're missing lunch."

He pointed at the screen with his pen. "I had a hunch about something, so I thought I'd run this routine to see if it'd help. So far, it's not panning out."

She glanced at her watch again. Scott was also supposed to be here this afternoon. Maybe he'd have some insight from a pilot's perspective. "Thanks for skipping lunch to think of that. I'll be in meetings the rest of the day, but text me if you come up with anything that can't wait. This is our top priority."

"Will do." He spun back around and plugged his earbuds back in.

She headed to her office. This avionics program was their top priority, though you'd never know it the way Gavin had been running her in circles ever since the fire alarm. First the financials and now he wanted her to pull and review everyone's personnel file in her department. He was convinced the problem was with one of her team members.

She was equally convinced it wasn't. And if the CCTV had been working—and whose fault was that?—it would prove it. Too bad *she* couldn't prove it. But anyone with the right clearance could have walked into her department. And that was a much bigger number of people.

She slipped inside her office and shut the door. She'd have ten minutes at best—if Kyle was late—to wolf down her food. Digging into her snacks, she logged back into her computer to see if what she was seeing had changed. She had spent all weekend going over her team's projects, which were within acceptable parameters like she thought. So she'd broadened her search to company-wide projects when she'd stumbled on this. A project that was assigned to her, but one she'd never seen. In fact, she only noticed it because of her status as VP, not as a member of the project.

A knock on her door startled her and almost made her choke on the cherry tomato in her mouth.

Danielle popped in. "Security just called up. Detective Taylor is here. As well as Lieutenant Commander Blake." Her eyebrows raised at that.

"They're both approved. Thanks." She stashed her food in her drawer and stood, wiping her hands down her skirt to remove any crumbs. So Scott had come with Kyle. Interesting. She hadn't expected them to come together, especially since Kyle was on duty and her appointment with Scott was later in the afternoon.

She pulled the door open the rest of the way and a moment later Kyle and Scott appeared wearing clipped-on visitor badges. "Thanks for coming. Come on in." She ushered them to a small, round table in her office. "Would you like something to drink? Coffee? Water? Soda?"

"No, thanks." Kyle shook his head.

"I'll take some water." Scott grinned at her.

Melissa turned to Danielle who hovered at the door. "Emergencies only." Danielle nodded and pulled the door shut behind her.

Melissa moved to her small fridge. "One water for the lieutenant commander coming up." She handed the bottle to Scott. "I don't think I ever knew your rank."

"I thought today it might be useful."

Kyle grinned. "Yeah, but his friends call him Superman."

Melissa frowned, confused. There was an inside joke here she was missing.

Scott elbowed Kyle. "It's my call sign. Anyway, Kyle and I were having lunch, and he mentioned coming over, so I hitched a ride. I hope my coming earlier than planned doesn't create a problem." A shadow crossed his features but was quickly replaced by his signature grin.

She joined them at the table. "Good thinking. So, Kyle, did you come up with anything?"

He met her gaze. "No prints."

"Could the alarm have been triggered from the central system manually? Adam Martinez, our head of security, said that the system allowed for that."

"He looked into it and told me that hadn't happened. Plus, when Joe's team checked the building, they found the alarm physically pulled, and they reset it."

She leaned back. "So someone pulled the alarm but didn't leave prints. That must mean they were wearing gloves. And combined with the CCTV being out in that area, that's starting to sound a lot like this was done on purpose. Or is there some legitimate explanation I'm missing?" Gavin was going to love this. He'd point the finger right back at her team.

Kyle shrugged. "I can't say that I know all that goes on here, but none of that sounds like normal day-to-day business practices anywhere. In a school, you could see why a kid might pull a fire alarm. Even in some buildings, it happens to serve as a distraction for something. If that's what's going on here, only you can decide that. But if you figure out who it is, I'd be interested in talking to them."

"It's a distraction all right. There are about twenty things I need to be doing other than chasing this down. Yet it's become my priority instead of security's because Gavin thinks my team is involved somehow." She pushed her hair behind her ear. "Sorry, not your problem. I was just hoping you'd have an easy solution." She gave Kyle a wry grin and then sipped her coffee. She had to rein it in. She had an image to protect, one that exuded control. Allowing these two guys especially to see that slip—no matter that they were friends instead of coworkers—just wasn't something she wanted to contemplate.

Kyle stood. "If you discover anything, no matter how small, let me know. Even bounce ideas off me. I understand the frustration." He glanced at Scott. "I'll let you two get to your top-secret business."

Melissa stood and walked him out to where Danielle could escort him the rest of the way. She sat back at the conference table to find Scott's gaze on her, steady. She brushed at her skirt. Business. She could talk about that.

She met his gaze. Big mistake. Those pale blue eyes seemed to suck her in like an undertow in the ocean. No wonder women fell all over themselves for him. He didn't even have to try.

She licked her lips. "Um, so we have a bit of a problem you might be able to help us with. Despite all the other problems going on around here, our top priority is the new, upgraded avionics system we're testing out with the Navy. You've probably heard about it."

His eyes turned icy, narrowing, and his face hardened. He gave a quick nod.

She swallowed. Okay. "Well, we're having some glitches that we can't quite nail down. I'm not a pilot, and I need feedback that I can trust, that isn't politically or career motivated." She clasped her hands on the table. "My budget is tapped out, so I can't pay you for your expertise. You'd be doing a personal favor for me. But—and this is confidential, even my team doesn't know—the company's finances are shaky. If we can't get this project to work and get the contract, we're going under."

Scott didn't say anything, his eyes as unreadable as ice.

Sweat trickled between her shoulder blades. Until this moment, she didn't realize how much stake she'd put in his help.

It might have been the biggest gamble of her career.

Scott couldn't believe what he was hearing. In the early days after the accident, people would say things and the meaning just wouldn't register. He'd have to concentrate for the words to make sense. But he was past that stage. He just didn't want to believe what he was hearing.

He kept his face impassive as a swirl of memories and emotions assaulted his brain. He knew what was coming but prayed it wouldn't, prayed he could muscle it away. His chest tightened and sweat soaked his shirt. He could never remember the crash, but it haunted his dreams. The fear. The pain. The heat. The loss of Jordan Newhart, his EWS, electronic warfare officer.

He concentrated on his breathing, the pain on the side of his head moving from a dull throb to sharp stabbing. He reached in his pocket for a couple of ibuprofen and washed them down with the rest of his water bottle.

"Scott?" Melissa's voice broke through his haze, her face furrowed with concern. "Are you okay? Maybe this isn't a good idea."

"You bet it's not. Your company is responsible for the crash of my airplane, my head injury, and the fact that I'm sitting here instead of flying right now. And those glitches? They killed one of my friends."

His accusations flew at her like missiles, and her face paled. He might have overdone it a bit, but for a moment, it felt good to throw the pain in someone else's direction.

He stood and his vision grayed, spots dancing before his eyes. He grabbed the table.

"Did you ride over here with Kyle?" Her voice sounded as if it were in a tunnel, distant and echoing.

He started to nod but remembered in time that that would hurt. He needed to keep his head still, lie down in a dark room with an ice pack. "Yeah," he croaked out.

She wrapped her fingers around his biceps. "Migraines are nasty things. I'll get you back to Joe's."

Following along as she guided him through the office, he slipped on his dark glasses, thankful he didn't have to talk to anybody or figure out where he was going. A short time later they were in her Audi with the AC blasting his face.

But one thought kept running through his head.

Her team was behind his crash.

MELISSA TOSSED HER PURSE ON THE CONSOLE TABLE IN THE entryway of her townhome and kicked off her pumps. She needed to give Gavin an update, but she needed a minute to catch her breath. She was still a bit shaken from her encounter with Scott. Maybe she should talk to Kyle about it. Or Joe, but she knew Kyle better. Trauma to the brain—and even a migraine —could alter a person's behavior, so she wasn't holding Scott's anger against him. But it made her wonder about the details of his accident. His accusation that her avionics was behind it... Well, she had to deal with Gavin first before she could even unpack that statement. But the very fact sat there hard and cold in her stomach.

The cool, dark hardwood floors felt good on her tired feet as she walked into the kitchen and pulled a bottle of Perrier from the fridge. She perused the other contents. Not much there. She hadn't had time to go to the store or even been home long enough to have groceries delivered. That and dinner would have to be solved tonight. But after she spoke to Gavin.

She grabbed a yogurt from the fridge, poured the Perrier into a glass, and plopped into her favorite upholstered chair and ottoman, propping up her feet. As she ate, she considered what to tell her boss.

All the evidence pointed to the fire alarm being pulled intentionally but without a clue as to who might have done it. Gavin would point toward her department, but who knew why the person picked that particular alarm? In fact, wouldn't someone choose an alarm away from their department?

The second bit of information was even more troubling, and she didn't know how to approach Gavin with it. It was the information she had run across earlier today. The project created in her name that she knew nothing about. There were significant charges made to that account that Gavin had signed off. As well as his son, Trent. Nothing about it looked good. And with the company losing money like it was, there was no room for a pet project that had nothing to show for itself.

If that's what this even was.

Scraping out the last of her yogurt, she got up and threw the container in the recycling bin and put the spoon in the dishwasher. No putting it off. She picked up her phone and called Gavin.

"Do you have information for me?"

She was a bit taken aback by his tone. Straight to business. Usually he asked how she was doing and about her team. He hadn't been himself lately. Maybe it was just the stress of the missing money, the Navy contract, and now the fire alarm. Hopefully what she had to tell him would help alleviate his stress.

"Uh, yes, actually." She explained about the project she'd discovered. "But what I don't understand is why your signature is there approving these expenses. Surely that's some sort of a mistake."

She heard him shuffle something around on his desk. "No mistake. Trent had waited too late to get the signatures from you, and he didn't want the vendors to wait until the next round of checks were cut to get paid. So I signed for it. You weren't around."

"I've never even seen this project before today." How did she get to be on the defensive? Everything with Gavin was backward lately.

"Melissa, this is your department. If you can't keep track of what's going on within it, then maybe I need to find someone who can."

What? A million words spun through her brain, but she couldn't stop any of them long enough to get anything out. She resorted to giving him the update from Kyle on the fire alarm situation.

"Like I said, it's someone in your department. You've got problems, Melissa, and you don't have much time to get things under control or I'm going to have to make some changes."

They hung up, and Melissa stared at the phone. Why was Gavin trying to blame her for this? It didn't make any sense.

Something was going on here, and it didn't look like she had much time to figure it out.

Scott had just dumped a bag of M&Ms into a vanilla cake mix when Joe walked in the door carrying something that smelled an awful lot like Charo Chicken.

Joe set the bags on the counter. "What're you making? Cake?"

"Fun cake." Scott slid the pan into the oven, closed the door, and set the timer.

"What's fun cake?"

Scott grabbed plates out of the cupboard and set them next to the food Joe was pulling out of the bag. Yep, he was right. Charo Chicken. "It's something my OT and I came up with. A boxed cake mix has easy-to-follow instructions and can be customized endlessly. I usually throw in some sort of candy and then frost it with whatever sounds good."

Joe nodded. "Sounds like my kind of occupational therapy."

They filled their plates with the citrus-infused chicken, rice, salsa, and tortillas, and took a seat at the table.

"Any particular reason you made a fun cake today? Other than your undying gratitude for me providing you a place to crash?" Joe took a bite of a filled tortilla as salsa dripped on his plate.

Shadow sniffed around the table then settled underneath it with a sigh.

"It's a way to focus on one thing that I can accomplish. It helps straighten out my thoughts." He took a bite of his own chicken-stuffed tortilla, chewed, and swallowed. "Kyle and I went to see Melissa today." He put the rest of his tortilla down, the food sitting like lead. "Kyle gave her an update on the fire alarm. No prints, no idea who pulled it. I stayed because she had asked for my help. Turns out her company was the one that pushed the software update to my Growler that caused the crash. She wanted me to help her figure out the glitches."

Joe's gaze was steady on Scott, not reacting. "Did she say her company was responsible for the crash?"

"No, but I was in that plane. I know how it was reacting, not responding to commands, doing bizarre things. It was fine until we were on the shake-out ride to test that software update." He wiped his mouth. "I know it wasn't her fault personally." He shrugged. "I might have unloaded on her a bit too much." He paused, and his voice dropped. "And the memories came back. Well, what passes for memories. Triggered a migraine."

"How'd she respond?"

His head heated as he considered what she must think of him. "She was actually pretty nice about it. She brought me back here. I owe her an apology."

The timer dinged, and Scott got up to take the cake out of the oven. The smell of warm, buttery cake filled the room and brought his appetite back. It had to cool before he frosted it with Nutella. He slid back into his chair and picked up the tortilla again.

Joe leaned on the table. "What's going to happen to the software? Are they still using it in planes?"

Scott shrugged. "There's a preliminary inquiry going on. It

should be obvious what happened. That software needs to be removed. She called it glitchy. It's way more than that."

"She respects you. That's the reason she asked for your help. Maybe it would be good therapy for you to work in a field you are familiar with, bring a different perspective to the table."

Not likely. As he opened his mouth, Joe held up his hand.

"Hear me out. I'm sure you're worried about your headaches coming on again and those ghost memories rising up."

Not hardly. Well, maybe a little.

"But you and Melissa can come up with a game plan for that. She did a great job today, didn't freak out, and was very understanding even if you were a total bear."

"Hey—"

"You forget how well I know you."

Scott conceded with a nod. "You have a point."

"Of course I do." Joe leaned forward. "What if you could prove what happened in the crash? What if you were part of the team that uncovered the problem and kept it from happening to other naval aviators?"

Heat and pressure built in Scott's chest, and the edges of his vision darkened. He concentrated on his breath, and the darkness receded, the pressure lessened. "Yeah." His voice was soft. "Maybe." Could he do it? Could he chase the ghosts away long enough to help Melissa figure out what went wrong? Was he still capable of that kind of analysis and thinking?

If he wanted his career back, he'd better be.

Joe stood and began clearing the plates and food. Scott waited a beat then joined him.

Standing in front of the sink, Joe scowled. "I thought the Navy had taught you how to clean up after yourself."

"Huh?"

Joe gestured to the sink with his hands full of dirty dishes. "You left a mess."

Scott slapped him on the back. "It'll be worth it when you taste my fun cake."

They got the kitchen back in order, one more reminder to Scott of how his brain didn't quite function all the way back to normal. He didn't even remember leaving the mess, but he was glad Joe didn't let those things slide. Didn't make him feel like a helpless infant, like Mom had by doing everything for him.

He grabbed the Nutella and frosted the cake with it then served up a couple of slices. He watched Joe take a bite. "What'd I tell you?"

"I'll let you stay."

Now if only Melissa was as forgiving.

Chapter Five

As soon as Melissa got to work the next morning, she pulled Danielle into her office and shut the door. She indicated the chairs at her conference table, and once they'd sat, Melissa held Danielle's gaze. She hadn't slept at all last night, debating with herself. Should she tell Danielle or not? If she did, it could change—even ruin—both of their careers. She let her breath out.

"I have to tell you something, but what I say can't leave this room. Regardless of what you decide to do when I'm done. Don't take notes." She nodded to Danielle's ever-present notepad.

Danielle's eyes widened, but she nodded. She'd been loyal no matter what Melissa had asked her to do, which, granted, hadn't been as crazy as she was about to reveal.

"Remember that missing money we've been looking for?"

Danielle nodded.

Melissa turned around and nudged her screen so Danielle could see it. "Here's what I found." Melissa walked Danielle through her discovery of the hidden project and the expenditures.

Danielle followed along intently. Her eyes lit with under-standing. She looked up. "Have you talked to Gavin about it?"

"Last night. It didn't go well. He basically said it was a project Trent was working on. He had waited too late to get the invoices approved, and he didn't want the vendor to miss the next round of payments. Since it was after hours and I was already gone, he went to Gavin."

Danielle raised her eyebrows. "It was that big of an emergency?"

"Exactly." She pointed out where her and Danielle's names were on the project. "We're on the hook for this. A project we know nothing about."

Danielle pointed to the expenditure lines on the screen. "So this isn't all the missing money, but it's a lot of it. What did it go for?"

"Not sure yet. We'll need to pull the invoices, but that requires getting finance involved. I'm going to talk to Gage DeSoto over there today, but it's pretty weird that I need to see an invoice on a project that I'm supposed to be supervising. I haven't thought through what I'm going to tell him without raising more red flags."

Danielle tapped her pen on her chin. "Tell him the vendors are doing an audit of their own system and need our help."

"That'll work."

"So did Gavin have anything else to say?"

"He told me it just proved my department was a mess, that I lacked control and communication. That Trent couldn't work with me, and that's why he had to go around, et cetera." She let out a breath. "None of that is true. Gavin was just grabbing for whatever excuses he could toss out. Which means he's in on this or he knows Trent's up to no good and Gavin's covering for him." She leaned back in her chair and looked to the ceiling as if the answers were written up there. *Please, God, some flaming message of direction would be helpful about now.*

"He's always making excuses for Trent. He feels guilty

because he was never around when Trent was growing up and never saw him after Gavin and his wife divorced. And you know how he dotes on Annaliese, his thirteen-going-on-twenty-one daughter and the spitting image of his second trophy wife." She dropped her gaze to Danielle's. "I didn't really say that."

Danielle grinned.

"Okay. So you can see the problem we have here. Trent's behind this. But Gavin's blaming us. I think the money chase, the fire alarm, all of that is serving as a distraction so we won't see what's really going on. Kyle said whoever pulled the fire alarm would be someone who wanted a distraction. So it makes sense." She paused. "But you can see the danger too. Going up against Trent and/or Gavin could cost us our jobs here and our careers anywhere else. So I'd understand if you wanted to walk away. I can find a good spot for you in another department."

Danielle met Melissa's gaze steadily. "I'm in. Yeah, it might cost us everything. But if we turn an eye and the company keeps hemorrhaging money, we'll go under sooner or later." She tapped her pen on her blank pad. "Which brings up the avionics testing. We need more hands on deck, but Gavin just cut our budget."

Melissa sighed. "Yeah, I thought I had a solution to that problem. But it didn't work out. I'll think of something."

"So what's our next move?"

"I'll pull the invoices from finance. I'll have you fine comb them. In the meantime, get Jeremy whatever support he needs for his debugging analysis. Get Diana and whoever else she wants to review the latest gripe sheets and reports from the Navy on the last software update. Avionics is our priority, so everything else goes on the back burner. I'll take the heat from Gavin and run interference." She put her hands on the table. "You're the only one who really knows what's going on, so let's keep it that way. And if you want to sleep on it, you can give me an answer tomorrow."

Danielle shook her head. "I don't need to. I'm in. It's the

right thing to do. God's got this, however it shakes out." She stood. "I'll take care of the personnel assignments. And—" she paused with her hand on the doorknob— "I'll be praying."

"That's our best strategy." Melissa smiled. A better conversation than she expected. She didn't know how Danielle would respond. And Melissa wanted to protect her. She'd kind of hoped Danielle would decide to move somewhere else. But the woman was right. This was the right thing to do. And they needed to pray.

She spent some time unloading her heart to her heavenly Father, more like an emotional brain dump, asking—no begging —for wisdom and protection, especially for her team. She needed to ask her small group to pray for her even though she couldn't give them any details.

Her phone buzzed on her desk, and she glanced at it. Scott was calling. Huh.

She swiped it on. "Hey, how's the migraine?"

"Much better, thanks. I appreciate what you did yesterday. I owe you an apology for my attitude." Regret laced his tone.

Her heart warmed. "I get it, Scott. You've been through a lot. It's understandable."

"You're too kind. But I was out of line. And I've had a conversation with Joe who showed me a different perspective."

She laughed. "Good friends do that."

He let out a breath. "Thanks for being so understanding. So can we start over? If you still want my help, I'll give it my best shot."

"Of course." *Thanks, God. That was fast.* "Can you come by tomorrow? I've got a fire here I'm trying to put out, but hopefully it'll be resolved by then, and I can give the avionics my full attention."

"That'll work. Let me take you out to dinner tonight. As a way of apology. I was a jerk."

A spark lit through her stomach. "Oh, that's not necessary. You're doing me a favor."

"Please. I want to. About six?"

Warmth spread from her stomach throughout her body. She'd have to rein in her attraction to him, or it was going to be difficult to work together. But it was just dinner, and they'd shared a meal before. "Okay. But I'll still be at the office, so meet me here." She glanced down at her wide-legged black pants and floral-print blouse. It would do.

"Looking forward to it."

After ending the call, she set the phone on her desk, far too giddy for the situation. Even just as friends—and that was all they could be— it would be a nice break. But for now, she had work to do.

SCOTT HUNG UP WITH MELISSA AND RUBBED HIS HAND over his face, glad he'd gotten that call out of the way. It had been on his mind all last night. And it had gone way better than he'd expected. The dinner offer had been spontaneous, but he was glad he'd made it. He enjoyed spending time with her. Not only was she attractive, she had a great heart and a great brain. Which, not for the first time, made him wonder why she wasn't with someone.

Though, she was an awful lot like him—married to his work. Still, he was looking forward to spending time with her. The challenge of figuring out her problem, helping her with it, and being around her. All of it was just up his alley. And maybe, this was part of the reason for his injury. Like Esther in the Bible, for such a time as this. He might be of real help, a kind of help she might not have access to. He had a hard time believing there was any purpose to his injury, but he'd grasp on to this thin wire of hope.

Joe was right, though Scott would never tell him. But there were a lot of positive things that he could focus on, and it was about time to start his workout. He had a whole list of exercises from his physical therapist to run through to improve his balance, strength, and increase blood flow to his brain. He could do all of this from Joe's condo, and he could run through the neighborhood. By the time he saw his physical therapist later this week, he was determined to show improvement and get signed off as soon as possible. And if he could help Melissa solve her problem quickly, it would be a win all the way around.

He went to his room and pulled out his recovery binder, flipping it to the physical therapy tab that listed his exercises. He ran through the list to refresh his memory and then got out his running shoes. He'd warm up with a run. He pulled on his shoes and set the app on his phone to record his run.

A knock at the door stopped him. A salesman? He peeked out his bedroom window that looked out to the front. A huge bunch of balloons blocked his view, but based on the heels and dress, he assumed they were being held by a woman. Probably the wrong condo. Who would be delivering balloons here?

He went to the living room and opened the door, not sure he could be much help with directions to the right unit since he didn't live in the complex. He nudged Shadow back with his leg.

Macy and a big bunch of balloons filled the doorway.

"Hi, Scott! I brought you a little get-well basket." Her bright smile lit up her face and flashed him back to a time when he'd kill to get that smile from her directed his way.

"But—" He didn't quite know what to say.

She pushed past him, the balloons whacking him in the face. "Sorry this is late. I didn't find out about your accident until just a few weeks ago. Then I didn't know where your parents had moved to. But now that you're living with Joe…" She turned and gave him that blinding smile. "I know where Joe lives."

Emotions swirled and chased each other through his chest, too fast for him to actually grab and name. Just when he thought he had a handle on them, they whirled in another direction.

Macy set the gift basket on the dining room table with balloons brushing the light fixture.

"Macy, why are you here?" There was always a plan behind that dazzling smile.

"I told you." She gestured to the basket. "A little something to cheer you up."

"I'm not sick." He heard the edge in his voice, regretted it, but not really. Macy didn't pay much attention to pushback. She just kept doing what she wanted.

She took a step toward him, put her hand on his arm. "What if I just wanted to come by and say hi? It's been a long time. I thought you might want some company."

He shook his head. Nope, she hadn't changed. "I was just heading out for a run. But thanks for thinking of me."

Shadow must have understood the word *run* because his head jerked up. It was fun having a dog to run with.

Her smile faded. "I'll let you get to your run. But call me. It'd be good to catch up."

He moved to the door and opened it. "Thanks for the gift basket."

She trailed her fingers along his arm as she passed him. "See you."

He smiled and closed the door behind her.

Wow. Now he really needed that run.

He did a few quick stretches, hooked Shadow to the leash, then headed out the door. He ran through the condo complex and then out to the street that looped around the neighborhood. He hit a good pace of rhythm of breathing and stride, Shadow right along with him. Then his phone buzzed in his pocket. He glanced at his fitness tracker to see what was coming in on his phone. A call from his CO. He stopped and steadied his breathing then pulled his phone out, trying to make his voice sound normal. Shadow sat and panted.

"Yes, sir."

"Commander Blake, just wanted to give you a quick update

on the preliminary inquiry before you got the official notice. They can't find any evidence of the computer controlling the plane the way you suggested. It still points back to pilot error." A bit of regret and maybe pity tinged his CO's voice.

"Sir. All due respect. It happened. The computer forced the nose down into a stall. I fought that with everything I had. Newhart and I"—his voice caught—"we did everything we could." He lost power in his voice.

"But Newhart isn't here to corroborate your story, and the data is reporting something different. It's now a Board of Inquiry investigation."

Scott was barely aware of his CO asking about his injury and how his therapy was progressing. He stuttered out some response, and his CO ended the call. He stood on the sidewalk holding his phone. The disciplinary results could range from retraining to the loss of his career. Everything he'd worked so hard for seemed to be crumbling under his touch.

He wasn't Superman. He never had been.

Chapter Six

S cott flipped the AC up on his Corvette, trying not to sweat through his ocean-blue button-down shirt, even though it was only sixty degrees outside. He'd made the mistake of stopping by his folks' house on the way out and picking up his mail. Which included a letter from the Navy. So his CO had given him some advanced warning but not much. The letter sat unopened on the seat next to him.

After the run-in with Macy and the call from his CO, he considered canceling with Melissa tonight. He just wasn't up to being his charming self.

On the other hand, the last time Melissa had seen him, he'd been a jerk. So there was nowhere to go but up. And it wasn't even a date. Plus, he could use the distraction. He glanced at the letter again.

After pulling into her company's parking lot, he texted her. He felt a little like a jerk for not going up and getting her, but with all of the security he'd have to go through, there really wasn't a point. One more glance at the letter, and he tossed it behind the seat.

She texted back and a minute later she exited the main doors. His heart kicked up a notch. Average height with pretty chestnut hair, there was something about her—her confidence, her intelligence—that made any time he'd spent with her enjoyable. However, they had a job to do. He had to keep that in the front of his mind.

He hopped out and opened her door. "How was your day?"

She made a face. "Let's just say I'm looking forward to dinner and not thinking about work for a while." She slipped into the car.

He shut the door and got in on his side. "Seafood sound good?"

"Sounds great."

"Good. I was thinking of Ironwood." He pulled out of the parking lot and headed toward the restaurant.

"I love that place."

So far, so good. But an awkward silence filled the car. It was the first time with just the two of them, other than when he'd been in her office accusing her of killing his EWO. Maybe this whole thing was a bad idea.

Melissa shook her head. "Sorry. Still thinking about work. Bad habit. Oh!" She pulled her phone out. "I got a text from Jaxon's mom. Remember? The boy whose grandpa had the heart attack."

"Yeah? Did the grandpa make it? Kyle seemed to think it didn't look good."

"He did." She read from the screen. "Thanks to the quick work of the on-scene help, my dad was able to get surgery in time to remove the blockage, and Jaxon had someone to look after him. The first thing my dad did was to ask about Jaxon. And Jaxon can't stop flying his planes around. We even got him a book at the library on making paper airplanes. If you don't think it's too creepy, I'd love to have your address so Jaxon can send you the picture he drew for you." Melissa grinned at him.

"Glad that worked out well. And nice to know my mad paper-airplane-making skills come in handy at those crucial moments."

"I was impressed."

A jolt shot through his chest at her words. He would have thought it would take a lot more than entertaining a small boy to impress her.

They pulled into the restaurant parking lot and went in. The hostess seated them at a secluded table in the back. They made small talk as the server took their food and drink orders. Things were easy and casual between them. For a moment, he could believe they were on a real date. An idea he found appealing. Impossible though it was. As soon as he got cleared, he was back on duty at Naval Air Weapons Station China Lake, and she had her job here.

All evening he knew he had to explain about his TBI, the traumatic brain injury, but he hated thinking about it. He didn't want her to see him as weak. In the early days of his recovery, he had to swallow his pride a lot, getting help doing simple things. Even now, living with Joe and not being able to do what he loved was bad enough.

Did he have to tell her? Part of him argued against it. He could skate into Broadstone Technologies, impress her with his flight knowledge, and she might never have to know what tormented him at night.

Yet, as he looked at her across the table, there was something more in her face, her openness and trust. And he wanted to respond in kind. The Superman image got to be heavy to bear at times. Maybe there was room for more than just Kyle and Joe in his life.

A certainty settled over him, like making the decision to jump off the high dive. If she was going to be working with him, she needed to know. Because next time he blew up at her, she might never speak to him again. And the thought of that twisted his chest. Not to mention he desperately needed her help. More so since the investigation into his flight accident had moved to the Board of Inquiry.

Once the server had brought dessert and coffee, he decided

to dive right in. He swirled his coffee around in the cup. "So the migraine yesterday was a result of the brain injury I got in the accident. I don't really remember the accident at all. I guess that's common. But somehow when I ejected, I hit my head. I had a pretty nice gash for a while." He touched the side of his head between his temple and ear. With his hair slightly longer than regs, it wasn't too visible anymore.

But Melissa's gaze switched to the side of his head, making him slightly self-conscious. When had that ever been a thing for him?

"Anyhow, I'm working with a physical therapist for balance, strength, things like that. But I still get tired eyes and blurry vision if I look at something too long. Bright lights bother me. And the migraines come on without much warning."

Her brow furrowed, a crease forming between her eyebrows. "That's got to be difficult for you all the way around. So different than the life you're used to living."

"Yeah." He met her gaze. "I'm hoping it'll all resolve sooner rather than later so I can get back to flying. But the brain heals at its own rate, or so they tell me." He took a sip of his coffee, the words coming a bit easier now at the openness in her gaze. No judgment or worse, pity. "At the beginning, I had a lot of outbursts, anger, crying, yelling. I guess it's normal, but it feels pretty awful to see your mom cry at what you've just said. Those don't happen much anymore. I usually can feel it building up, but occasionally it takes me by surprise. Like with you yesterday. I think learning about the avionics brought back flashes from the crash, triggered the migraine, and it all became a catastrophic system failure." He gave her a rueful grin, feeling a bit lighter.

She reached over and took his hand, and her touch zipped up his arm and into his chest. "Thanks for telling me. I could tell you weren't yourself yesterday. I just wasn't entirely sure how to help you."

He nodded. "You did the right thing. Just getting back to

Joe's and getting to a dark room helped a lot. It's been good to be there. I love my folks, but Mom can hover."

A flash of sadness crossed her face and then was gone. What was that about? "Tell me about your family." He wanted to get the focus off of himself.

She slipped her hand from his and leaned back. "Well I'm the oldest. In case you couldn't tell." She smiled. "Then there's my sister Allie. She's a real estate agent and relocation specialist. She's actually helping Kyle's sister, Kim, find a house right now. We're close. Then there are my two brothers, Daniel and Matthew, and the baby is Brittany. My mom moved to Arizona right after Brittany graduated from college, and I haven't seen my dad since I was eleven, shortly after Brittany was born." She pushed her coffee cup around. "What about you?" She took a sip.

"I have a sister, Jessica, who's ten years younger than me." He paused. "I had an older brother. He was a high school football star, killed by a drunk driver when he was seventeen and I was seven."

The furrow appeared again. "That must have been devastating to all of you."

"It was." He pushed back his cup and picked up the check. "Sorry to bring the energy down." He pulled out his wallet and tossed a card on the table.

"I'm glad you told me. And now you know my family isn't perfect either. But it's all part of who we are."

The server came and took his card and their plates. Scott thought of the letter sitting in his car, what his CO had said. He hadn't told anyone, not even Joe. But if anyone could help him clear his name, it was Melissa. But clearing his name meant proving that her company's avionics program was faulty. What a great way to end a pleasant evening.

The server returned Scott's card, and as he was putting it away, he noticed Melissa watching him.

"Thanks for dinner. You didn't have to do that." Her gaze was steady, studying him.

He slid out of his seat. "My pleasure." And things were back to being awkward, but that was his fault.

They left the restaurant, and he opened her car door before sliding into his side. But he didn't start the car. It was like the letter had a homing beacon.

If he was going to be working with her, he'd better put all his cards on the table. Find out if she was willing to help him or not. Stakes and all. Another jump off the high dive. He did it once and survived. He could do it again.

He reached behind the seat and grabbed the letter. "I got a call from my CO today giving me a heads-up about this." He tapped the letter on his thigh. "Apparently the initial investigation says it was pilot error. Now, they always say that. But in this case, I know what happened. Newhart—he was my electronic warfare officer—and I were fighting with the plane. We were getting weird error messages that made no sense. The computer was overriding our commands, pitching the nose down. We had to eject." He shook his head. "Newhart didn't make it." He hoped she didn't notice how his voice cracked. "I don't remember anything after pulling the ejection handle until I woke up in the naval hospital in Balboa.

"I thought for sure the preliminary inquiry would clearly show that there was a computer malfunction. That the latest update had done something screwy. But my CO says they can find no evidence of what I said happened is true." He shook the letter. "This is supposed to be the official notification of that. I just can't seem to open it." He met her gaze. "If I can't prove what happened *actually* happened, then I'll never fly again." He swallowed. And who would he be if he wasn't a naval aviator?

"I believe you."

It took a minute. "What?"

"I believe you. We've been having problems with that software update. I don't know the extent of them. I thought they were just odd glitches." She let out a breath. "This could ruin my company. But I can't let another pilot get killed. We have to get to the bottom of it." She glanced at the letter in his hand. "Why don't you open it while I'm here, and we'll figure out a game plan?" She squeezed his hand. "We'll find the truth together."

AS SCOTT PULLED INTO MELISSA'S COMPANY PARKING LOT, a heaviness filled her stomach. It had been an enjoyable evening, and she hated to see it end. The fact that he'd opened the letter from the Navy with her and wanted to work with her to discover the truth had created a bond that she hadn't expected and couldn't quite explain.

"Where are you parked? I'll drop you off at your car."

"Oh, I've got to go back inside and finish up some work tonight."

"Seriously? Are you sure that's a good idea? Scratch that. It's none of my business. I get putting in long hours."

She gave him a soft smile. "I won't be long. I just need to check on something so I'll be ready for tomorrow. If I get this thing off my plate, then we'll be able to move forward with the testing."

He nodded. "I get that. I feel weird about letting you walk back into your building alone, but I know you've got security. I'll still watch to make sure you get inside the building safely."

Her heart warmed. "I'd appreciate that. That's sweet."

"My pleasure."

She opened the door and got out. "Thanks, Scott. I had a great time."

"I did too. I'll see you tomorrow bright and early."

His grin about melted her heart. She knew why Kyle and Joe joked about women following Scott around.

She closed the door behind her and strode towards the main entrance, taking the security badge out of her purse. She pulled the door open and turned. Scott was still watching her. She gave him a small wave.

Tonight had been better than she had expected. Not that she expected it to be bad, because she had always enjoyed Scott's company, whatever little of it she actually experienced. But it never had been just the two of them, and she was surprised that he opened up to her. And that *she* had opened up to *him*.

Plus the attention of a good-looking guy never hurt. Their waitress was giving him the eye all night, and he certainly turned heads wherever they went. But underneath that cocky, fly-boy exterior was a sweet guy and a good friend. Given what she knew of Kyle and Joe, she really wasn't surprised.

Once she got past security and up to her office, she saw the files that Danielle had left for her. She had called CFO Gage DeSoto earlier that day, and he had assured her it wouldn't be a problem for Danielle to request the invoices to be pulled. She leafed through them and saw Gavin's counter signature on every single one. Her stomach sank. She had known this would happen, but there was something about seeing the proof in black and white. His signature. She'd seen it on so many documents, including ones that had benefited her. Like a letter of recommendation for her MBA program and reviews and raises.

It had to be Trent. That was the only reason she could come up with for Gavin to be in on it. Whatever this was. He'd always had a blind spot when it came to Trent. And while she wasn't a parent, she knew what it was like to want to make things easier for her younger brothers and sisters. She could only imagine how Gavin felt. But this was taking it too far. At some point you still had to do the right thing.

She needed to talk to Gavin. He'd always listened to her, respected her thoughts and opinions. It wasn't unusual for him to stay late, so she gathered up the invoices and headed to his office to see if his light was on.

As she rounded the corner of the hallway, light spilled from his office. Every office had glass sidelights that allowed anyone to see inside. You could see if someone was in their office or not, and it served for security purposes as well. No one could misbehave behind closed doors.

She heard voices and paused. Was Gavin on the phone? But then there was a second voice. Trent. As she got closer, she could make out the strained tone and heated words. Unsure if she should continue, she waited and listened. She didn't want to eavesdrop, but she did need to see Gavin and didn't really want to speak with him if Trent was around. Maybe she could figure out if it sounded like he was going to leave soon.

Trent's voice. "Dad, you're in this as deep as I am. You can't cut me off now. You know they'll kill me."

Kill him? Surely she didn't hear that correctly.

Gavin's voice, angry. "She's getting too close. I can put her off, but you need to take a vacation. I can't keep covering for you. You're going to cost me my company. If it gets out that you've got a drug problem, you'll lose your security clearance and I might too. I'll get you into rehab."

"I'm not doing another rehab. And this is not just about drugs, and you know it."

"You'll destroy us both."

"Dad, you're in it as deep as I am. You have no choice. You'll have to do it my way now."

There were footsteps, like someone was heading for the door. Melissa's legs turned to jelly. She forced herself to hurry back down the hallway to her office, hoping she hadn't been seen. Easing her door closed, she locked it, the snick of the lock sounding far louder than it probably was.

This was far worse than she had suspected. She'd figured Trent had been into drugs when he was younger based on a few things Gavin had said. But she'd also thought he'd straightened himself out. Otherwise why would Gavin give Trent a job? Yes, it was more of a figurehead position than a real job. He didn't manage any people. But he did have security clearance, and that required a certain level of responsibility. Gavin wouldn't risk his whole company over finding Trent a job. Would he? No, he could have pulled favors at a number of places, if that were the case.

She paced her office then sat, trying to slow her breathing. She couldn't go to Gavin now. Maybe later. She needed to think. The whole thing about someone killing Trent—and this not just being about drugs—caused the hairs on the back of her neck to rise. She didn't know what she'd stumbled on, but it wasn't good.

The best thing was probably to go home. But could she get out without Gavin and Trent knowing she was here? If they pulled the security footage, they'd see that not only had she come back to the building, she'd been in the hallway outside Gavin's office. Hopefully, there was no need for them to pull that footage.

She picked up the desk phone and dialed security. "Hey, George. It's Melissa Ellis. Did you happen to see if Gavin or Trent has left? I thought they were working late and needed to ask them a question."

"Hey, Ms. Ellis. Trent just left about two minutes ago. You just missed him. I haven't seen Mr. Broadstone this evening though."

"Thanks, George. I'll call it a night myself."

"You always do work too hard." He chuckled, a deep rumbling bass.

"Well, if I had a household of grandkids to come home to, I might be more inclined to do so." George had pictures of his eight grandkids taped to his workstation, and Melissa tried to always ask about them.

"Uh huh. I'd better see you down here in a few minutes."

"On my way." She hung up. If she took the back stairs, something Gavin never did, she should avoid him even if he decided to leave.

She locked the invoices in her desk, grabbed her purse, and headed out. As she tiptoed down the concrete-and-metal stairs, she was careful to make as little noise as possible in the echoing space. And yet she couldn't help but feel like a mouse trapped in a maze. She reached the bottom floor, her heart rate far faster than it should be for just a trip down the stairs. Easing open the door, she scanned the lobby. Empty except for George. She let out a breath and hustled over to check out with him, a requirement for after-hours visits.

Handing him her badge, she smiled.

"Working awfully late tonight. Sure you don't want an escort out to your car?"

She hoped her voice wouldn't shake. "I'll be fine. Remember, I took those self-defense classes you nagged me about." She winked, the familiar banter easing her nerves.

He scanned her badge and handed it back to her. "Never can be too careful. Have a good night, Ms. Ellis."

"I will." She strode to the front doors without seeming to be anything more than eager to get home. Pushing them open, she peered out to the parking lot. Trent's Maserati was gone, but her Audi looked lonely across the far-too-wide parking lot for her comfort. As she started toward her car, keys out and ready, she couldn't help but wish Scott had taken her to her car instead.

Chapter Seven

Scott got up before Joe and hustled through his PT routine, taking Shadow with him on the run. At this rate, that dog was going to be in better shape than either of them considering he ran with Scott and then walked with Joe and Sarah and then ran with Joe. No wonder the dog slept all day.

He still struggled a bit with his balance exercises on the Bosu ball. He would have run through them again, but he had to meet Melissa. His PT appointment was tomorrow, so he wanted to show good progress.

Was he doing the right thing in helping her? Or was she helping him? He hopped in the shower. This whole thing could backfire on both of them. He ran down what he knew. She had said their software had glitches. What that meant, he didn't exactly know. Because what took down his plane seemed like a lot more than glitches. They needed to do more digging, and if he could point them in the right direction, they'd find the answers that much sooner.

He dried off and shaved. The fragments of memory about the crash were always just out of reach. If he could remember more clearly, he could explain to her what happened, what he saw, see if she could narrow it down in their program.

But then, the initial inquiry didn't find any computer error. So where was the proof? He dropped the razor in the sink and stared at himself in the mirror.

What if he *was* at fault? What if his work with Melissa just uncovered proof that he was responsible for Jordan's death and ditching a multi-million-dollar plane?

He met his own gaze. Was he man enough to face that?

Worse, what if he uncovered something that put Jordan at fault?

Shakily, he wiped off the shaving cream and headed for his closet, pulling on a shirt. The only way forward was through this. He knew in his gut what happened. Now he had to prove it.

And if what he turned up proved that he was responsible for his friend's death?

Then he'd face that too.

DANIELLE SLIPPED INTO MELISSA'S OFFICE AND SET A CUP of coffee in front of her, doctored up just the way she liked it with a lot of creme brûlée coffee creamer.

Melissa looked up. "Thanks. You always can read my mind." It would be her third cup, but nothing was working this morning. Considering she had tossed and turned all night thinking about what she had overheard in Gavin's office, she'd be surprised if she'd even gotten two hours of sleep. It was the second time this week she hadn't slept well. Coffee couldn't help that kind of tiredness. Scott was sure going to think she was on top of things today when he saw how she couldn't even form words come this afternoon.

Danielle leaned against the desk. "You worked too late last

night. I thought you were going to dinner with Scott." She raised her eyebrows.

"I did. But I came back here after. Scott has agreed to help us, and he's coming in today." She glanced at her watch. "He should be here any time." She let out a breath. "I came back here after dinner and saw the invoices you left. Gavin was still here, so I went to talk to him, but Trent was in Gavin's office. They were arguing, and I didn't want to interrupt. I got the sense that there's something bigger going on here. Maybe I need to spend some time thinking about what that might be before I show the invoices to Gavin."

The desk phone rang. Danielle answered. "Melissa Ellis's office. Danielle speaking." Pause. "Yes, send him up." She hung up. "Scott's on his way up. Or should I say Lieutenant Commander Blake." She gave Melissa a sassy grin. "I'll have the team assemble in the conference room, and we can get started."

They both left Melissa's office just as Scott arrived. Danielle shot Melissa a look with raised eyebrows and then scurried off.

Melissa ignored Danielle's coded message and smiled at Scott. "Good morning. Thanks for making it. Can I get you some coffee?"

Scott raised his eyebrows at her. "Sure." He glanced toward where Danielle had disappeared. "Did I interrupt something?"

"No. Danielle and I were just discussing some of those developments I was working on last night." They headed toward the break room.

"Did you get everything wrapped up?"

"No." She let out a sigh. "Things just got more complicated." She put a cup under the machine for him. "I'm on cup number three."

He grimaced. "Not much sleep last night, huh?"

She pulled the cup out and handed it to him. "Nope, but between you and Danielle, I'm sure we'll accomplish everything we need to today, whether or not I'm actually conscious."

They grabbed their coffees and headed back to the conference room. She introduced him around, and they got started.

The morning was actually quite productive. Scott got along well with the rest of the team and gave Jeremy some ideas of where to look for problems within the code that corresponded to the systems where Scott and his electronic warfare officer had noticed problems.

Danielle had leaned over at one point and asked Melissa if she wanted to order in lunch for the team so they wouldn't lose their momentum, but Melissa thought they'd all be better off taking a break and getting out of that conference room.

The team disbursed for lunch, and Melissa touched Scott's arm. "Thanks so much for today. We've gotten more help from you than from any of the gripe sheets from the other pilots. What sounds good for lunch for you? The company is buying."

"Want to grab a couple of sandwiches and go to Mason Park? We can get a little fresh air and walk around a bit."

"That sounds like a great idea. I'll need some fresh air if I want to stay awake this afternoon."

They headed out to Melissa's car and over to the sandwich shop. Danielle had called in their orders, so they were waiting. Scott ran in and grabbed them, coming out a few seconds later with a bag and a couple of drinks. Once at the park, they found a picnic table in the sun.

Scott pulled out the two sandwiches and a side salad. "This must be for you?"

Melissa frowned. "I didn't order a salad." She peered through the plastic top. "And if I did, it would have a lot more than lettuce and tomatoes on it. Must be a mistake. Did you get the sandwich you ordered?"

"Um hmm." He'd already bit into it.

Melissa unwrapped her sandwich and took a bite of roast beef and provolone on multi grain. She about sighed with pleasure. Between the food and the sun ,with just a little bit of breeze, she might actually be able to rally.

"So what happened last night? How can something get more complicated after business hours?" Scott took a bite of his sandwich and looked at her with raised eyebrows.

Melissa shifted, not sure how much to tell him, but he probably needed to be warned about what he might be getting into. "I told you that the company was having financial problems. Danielle and I figured out that a lot of money is going to a project that no one seems to know anything about. It's headed up by Gavin's son, Trent. I went to talk to Gavin about it last night—since he had signed off on the invoices—and he and Trent were arguing. I didn't hear the whole thing, but it sounded like Trent has gotten himself in deep with drugs and maybe drug dealers. He said something about they were going to kill him."

She took a sip of her drink before continuing. "Gavin has always had a blind spot when it comes to Trent and has bailed him out more times than I can count. But somehow he's working for Gavin and has a security clearance even though he's more of a figurehead than anything. Nobody expects him to do any real work. But if he's into something and Gavin's funding it, that could be a real problem for all of us."

Scott studied her while he chewed his sandwich, and she resisted the urge to be self-conscious about it. "There are terrorists who use drugs to fund their activities. If somebody's got something on Trent, and there are any terrorism connections, it could become a problem real quick."

Melissa hadn't thought about terrorism. Heavy lead filled her stomach.

Scott popped the lid off the salad and picked up the plastic bowl. "Come on."

She looked at him; her eyebrows rose. "What are we doing? Why are you carrying the salad like a football?"

He tilted his head to the side. "We're going to do something fun before we go back to the office. I think you need it."

"Okay." She followed him as they headed toward the pond in the center of the park. Almost too late, she remembered her

Jimmy Choo shoes and watched where she stepped as there was plenty of duck and geese poop on the sidewalk. In the spring when the goslings hatched, the geese could get aggressive. Now, most of the ducks scattered away from them into the water, but a few geese wandered in their general direction, either curious or warning them away.

Scott ripped up pieces of the lettuce. A few ducks turned and swam toward them. He threw bits of lettuce, a few pieces at a time, on the water.

"Here." He handed her the cherry tomatoes.

She took them reluctantly and began tossing them in self-defense as soon as the geese noticed she now had food. Her attempts didn't land very far, and she had to back up to keep from being trampled by them.

Scott laughed. "They like you better than they like me."

"That's just because I throw like a girl, and I'm an easier target. At least we have good food for them instead of bread. Did you know you aren't supposed to feed bread to ducks? It's bad for them."

"I didn't know that. So the extra salad is fortuitous. Though, I don't think we would have had any leftover bread to toss them anyway." He reached into the salad bowl for more lettuce.

"It can lead to deformed wings, something they call an angel wing. But it keeps them from flying."

Scott handed her the last of the lettuce. "Yeah, I kinda know how that feels." He tossed his handful out across the water, his expression unreadable.

Yeah, he probably did. She held up her hand, now empty. "Look, I don't have anymore." The ducks didn't believe her and kept moving toward her. She backed up and ran smack into Scott.

He grabbed her around the waist.

At his touch, she froze. "Sorry." She half turned and was eye level with his chin. Slowly, she tilted her head.

His gaze was intent on her face. The heat of his hands on her waist seeped through her blouse. His gaze darted to her lips and back to her eyes.

The sound of slapping webbed feet on the sidewalk broke their connection.

"We'd better get out of here." Scott grabbed her hand and tugged her along toward the parking lot.

"Here we are on the run from an attack of the killer geese. We are out of lettuce-slash-ammo so we have to retreat. Did they teach you this in the military?" She was breathless from laughing.

He laughed. "They taught me better tactical planning than this. I feel like I let you down with my lack of anticipation of the enemy's counter assault."

The geese had lost interest and wandered off in search of an easier target. She leaned against the car to catch her breath. "Thanks. I needed that. Even if I did almost die."

He bumped her shoulder with his. "Die? Not with me around." But his voice had lost its humor. A shutter came over his eyes, and she could immediately read his thoughts. His friend had died with him around.

She nodded. "Yes. I believe that." The accident hadn't been Scott's fault. And she would help him prove it. No matter what it cost her or her company.

He didn't deserve to carry around a burden of guilt that wasn't his.

Chapter Eight

Scott sat on the table at the physical therapist's office, the paper covering crinkling under his weight. He'd rather be helping Melissa figure out the software problems in the avionics so he could clear his name. Yet, if he didn't get signed off from his physical therapist, he wouldn't be cleared to go back to flight duty. But today was his re-evaluation appointment. Man, he hoped he'd made enough progress so he'd only have a few more weeks of this.

Matt came in carrying Scott's folder and shook his hand. He took a seat on a rolling stool, flipped the folder over on itself, and balanced it on his knee. "How've you been sleeping? Difficulty falling or staying asleep, excessive daytime sleepiness, or unusual events during sleep?"

Scott shrugged. "Some, but it's not too bad. I can get back to sleep most nights. I'm not too sleepy during the day."

Matt jotted down notes. "Are you tracking it in your planner and following your sleep hygiene plan?"

"Yes."

"How have your headaches been? Any migraines?"

"I had one earlier this week, but I was able to manage it."

More notes. Scott shifted, the paper's movement sharp

against the sound of Matt's pen scratching out notes. "How's your vision been? Still having some light sensitivity?"

"Most of the time it's fine. I wear dark sunglasses when I go outside." He paused. "I still get tired eyes if I spend too much time reading or on the computer. I helped a friend with a work problem where I have some expertise. I didn't think I had spent that much time in front of a computer, but I did notice at the end of the day, my eyes had trouble focusing. But they were fine after a break."

"Emotional outbursts or irritability?"

He shifted again. "I think it was related to the migraine. I was a little short with someone when the migraine came on." He was grateful Melissa had accepted his apology and didn't seem to hold it against him.

Matt finished writing and then set the folder on the edge of the table. "Let's run you through some assessments." He held out his hands. "Grip my hands as hard as you can."

Scott complied.

"Okay. Now stand up with your arms straight out, palms up, and close your eyes."

He slid off the table and did as he was told.

"Okay. Now put your arms across your chest—touching your shoulders—and stand on one leg."

Scott took a deep breath and let it out. Focus. He picked a spot on the wall and willed his body to be still as he lifted one leg.

"Now close your eyes."

He imagined the spot on the wall as he closed his eyes. A few seconds later, his hip connected with the table and his eyes flew open.

Matt grabbed his arms. "You okay?"

Despair drained through him. No, he wasn't okay. "Sure."

They ran through some further tests with Matt moving his fingers in different directions. Toward the end, nausea hit Scott as a headache built behind his eyes.

"Okay, let's take a break." Matt brought him some water, which helped. After a few minutes he was ready to finish his normal physical therapy session.

As he was wiping the sweat off the back of his neck with a towel, he turned to Matt. "So how much longer before I'm back on duty?"

Matt shook his head. "I can't really say. The brain heals at its own rate. But you have made progress, so keep at it. I know you want to keep busy and feel useful, but the fact that helping your friend affected your vision means it's too soon. You need to wait before you get back to that kind of work."

Scott didn't say anything. Matt reviewed his at-home exercises and gave him a few more to do. Scott threw the towel into the laundry bin and grabbed his keys. "See you next week."

He slid into his car and sat there a moment before leaning his head on the steering wheel. Great, so the one thing he needed to do to clear his name—help Melissa—could also be the thing that kept him from healing enough to get cleared for duty.

He heard a car pull up. Not wanting anyone to think there was something wrong, he started the car and headed back to Joe's.

God, why? Why haven't you healed me yet? I know you gave me gifts and talents to use, and I use them best in the Navy. I'm a light to those around me. I just don't understand. I know you are good, but right now, I'm having a hard time seeing it.

MELISSA ATE HER VERY LATE LUNCH AT HER DESK AND couldn't help but compare it to the lunch she'd had with Scott at the park. She really should get outside and take a break. But Scott wasn't here to make her. She smiled at that.

Scott had an appointment and wasn't working with them today. But he'd given them enough to work with based on what they had already accomplished. Things finally seemed to be breaking through. At least they had a direction to go in to look for answers. And since the team was busy, Melissa was free to get through some of her own backlog.

Today, the roast beef on multigrain that Danielle had ordered in for her wasn't quite the same as it had been yesterday. She appreciated Scott's perspective, his ability to help her take a break and have some fun. Even if they did get chased by crazy geese. She laughed. It was good for her to be around him. Other people had encouraged her to take breaks and rest, but they didn't understand the pressure and her stress. He did. It allowed her to trust his advice.

How was his physical therapy evaluation going today? Maybe she'd call him on the way home and find out. For his sake, she hoped it was good news. But the sooner he was back on duty, the sooner she'd lose his help.

It seemed like his help was full of contradictions. They were out to prove different things. He wanted to prove her avionics caused his crash. She really hoped they hadn't. Scott was a good pilot, though, and unless there was some rare solution that exonerated both of them, one of them was going to be wrong. As much as she didn't like being wrong—hated it—she didn't want anyone else to die. And that meant the product had to work correctly. She needed his help to make that happen.

Just to add to the complications, she was growing more attracted to him than she should be. He was honorable and honest. But he had a life based around NAWS China Lake, and she had one here. The more they spent time together, the more she risked getting her heart involved. Even if she wanted to make the three-hour drive to see him once he was back at work, how was that sustainable in the long term?

She finished her sandwich and threw away her trash. That was borrowing trouble way down the line. Her ability to forecast long term and to see potential problems was great in business. Not so much in her personal life.

Besides, she had more pressing issues. She had to talk to

Gavin. While she thought she knew what he might say, she couldn't take any next steps without talking to him first. She owed him that much. Maybe he'd surprise her. In a good way. Because lately her surprises had all been negative.

She unlocked her desk and pulled out the invoices. Might as well do it now. If it blew up in her face, she could always head home. Or the pottery studio. Some time with clay under her fingers sounded like just the thing she needed to get her mind off work and release some steam.

On the other hand, Gavin had always been fair and respected her opinions and heard her out. She had no reason to believe this time would be different.

Except that it involved Trent.

She stuck the invoices in a folder and stepped out of her office, letting Danielle know where she would be.

She headed toward Gavin's office.

Through the side lights, she could see he was at his desk. His admin, Shari, smiled at Melissa as she walked up. "I'm sure he has time for you. Just let me check." She picked up the phone. "Melissa's here. Do you have a few minutes?" She hung up. "Go on in."

"Thanks." Surreptitiously, she wiped her hands on her pants before opening his office door.

"Melissa. Have a seat. What can I do for you?"

She took the seat in front of his desk. He always got right down to business. Few if any pleasantries. Normally, it was a trait she appreciated, but today she would have liked a little time to get her thoughts together. But, might as well jump right in. She summarized what she had discovered so far about the missing money. She skimmed over what he had told her on the phone about Trent. Then she opened the folder and handed him the invoices, telling him where they came from. "This is a pattern much larger than just paying a late invoice. Your countersignature is on every single one of these. Normally, that would be me. So I'm surprised Trent didn't come to me, at least for most of them. But like I said, he hasn't told me anything about this project, and I'm a bit in the dark as to what it's all about. Or why Danielle and I are on it."

Gavin grabbed the invoices and studied them, his face darkening. From past experience, she knew a storm was brewing. But who would bear the brunt of it? Her or Trent? She wanted to call him a liar, countering his excuse from their phone conversation.

The silence dragged out. He tossed the invoices on his desk. "How's the avionics program coming? I can't believe you have time to stick your nose in other projects when your team has enough of its own problems to deal with. Focus on that. If there are any problems or any complaints from the Navy when we run our second round of tests, I'll fire your whole department."

She forced herself to meet his gaze boring into her. She had done nothing wrong. But the anger burning in his eyes made it difficult not to flinch.

"If this is all you have to complain about, then get back to work. Your whole team is running on borrowed time. If they lose their jobs, it'll be your fault."

Melissa rose on shaky legs. She wished she had something brilliant to say that would acquit her and her team in his mind. But nothing came to her. She gave a brief nod. "I see." Turning, she left his office, tossing Shari a tight smile.

Once around the corner, she realized he hadn't given her back the invoices.

SCOTT STARED INTO THE REFRIGERATOR. HE'D BEEN moping around the house since his PT appointment. Joe was gone, off doing something Scott couldn't remember, but was heading over to Sarah's later. So the house would continue to be empty. He should probably get out and do something to shake this fog of depression. The answer likely wasn't in the fridge either.

His phone rang. He closed the fridge door and grabbed his phone, though he didn't really want to talk to anyone. It was Melissa. He hesitated, then swiped the phone on.

"Hey, how'd your PT appointment go?"

Not what he wanted to talk about. "Are you in the car? Heading home already?" He could hear road noise, but it was early for her to be cutting out. Especially since she tended to stay late. And it was a way to avoid talking about his appointment.

Her sigh came through the phone. "Yeah. I talked to Gavin. It didn't go well." She gave him a quick rundown. So they'd both had pretty bad days.

"He kept the invoices, but I have copies in my desk. I hate to think that he might try to destroy them, but I wanted to be prepared."

"Good thinking." He paced the hallway, from the living room back to Joe's bedroom and back again. It wasn't that long of a hallway, but he couldn't sit still. "What's going to happen next?"

"Well, with your help, I think we'll get the avionics system nailed down. I can't even conceive of my whole team getting fired." A hitch caught her voice.

She was a good boss, cared about her team more than herself or her standing in the company. A rare thing.

"But I have to go to the board about Gavin. I've been thinking about what you said about the terrorists and drugs. I don't know what Trent's into, but it's affecting Gavin and the company. Something has to be done to protect the company. I can't let Trent's bad choices and Gavin's defense of them take down Broadstone Technologies. The board should know."

"Whew. That's throwing down the gauntlet. Are you worried about the repercussions?"

"Yep. That's why I'm heading to the pottery studio for a while. I need to do something physical and not think about work for a bit."

"Ah, so you do know how to have fun even when I'm not around."

Her laugh sent sparks down his spine. "I've managed without you, flyboy."

"Oh, you wound me."

"Enough about me. I called to see how your PT appointment went."

He stopped pacing. There was no avoiding her question. "Well, not as good as I hoped. Tell you what, want to head over here after the pottery studio and we'll grab something to eat? I'll give you more details then." Why did he just offer to spend more time with her? She was already getting under his skin, a situation that would grow dangerous if left unchecked. There was no way they could have a future. Their paths were taking them different directions. Yet something about spending the evening with her, sharing their rough days, seemed like the best thing he could think of. And he knew he needed some company. The verse from Isaiah fifty-eight about the best healing coming from helping others spun through his mind.

"If you don't mind me in grubby clothes, that sounds like a great plan. I'll call you when I leave here. I just pulled up to the studio."

They hung up, and he set his phone on the counter. He searched the cupboards for a cake mix and toppings and got to work. Takeout would only be improved by one of his fun cakes. And it would keep his mind from spiraling where he didn't want it to go.

Chapter Nine

Melissa hung up her clay-spattered apron and studied the vase she had made today as it sat on the shelf to dry. Not too bad. It would air dry, then get fired, and she'd come paint it. So different than what she did for work, but so satisfying to see something beautiful come from a gray, wet blob. *Kinda like what you do with us, huh, God?* Though there were days she didn't feel too much removed from a lump of clay.

Her old jeans and shirt didn't look too bad. She kept them in the car just for this purpose. It was one less obstacle to overcome when it came time to do something good for herself. She grabbed her purse, waved to the store owner, Dominique, and headed out the door. The late afternoon winter sun had been headed to bed when she'd pulled up, and the parking lot had been crowded. Now, the early evening was fully dark, and her car was around the corner. She pulled her keys off the clip on her purse.

And just like that, the day's events covered her again. It would be helpful to talk about a game plan with Scott. He had good ideas. Going to the board would set off a bomb in her relationship with Gavin. He could no longer be her mentor. The thought halted her mid-stride. He'd been so instrumental in her getting where she was now. It was hard to believe that he was the same man she was going to bring before the board of directors.

She started walking again. There was her car. Off by itself.

She'd talk to the chairman of the board first—maybe in person—before getting on the agenda. Gavin was on good terms with all the board members, so she'd have to carefully lay out her case. But the company was in jeopardy, and the board deserved to know. Not to mention her whole team was in danger of being fired at Gavin's whim. While she wasn't certain he'd—

Something wrapped around her upper arm, and a hard object poked her in the back. She started to turn her head, but a deep, rough voice said, "Keep looking forward. Keep walking, and you won't get hurt. Understand?"

She nodded, not sure she could get her voice to work. Her legs wobbled like rubber, and she was grateful for her tennis shoes instead of heels. Her self-defense training flew through her mind, but with a supposed gun at her back, it was best to bide her time and look for an opportunity to act.

When they reached the back of her car, the person yanked her arm to a stop. No, not the trunk. She'd die before she'd let them put her in the trunk. She waited for a moment of distraction to act.

"I've got a message for you." The voice was close to her ear. "Keep your nose out of things that don't concern you. Got that? Do what you're told. Forget we ever had this conversation. Understand me? Or I'll visit you again. And you won't like it."

She nodded, swallowing. Her mind raced. If she could get away, where was the safest place to run to? Was there anything around she could use as a weapon? Anything?

"Count to fifteen so I can hear you. Look straight ahead until you're done."

Okay? "Um, one." The object in her back disappeared, and the grip on her arm released. The presence behind her seemed to move away. "Two. Three. Four . . ." She listened intently for footsteps, a car that might be heard above the general traffic noise of the street while she counted. "Fourteen." She took a step closer to her car and nothing happened. "Fifteen." She looked around.

The parking lot was empty.

She scrambled in her car, locked the doors, and started it, ready to take off from the parking lot. With a shaking voice, she used voice activation to call Scott.

SCOTT PACED JOE'S HALLWAY, WISHING HE HAD ingredients to make another cake. The one sitting on the counter was a chocolate poke cake with caramel sauce and toffee bar crunch topping. But he needed to get more supplies before he could make another.

Listening to Melissa's trembling voice had just about done him in. It was all he could do not to jump in his car and go after her.

But she was coming here instead of going home. And Kyle was coming over too. Scott had called him right after Melissa assured him she was okay to drive.

He peered out the front window, watching for her headlights. It couldn't be a coincidence that someone grabbed her after she'd talked to Gavin. Though he wasn't sure she was ready to hear that yet. And if this guy was connected to Gavin, then he knew where she lived and worked.

He ran his hand through his hair, longer than he'd had it since high school. Just another sign that his life had taken a drastic turn. But in the meantime, he could help Melissa. Which now seemed to include keeping her safe.

The next set of headlights turned toward Joe's condo instead of driving past. He sprung out the front door and was by her car door the moment she opened it. "You okay?"

She nodded and stepped away from her car. "He didn't—"

Her voice broke and tears pooled in her eyes. He pulled her into his arms, tucking her head under his chin. She trembled, and he tightened his arms around her. "It's going to be okay."

He lifted his head and scanned the area around them. It wasn't wise to be out in the open like this. Who knows if she'd been followed or not. Even so, he was reluctant to break his hold. "We should go inside." He eased her back. "Got your purse and keys?"

She nodded and wiped under her eyes. "Sorry. I'm not usually like this." She gave him a watery grin. "You shouldn't be so nice to me."

He flashed his most charming smile and placed his hand on her lower back, heading them toward the house. He scanned the area one more time. Anyone could be out there, hiding in the dark and the landscaping.

Inside, he locked the door behind them and guided her to the couch. "I'll get you some water. Kyle should be here any minute."

She nodded, her hands clasped in her lap, her body folded in on herself. The confident woman he normally saw had shrunken. His heart twisted a bit at her vulnerability.

"I don't know that there's much I can tell him. It's kind of like the fire alarm all over again."

Scott handed her a bottle of water. "It's good for him to know, regardless. At some point, there will be a pattern or a slipup. We'll figure it out."

A pattern of raps sounded on the door. Kyle. Their old code from high school when they'd tap on each other's bedroom windows and then sneak out. It brought a half smile at the memory. Scott opened the door.

Kyle had come straight from work, badge and gun still visible.

"Thanks for coming so fast. I'm going to order some food. Want some?" Scott closed and locked the door behind Kyle.

"Thanks, but I'm heading to Heather's after this. She's cooking tonight."

Scott raised his eyebrows. "When are you two going to make it official?" Then he wished he could suck the words back in. They'd been friends a long time, but Melissa was there, and if he were in Kyle's shoes, he wasn't sure he'd want to have that discussion now. "Forget I said anything."

Kyle shrugged. "I'd take her to the courthouse tomorrow, but she deserves to figure out if she can be married to a cop. She says she can, but I want her to have plenty of practice so she's sure." He had been engaged once before to Christa. Who had decided after they'd planned the wedding that she didn't want to be married to a cop. So his caution was warranted. He raised an eyebrow and nodded to the dining room table.

Scott turned. The stupid balloons from Macy. He and Joe had raided the gift basket of the candy bars and popcorn, but he hadn't had the heart to pop the balloons. But he wished he would have. It would have been less painful than the explanation he was going to have to give.

"Uh, Macy stopped by the other day."

Kyle's eyebrows flew even higher. "How did she know where you were?"

Scott shrugged. "Beats me. She's got some intelligence network that rivals the FBI's. She always knows what everyone is up to."

"You two keep in touch?"

"I hadn't seen her in sixteen years, but Joe said she kept in touch with one of his sisters."

"Must have been an interesting conversation between you two."

Macy had been the source of conflict between Joe and Scott in high school. She'd been Scott's girlfriend until he broke up with her to concentrate on their winning football season. But then she'd come on to Joe and spread some rumors that Scott had stupidly believed and had damaged their friendship for much longer than it should have. "We're cool. Macy's just… Macy."

Melissa watched their exchange, her face pale and confused. They did not need to be talking about Macy. He grabbed a seat on the couch next to Melissa. "Sorry. Just an old high school friend who stopped by."

Kyle sank into the recliner and turned his attention to Melissa. "Hey, heard you had a rough night. You okay now?"

She nodded and let out a breath. "Yeah, just a little shaken. I think maybe even more than if it had been some random guy. I know what he meant and likely who is behind it. That's what scares me more than anything."

Kyle punched an app on his phone and placed it on the coffee table between them. "Tell me everything. Start at the beginning. Anything you've discovered since the fire alarm incident."

She told him all that they had uncovered about Gavin and Trent, including her confrontation with him today and his threat to fire her team. Her voice was steady, and her recall clear. "As to the guy tonight, there's not much to tell you. His voice was rough, but he might have been using a modulator. He seemed about Scott's height, based on where his voice was relative to my ear. He could have been bending down. Beyond that, I don't know. But somehow he knew I was going to the pottery studio."

"Did you tell anyone where you were going?"

"I told Danielle when I left the office early. I don't think she would have told anyone else, but it's not a big secret. A lot of my team know I sometimes go to the pottery studio after work. It would be a reasonable guess. I can ask Danielle tomorrow if she let it slip to anyone. Or I could have been followed. I'm concerned about this incident getting around. We don't have any proof of anything other than a few invoices. But if you come into the building flashing your badge and asking questions, I'm afraid things will escalate."

Kyle nodded. "Your concern is warranted. Are you still planning on going to the board?"

"I have to. That's a business decision and a moral one."

"If they remove Gavin, it might take the pressure off you. Or it might make it worse. Either way, be extremely careful. Don't go anywhere alone. Stop working late at the office."

She leaned her head back against the couch, and Scott could see her mind whirling. She was thinking about the avionics program, how much there was to do, and the security of her team's jobs. Because that's exactly what he'd be thinking about.

Scott touched her shoulder. "I'll help. If you need to stay late, I can be there."

The tension eased from her shoulders. She opened her mouth, and he expected an argument but all she said was, "Thank you."

Kyle stood. "Keep me in the loop. I'll poke around quietly. You have an alarm at home?"

"Yes, because of my security clearance."

"Good." He shook Scott's hand then left.

Scott turned to Melissa. "Change of subject. Pizza sound good? We can have it delivered so we don't have to go anywhere."

"Sounds great. I'll eat anything on it, so get what you like."

He brought up the app on his phone and placed the order. "And for dessert, I made a special cake."

She grinned. "Oh really? You don't strike me as the baking type."

He shrugged. "It's good therapy. Now these are my own special creations. Box cake mix with whatever candy seems like it would be good to stir in and frosting that could be considered creative."

She laughed. "Well then, this I gotta see."

He stood and tugged her up from the couch, leading her to the kitchen. "Wah lah! Chocolate poke cake with caramel poured over and toffee candy bars crumbled on top."

"Sounds like a diabetic coma waiting to happen. Can't wait to try it." She leaned against the counter. "Okay, my drama is done. Tell me about your PT session before the pizza gets here."

He was amazed at the way she was able to shift gears. She'd done what she needed to do and then moved on. He gave her the rundown of his appointment. "So, no return to duty date yet." He paused. Should he tell her about his eye problems? He didn't want to add to her burden, but they'd been pretty open with each other.

The doorbell rang. Pizza. He didn't have to decide right now. He checked the peephole before opening the door. The smell of garlic and hot cheese made his stomach growl. He hadn't realized how hungry he was.

He brought the pizza inside. Melissa was already getting out plates. As they scarfed down a pizza with everything on it, the conversation kept mainly to light topics. But his mind spun to the rest of the night. She'd need to get home safely. And alarm or no, he wanted to check out her house first.

After a piece of cake with decaf coffee and a debate about what to name his fabulous creation, he broached the subject. "I'll follow you home. I want to make sure you get there safely, and I want to check out your house. Make sure there aren't any surprises."

She hesitated and then nodded. He wasn't sure he liked that she agreed so readily. She was more shaken up than she was letting on.

MELISSA IDLED HER AUDI IN FRONT OF HER TOWNHOME while Scott parked his Corvette. While she normally pulled into her garage and entered the house that way, Scott didn't want her doing that alone. He hopped in her passenger seat holding a paper plate. "I brought you a slice of cake. Joe will take the rest to the station, and we'll never see it again, but I figured you should have another chance at tasting greatness." He flashed her his signature grin.

She laughed as she pulled into the garage. "Is there anything you don't think you're fabulous at?"

He furrowed his brow and tapped his head like a cartoon character. "I'll have to get back to you on that."

"Uh huh. That's what I thought." She parked the car and shut it off. Everything looked normal.

"Stay here." Scott handed her the paper plate and got out of her car. He scanned the garage door and the door to the house then waved to her.

She got out and grabbed her bags, juggling the cake. Then entered the alarm code and unlocked the door to the house. Scott again made her wait at the door until he searched the house.

She dropped her purse and keys on the console table by the door. But holding the cake and her bag with her work clothes was getting tiresome. She simply wanted a hot shower and bed.

He came back down the stairs and gave her the all clear. She put her cake in the fridge and dropped her bag at the bottom of the stairs.

"One more thing. Let's add you to my Find Friends app so I'll know where you are." His gaze met hers. "It's not creepy. Okay, it kind of is. But at least I'll know where you are if I need to find you."

She laughed. "Okay." They made the adjustments on their respective phones. She realized he would leave any minute.

And she then would be alone.

She liked being alone. Right? And yet... a weird prickly sensation came over her. She set her phone on the console table.

"Hey." Scott put his hands on her shoulders. "Are you going to be okay?"

She nodded and looked away, not trusting her voice to speak.

He pushed her hair behind her ear, his touch trailing heat

across her skin. His eyes deepened their shade of blue. He slipped his hand behind her neck, his gaze darting to her lips and back up, his eyebrows raising slightly.

Her heart rate ticked up, and she leaned toward him as if pulled.

He lowered his lips to hers and skimmed his other hand down to her waist, pulling her close.

For a moment, all she felt was safe and cherished. Instead of being a boss or coworker, she was a woman. All the reasons why this wasn't a good idea drifted away, and she lost herself in his touch.

Too soon he eased back, his gaze a turbulent blue, reflecting the swirl of emotions she reeled from. He trailed his fingers through her hair. "I, uh, I'd better go." He traced down her arm, raising goose bumps. He squeezed her hand. "Call me. Anytime. I'm up a lot in the night, so you won't be bothering me. Promise?"

She nodded.

He kissed her forehead and then opened the front door. "Set the alarm behind me."

She nodded again. He was going to think she was a bobble-head doll. "Okay. Thanks for everything."

He gave her a heart-stopping grin. "Of course."

She locked the door and leaned against it.

What had just happened?

Chapter Ten

M elissa hit off the alarm on her phone and groaned. Church. It seemed like no matter how early she went to bed, she never felt like she was getting enough sleep. Probably because her mind worked all night trying to solve the mess she was in.

She eased out of bed and padded downstairs to the coffeemaker. While waiting for it to brew, she put a bagel in the toaster and thought about what to wear.

There was a barbecue at Kyle's house after church. His sister, Kim, was finally moving out. Melissa's sister Allie had helped her. Allie was a real estate agent who specialized in relocating executives for companies, so helping Kim was a bit of a favor. But Allie was so sweet; she'd help anyone.

Melissa dosed her coffee with creme brûlée creamer and slathered butter and cream cheese on her bagel, then hopped up on a red industrial-style barstool to eat.

Kyle had a nice patio, so they might end up out there. And California or not, it was November. She settled on skinny jeans with a deep plum long sweater, a long necklace, and ankle boots.

And of course, Scott would be there. He'd texted her a few times yesterday to see how she was doing. She'd assured him she was fine and raved about the second piece of his special cake. But they'd avoided the one subject that kept replaying in her mind: their kiss.

Of course, with as many women that followed him around, kissing a woman probably didn't mean anything to him. Might even have been more like a reflex to soothe an overwrought woman.

She had awakened a lot Friday night with fears about the man who'd grabbed her. Would he try to find her at home? But Saturday she was able to focus on what really needed to be done like bills, grocery shopping, laundry, cleaning. Routine things that soothed her with their normalcy.

She'd called Danielle and discovered that Gavin had asked where Melissa was on Friday. Apparently he'd come looking for her, and Danielle told him that she'd left early to de-stress and brainstorm. Danielle hadn't told him exactly where she'd gone, but Gavin knew that she liked to go to the pottery studio to unwind and think. That news sent a shiver.

While she found it hard to believe Gavin sent somebody to scare her, much of what she'd seen of Gavin's behavior lately was completely unexpected. On the other hand, if Gavin was behind the man who threatened her, then maybe she really didn't have too much to worry about. She couldn't imagine him actually hurting her. He just wanted her to leave him alone when it came to Trent. Too bad she couldn't do that.

After loading her dirty dishes into the dishwasher, she headed for her bedroom to finish getting ready. She might as well be slogging through mud, but maybe after Kyle's she'd be able to take a nap. It would be nice to have one day where she didn't have to think about work. Going to church, focusing on God, reminding herself that he was in control, and being surrounded by friends sounded just like what she needed.

She finished getting ready, grabbed her purse and Bible, and headed out to the garage, careful to lock the door and set the alarm behind her. She opened the garage door and backed out, but when she closed the garage door, she saw a note plastered to it. Which wasn't that unusual. Sometimes people would leave flyers and advertisements rubber banded to the handles of the garage doors. But this one was taped. Sometimes the homeowner's association taped up notices if they were going to be doing painting or repairs or changing out landscaping. Usually they also sent something in the mail. She glanced around the other garage doors. They were empty.

Her legs turned to liquid. Should she call Scott or Kyle? She grabbed her phone, scanned the area around her. The place was empty, as she would expect on a Sunday morning. She took a picture of the note from faraway and then another one up close. Using the edge of her sweater, she tugged the paper loose and slid into her car, tossing it on the seat next to her.

It simply said, REMEMBER WHAT I TOLD YOU.

SCOTT CLIMBED OUT OF JOE'S TRUCK IN THE CHURCH parking lot. There was no point in their taking separate cars since they were going to the same places all day. The air was cool, but the sun was out and warm. It would be a nice day to hang out with friends at Kyle's.

And Melissa would be there. He had mixed emotions. Why had he kissed her? He'd wanted to do it for a long time, but he prided himself on self-control. And kissing her was a bad idea. He told himself that a thousand times. So why had he given in? It had to be something about the normally confident and competent Melissa looking vulnerable that had twisted something in his chest. He wanted to gather her in his arms and protect her.

But that would only end up hurting them both. It wouldn't happen again.

He and Joe waved to people as they walked across the parking lot and onto the church courtyard. They went inside and found Kyle and Heather already saving seats for them. He and Joe slid in. His eyes couldn't help but scan the congregation to spot Melissa.

And there she was, coming down the aisle, her brow furrowed, biting her lip. Something wasn't right. He was on his feet before he even realized it and met her in the aisle. "What's wrong?"

She shook her head. "I'll tell you after church. There's nothing you can do about it now." She plopped into an empty seat.

He eased into the seat next to her. "Now I'll wonder what it is throughout the whole sermon and won't be able to pay attention." He gave her a grin.

She rolled her eyes. "You have no patience."

"On the contrary, I have a full complement of patience."

She met his gaze, her eyes dark and stormy. They were no longer talking about what was upsetting her, and they both knew it.

Breaking eye contact, she pulled out her phone and swiped it open to show him a photo. "This was on my garage door this morning."

His stomach turned to lead. He passed the phone to Kyle who was now interested in their conversation. Kyle's lips thinned into a hard line. He handed the phone back to Melissa.

Ryan, their worship leader, came out front and welcomed everybody. Church was about to begin.

Kyle leaned over. "We'll talk about this after church." He gave Melissa what was meant to be a reassuring smile, but Scott had known Kyle long enough to know there was tension and concern underneath the surface.

It was going to be a long service.

MELISSA STOOD ON KYLE'S PATIO TALKING TO HIM AND Scott about what she found on her garage door that morning. She hadn't been able to keep her mind on the sermon much, though she tried. It didn't help that Scott sat next to her, and she could feel heat radiating off him.

Sarah and Heather were busy setting up food in the kitchen. People were arriving, and Kyle needed to play host, not detective. But she got it. She couldn't shut off work either.

She explained that Danielle had told Gavin she'd left early on Friday. "He's not going to hurt me. He just wants me to butt out. Unfortunately, I can't do that."

"I don't like this at all." Kyle held Melissa's phone, zooming in on the photo. "You have the note in your car?"

She nodded. "I used the edge of my sweater to grab it so my fingerprints shouldn't be on it."

Kyle's eyebrows rose. "Smart thinking. He probably used gloves, and we won't find anything. But it was still good thinking." He handed the phone back to her. "I'll grab an evidence bag and get the note out of the car. Then let's enjoy ourselves and forget about work for a few hours." He squeezed her shoulder and slipped through the patio sliding door back into the house.

She looked up to find Scott's gaze on her. "You okay?" He rubbed her arm in the same spot Kyle had, but his touch felt much different.

"Yeah. I don't want to ruin anyone's party. Plus, Gavin won't hurt me. He thinks of me like a daughter."

Scott didn't say anything, but his gaze turned dark.

Their kiss flitted through her mind. It was a bad idea, but boy did she want to do that again. To forget—just for a few minutes—all the problems that swirled around her and get lost in his touch. "Um, I'm going to find my sister. She should be here any minute." She slipped back inside the house. Being alone with Scott was too dangerous. She wanted too many things that could never happen.

The front door opened just as Melissa headed toward the kitchen, and Allie slipped in. Melissa hurried over to hug her. "It's been too long. We need to do lunch. I have things to catch you up on." She couldn't help her glance out the patio door where Scott stood, watching her.

Allie patted her shoulder, missing where Melissa's gaze had landed. "Yes, we do. I'm going to Arizona to visit Mom next week after Kim is all moved in." She pulled back and lifted her bag of food. "Kitchen with this?"

The front door opened behind them, and a man stepped in who looked familiar, but she couldn't quite place. Broad shouldered like a football player, his dark hair had a wave to it that looked like it could get wild if he let it grow much at all. He must be a friend of Kyle's. He carried himself like a cop.

Allie fumbled her bag, and the man grabbed it. Allie blushed while she gave a winning smile. "Thanks."

Interesting. Allie knew him. And given the blush and the smile, probably had a crush on him. Ah, the joys of knowing everything about her little sister.

"Allie Ellis? Is that you?" The man handed her back the bag of food.

"Yep. Hi, it's been a long time." Allie rocked back on her boot heels, smiling brightly. She must really be uncomfortable.

Melissa gave her sister a discreet nudge.

"Oh, uh, this is my sister, Melissa. Melissa, this is Steve Collins. We went to high school together. I didn't know you were still in the area. I thought you'd gone out of state for college."

She shook Steve's hand. Melissa had gone to a different high school than Allie. Their family had made one of their many moves, and Melissa was determined to finish her senior year at her old school. So she made the forty-five minute drive each way, and Allie started at the local school.

"Nice to meet you, Melissa. You're in Bible study with Kyle, right? I'm his partner." He turned back to Allie. "I did, but I came back after and eventually got hired on at Laguna Vista PD and got stuck working with that guy." He pointed to Kyle who'd just come back inside.

Kyle came over and shook his hand. "Make yourself at home. I'll get some burgers on the grill in a minute."

Allie slipped behind Kyle and turned as if to go to the kitchen, but Kyle squeezed her shoulder. "This one here has been a lifesaver. Somehow she convinced my sister to leave my house and found a perfect place that she can't stop raving about. You should ask her to find you a place so you can stop throwing away your paycheck on rent."

Allie's smile looked so brittle Melissa thought it might break. Really odd. They definitely needed to do lunch.

"Sure. Happy to help." She held up the bag. "Better get the food to the kitchen." She scooted off.

To take any attention off Allie's abrupt exit, Melissa jumped in. "So what are you going to do with Kim's room?"

Kyle shrugged. "That's Heather's department. I just live here."

Melissa smiled. "I see how it is. I'd better go help in the kitchen. Nice to meet you, Steve."

"Same here." He lifted his hand.

Kyle looked between the two of them. "I can't believe you two haven't met before now."

"Yeah, that's odd." She shrugged and headed toward the kitchen. Other people's drama was much more interesting than her own. Which currently stood on the patio, she couldn't help but notice. Joe had joined him out there.

In the kitchen, Heather, Sarah, and Allie were putting food out on plates, but mostly talking. Cait Bellamy was there too, her engagement ring sparkling in the light. Melissa hadn't seen Grayson, Cait's fiancé, but he had to be around someplace.

Melissa snagged a baby carrot and squeezed Cait's shoulder. "You guys set a date yet?"

Cait turned, beaming. "We're thinking March. But it's hard

to find a venue, even with all my connections in the restaurant industry." Cait was a marketing director for Samashima Farms, and their farm-to-table program was a big hit with local restaurants. "I want to do it at my house, but there's just not enough room for a ceremony and reception." She owned a Victorian farmhouse that she had painstakingly restored, and it was gorgeous inside.

"It'll be here before you know it. Lots of details to take care of. Let me know if I can help. I'm good with details." Melissa grinned.

"You might regret that offer."

Melissa laughed as Kim walked in.

"Hey, Kim. Congratulations on your new place." Melissa gave her a hug. "You must be so excited."

"I owe it all to Allie. She convinced me that my own place would be so much better than living with my brother. And since there's an extra bedroom, I can use it as my closet and never again worry about Kyle giving me grief about how many clothes I own."

"The joys of being in the fashion industry." Melissa stole another baby carrot from the tray where Allie studiously laid them out.

"Well, Saturday is the big day. We close this week, right, Allie?" Kim looked over at Allie.

Allie glanced up from the veggies. "Yes. So far there have been no snags, so everything should go as planned."

"Good. Then that means Saturday you all can help me move." She snatched a bite of broccoli from Allie's tray. "I love that my brother has so many strong friends."

The women giggled.

Sarah nudged Heather. "What are you going to do with Kim's room?"

Melissa laughed. "I just asked Kyle that question, and he said to ask you."

Heather shook her head. "It isn't my house."

"Not yet, but soon. You did paint every room in it." Sarah set a bowl of dip on Allie's veggie tray.

"I needed a distraction." Heather had been a witness in a gang initiation robbery gone bad earlier this year and spent a lot of time in protective custody. But she and Kyle seemed stronger than ever. Interesting how difficult circumstances could drive people together or apart.

Melissa glanced out to the patio again. She needed to stop doing that.

Sarah leaned in and lowered her voice. "So, no ring yet. When are you guys going to make it official?"

Heather sighed. "Kyle wants to make sure I can handle being married to a cop. But nothing could be worse than what I already went through. We survived that." She nudged Sarah. "What about you and Joe?"

Sarah shook her head. "It hasn't even been six months. Give it some time." But a faint blush stained her cheeks. "All right, Melissa. Your turn."

"I can't say much, you guys know that from Bible study. But the work situation I asked for prayer about is not getting better. Scott is helping me, but I had to bring Kyle in too."

The kitchen got quiet. Then Heather spoke up. "I'm sorry you have to go through that. If you are in danger, you know you can always stay with either of us. Or Kim, now that she has a place." She grinned at that last bit.

"Thanks. I know you both have been through a lot, so you get it. I don't think I'm personally in any kind of danger. But I'm glad I've got Scott and Kyle to help me work through it."

Sarah reached out and touched her arm. "Just be careful, okay? Things can escalate quickly."

Melissa glanced out the patio door, this time meeting Scott's gaze. "Yes, they certainly can."

Scott missed whatever it was Steve had just said to him. He broke his gaze from Melissa's. She seemed so relaxed and at home with the other women. Of course, she had organized the Bible study that they were all in, so they had a history. But he was glad to see her relax. She needed a break. And even if she didn't think Gavin would hurt her, Scott wasn't so sure. But for now, she was safe and enjoying herself. Monday they would focus on the task at hand and keep the personal to a minimum. His stomach flipped a little at the thought, but it was for the best.

He turned to Steve. "Sorry. What?"

"I was just mentioning to Kyle that I thought it was funny I hadn't run into Allie before now. We went to high school together."

Scott nodded. He needed to do something to keep from staring at Melissa. "Kyle, want me to handle those burgers while you entertain your guests?"

"Sure. I need to get more ice. And we certainly don't want Joe manning the grill."

"Hey, I'm around fire every day!" Joe lunged to swipe the barbecue tongs.

"Doesn't mean you know how to grill." Kyle used his height advantage to move them out of Joe's reach and toss them to Scott. Just like on the basketball court. Suddenly, Scott was itching to play, but it was still off limits. Another thing that frustrated him. And that was his favorite way to blow off steam. Still, shooting free throws would be fine. He hip-checked Joe out of the way and took up his station in front of the grill.

"Hey, Steve. You play basketball?" Scott said over his shoulder.

"Yeah, some. Football was mostly my game back in high school. Got a partial college scholarship. But I like shooting hoops."

Scott nodded. "Kyle probably told you that we took our high school football team to the championships twice. It was a pretty cool experience. But I was the only one who played any college ball." He flipped a few of the burgers. "When the three of us play basketball, we usually have to scramble to get a fourth. We'd have to go easy because of my head." He shot Joe a pointed look.

"As long as we're not playing Ryan, I'm cool."

Ryan was their church worship leader who had briefly dated Sarah before Joe. He and Joe had met on the basketball court, and it had gotten rough. Scott hadn't been there, but he'd heard all about it from Kyle.

"Anyway, think the four of us could shoot some hoops one night?"

Steve nodded. "I'd like that. It'd be a break from the paperwork that usually keeps me occupied."

Kyle slid open the patio door. "More ice for the ice chest. And Scott, Jessica's here." Kyle's gaze narrowed then he turned and dumped the ice into the ice chest.

Scott suppressed a sigh. "I need to see her?"

"Yep." Kyle didn't look up.

Scott handed the tongs to Joe and headed inside. His sister sprawled on Kyle's couch in the den. Drunk. Again. She and Kim were friends mostly because they both wanted to tag along and annoy Scott and Kyle when they were kids. They bonded over torturing their brothers. But whereas Kim had grown up and found a career she loved, Jessica... had not.

Scott sank into the couch next to her. "Why are you here?"

Her heavily made-up eyes slid his way. "Hey, big brother. Kim invited me."

The smell of alcohol washed over him. "Did you drive?"

"How else would I get here?"

Her purse was on the floor next to her feet, keys next to it. He snatched them up.

"Hey!"

He cut his voice low. "You're not driving. Don't you dare put Kyle in that position. Not to mention you're a danger to yourself and everyone else out there. What were you thinking?" Why did he even ask? She wasn't thinking. She never was. She'd hadn't been born yet when Christopher was killed by a drunk driver. Scott had idolized his football-star big brother. And their parents had never been the same since. Of all people, Jessica should know better.

Pushing to his feet, he held out his hand. "Let's go."

She shook her head even as it lay against the couch, her blonde hair flopping in her face. "Nuh uh. I just got here."

"Jessica." He practically growled. "Do not make a scene."

Kim walked into the den, stopped a moment, then pasted on a smile. "Hey, Jessica. Thanks for stopping by." She perched on the arm of the couch and looked at Scott, eyebrows raised.

"I'm taking her home. Sorry."

Kim patted Jessica's shoulder. "Why don't you come see my new place next week? We'll get some pizza and hang out."

Scott mouthed "thank you" and reached for Jessica's hand. This time she didn't resist and let him pull her to her feet. He put his arm around her waist and escorted her toward the door. Once he got her back to his parents', how could he get her in without them knowing? With his dad's heart condition, he wanted to avoid stressing them out when possible.

Also, his car was at Joe's. He could drive Jessica home in her car, but he would still have to get back to Joe's. He wasn't going to ask Kim. This was her party. Same with Kyle.

Melissa came around the corner. By her glance at Jessica and then him, she took in the situation accurately. "Need a hand?"

"Can you get the door?"

"Sure."

"Hey, Kim? Thanks. You've been a good friend to Jessica. Sorry she showed up this way. Will you let Joe and Kyle know? I'll figure out a way to get home."

"I'll drive you," Melissa said. "Let me grab my purse and keys."

Scott started to protest but didn't have the energy. "Thanks."

She disappeared and came back shortly, purse over shoulder. She met Jessica's gaze. "Hey, I'm Melissa. Scott's friend."

"Nice to meet you, 'Lissa."

Outside, Melissa shut the door behind them. "Coffee or sleep?"

Scott stopped. "I hate to have my parents see her like this. They worry, and my dad has a heart condition." He didn't have to add they still worried about him.

She nodded. "She can come to my place. It's not far, we can either dose her up with coffee or let her sleep it off."

"Good plan." They got Jessica in the passenger seat of her car, Scott in the driver's seat. He followed Melissa to her house.

For a woman he was trying to keep at arm's length, she knew every way to get under his skin. Without even trying.

Chapter Eleven

Melissa slipped out of the conference room on their lunch break, her mind barely on the agenda they'd covered. Every Monday morning Gavin ran the meeting of all the vice presidents; today, he'd ignored her. She had little energy for the initiatives covered. Maybe because she had a bad feeling about where the company was headed. She had a team meeting in the afternoon. Tomorrow they'd tackle avionics again, but now, she had a call to make.

She got a hold of Carl Crocker. He must have recognized her name—she had presented at several of the board meetings—and his secretary put her through to him. After a few pleasantries, she got to the point, summarizing what she had learned, careful to keep to the facts as she knew them and not offer speculation. But she didn't need to. Carl had run his own successful business for thirty years. He could see where she was going.

"This is serious stuff. And you haven't talked to Gavin beyond what you told me?"

"No, sir."

"I hate to sandbag a man at his own board meeting."

"That was my feeling too. However, I have concerns for the company's viability that need to be addressed immediately."

His sigh came across the phone. "Yes, I see." He paused. "I'll get you on the agenda. It goes out ahead of the meeting, so if I include your name, Gavin will know something is up. I'll include it as a financial report. That work for you?"

"Yes, sir. Thank you."

"I hope you're wrong about this."

"Me too." Embarrassment in front of the board would be painful, but if it meant that Gavin had a reasonable explanation that he was willing to give to them, she'd endure it if it meant the company was okay. Unfortunately, that wasn't too likely.

She hung up the phone at Danielle's signature knock-and-enter. Danielle carried a take-out bag that she sat on Melissa's desk. "For you, since I didn't think you'd have time to eat."

"You're a lifesaver, as usual." Melissa pulled out a sandwich then reached into her small fridge to pull out a bottle of water.

Danielle leaned against the desk. "How was your weekend? Did you spend time with our yummy pilot friend?"

Melissa's face heated before she could gain her composure, their kiss springing to mind unbidden, as it had been doing far too frequently. No way she could play this off. Danielle had worked with her for too long.

Danielle gasped. "Ooh. Sounds good. Details!"

"Nothing to tell. He helped me after my incident on Friday." She scanned the area beyond her open office door to make sure they were alone, lowering her voice anyway. "So Friday Gavin just came over and asked where I was? I wonder why he didn't have Shari call you."

"Yeah. It was kind of odd. I was surprised he even knew where your office was. He never comes over here. If I hadn't stayed late to finish a few things up, he wouldn't have seen me either."

Maybe he didn't want Shari to know what he was doing. Or Danielle. A chill washed over her. If he wasn't expecting to see Danielle, what was he doing over here? His badge would let him into her office. He had security permissions to be anywhere in the building. Even she didn't have that.

She scanned her office. Nothing looked out of place. Danielle had been here, but he could have come back later. Or even on the weekend. She could ask security about that, if she could think of a good reason to want the info.

On the other hand, if he'd sent the guy to scare her, maybe that was enough. She rubbed her forehead. This was all too much. Right now, they had work to do.

"I'm on the agenda for the board meeting, so we'll see what's up after that."

Danielle squeezed her hand. "Be careful."

"I will."

"I'll let you eat and have a few minutes of silence before the next round of meetings." Danielle scooted out and shut the door behind her. The silence was bliss.

Melissa ate her sandwich and let her mind drift back to yesterday with Scott.

They'd taken Jessica back to Melissa's house, where Jessica proceeded to sleep for two hours on Melissa's couch. She and Scott had watched a movie that she could remember nothing about. Once Jessica woke up and had a cup of coffee and some ibuprofen, Scott drove her back to their folks' house while Melissa followed. He parked Jessica's car in the driveway and got out. Jessica came around and gave him a hug, and then he hopped in Melissa's car.

"You don't need to go in and say hi to your folks?"

"Nah, it'll just raise too many questions." He turned to her. "Thanks for doing this."

"I'm happy to help. You've helped me. It's what friends do." Her voice caught a bit on friends, but she hoped he didn't notice.

He ran his hand through his hair, the curl starting to be more obvious now that it was longer. "Jessica's always been a wild child. Some of it is my parents' fault. They indulge her way too much. I had an older brother, Christopher. Big high school football star. He was so good there was talk of college scholarships and him going pro. He was killed by a drunk driver when he was seventeen, and I was seven. Jessica wasn't even born. It devastated my parents. And then they had Jessica, and I think they just didn't have the heart to discipline her. So I pull her out of scrapes whenever I'm around. When I'm deployed, she usually calls Joe or Kyle. But with as much worry as my parents have about me, they don't need to worry about her. I don't know why she can't see that. It's like she doesn't care about them at all."

He leaned his head against the window.

Melissa reached for his hand. "I know a little bit about that. I've been taking care of my younger siblings most of my life. It's exhausting to have that much responsibility so young."

He'd squeezed her hand, but they'd pulled up in front of Joe's condo. Scott thanked her for her help and said he'd see her on Tuesday.

She'd never gotten that nap she'd wanted, and Scott continued to invade her thoughts. What he shared had drawn them closer together, much more like friends. Which was fine, wasn't it? You could never have too many good friends.

Tomorrow, he'd be here to help them with the avionics again. It was something to see him work with her team. She had to continually remind herself that this was only temporary.

Her phone beeped an alarm. Time for the team meeting. She wadded up her sandwich wrapper and threw it in the trash.

She walked to the conference room, pausing before she entered, watching the team chat and joke around. They all enjoyed team meetings—and each other. They worked well together with very little drama, each excelling at their job. She was proud of them.

Her mind flitted to the board meeting, the financial problems. All of their hard work could be down the drain soon. She looked at each face. They were depending on her for their very jobs and didn't even know it.

She had to do the right thing.

"You ready?" Scott tossed the basketball from hand to hand, relishing the familiar feel of it.

Joe sat on the couch, pulling on his shoes. "Almost. Grab us some waters, will you?"

Scott went to the fridge and pulled out a couple of bottles. He tossed one to Joe.

It had been weird having Joe around the house today, even though it was Joe's house. Scott was used to Joe being at Sarah's most of the time.

Joe hadn't said much about Jessica, other than to ask if Scott and Melissa had gotten her home okay. Jessica had called on Joe and Kyle on occasion when Scott was deployed and unreachable. As much as he hated her bothering his friends, it was better than his folks dealing with her. He didn't know how much they knew about her wild ways or how much they chose to turn a blind eye to. It wasn't something any of them discussed.

"Let's go." Joe held the front door open.

They headed out, walking to the park not too far from Joe's condo complex. It was overcast, but once they got warm, it'd be fine. Kyle and Steve were supposed to meet them there if they didn't run into any emergencies. It'd been a long time since all three of them had played together, though Joe and Kyle shot hoops quite often. Scott hadn't played since before the accident. Seemed like his life was divided into before and after the accident.

Surprisingly, there was an empty court. Joe and Scott shot around a bit, warming up, until Steve and Kyle arrived. They'd never played with Steve before, but it seemed wise to break up Joe and Kyle. They played a little two-on-two with Steve and Kyle against Joe and Scott. It didn't take long for the rhythms to come back. And the memories too. Hot summer nights shooting basketball into the wee hours, bugs flying around the outside lights. The smell of orange blossoms and the songs of crickets.

"Heard from Melissa today?" Kyle asked Scott as he screened him.

Scott dribbled, pivoted, then passed to Joe. "Nope. She had meetings all day. I'll be there tomorrow, though."

Joe went in for a layup, which Steve blocked. He was a better basketball player than Scott had expected. It made for a good game. The guys were going easy, though.

Scott caught the rebound and sank it, then tossed the ball to Kyle.

Kyle dribbled in. "I checked in with vice. There are definitely some drug runners they believe are being backed by terrorists actively working in the area. If her boss's son is mixed up in that, things could get really bad. She won't just get a warning." He passed to Steve.

Joe tried to swipe the ball away. "Ever figure out what was up with the fire alarm?"

"Nope. Just one of many pieces that don't make sense." Scott lunged for the ball just as Steve pivoted away. Scott's foot tangled with Steve's, and Scott landed hard on his hands and knees.

"You okay?" Steve offered him a hand up.

Scott sat back and blinked, took a deep breath. "Yeah, I'm fine." He took Steve's hand and got to his feet.

"Let's take a water break." Joe headed to the bench and grabbed their water bottles, handing one to Scott. "Hands and knees okay?"

Scott looked down. One of his knees was scraped up but not bleeding. He'd taken far worse dives. Why was everyone treating him like he was an old lady? He hated it. "I'm fine." He chugged the water.

Not even a pickup basketball game felt the same. When would he ever get his life back?

Chapter Twelve

Melissa entered her office, Danielle on her heels, and tossed her purse in her desk drawer before grabbing her coffee cup. "Are the bagels ordered for the team?"

"In the conference room waiting for us."

"Excellent as always. What would I do without you?" Melissa nodded toward the door, and they headed to the break room.

Danielle raised her eyebrows. "Let's hope we don't have to find out."

Once they were at the coffee machine, Melissa stuck a mug under the dispenser. "The board meeting agenda went out last night. Any sign of Gavin?" She wasn't sure if Gavin would wonder what the financial update was about or if he even looked at the agenda. But it made her stomach this.

She handed the full mug to Danielle who took and doctored it. "Nope. But it's early. Shari says he doesn't roll in until ten at the earliest, later if he can get a golf or tennis game scheduled."

Melissa filled her own mug and added creme brûlée creamer. She bought the industrial-sized containers at the restaurant supply store and shared them with the office. Based on how quickly they went through the bottles, at least four other people were addicted to the stuff like she was.

They headed back to their offices, and Melissa glanced at her watch. Scott would be here any minute. "Let's assemble in the conference room as soon as everyone gets here. They can start snacking, and we'll begin in fifteen minutes."

Danielle nodded, her phone ringing. She touched a button on her Bluetooth headset. "Send him up. Thanks." She grinned at Melissa. "Your hot pilot is on his way up. I'll send him to your office first." She sashayed away, closing the office door before Melissa could correct her.

Today should be interesting. If she could keep her mind on what they were doing and not the board meeting. Or Scott. A knock sounded on her office door. She wiped her hands on her pencil skirt and pulled the door open. As if she had conjured him with her thoughts... Scott. Looking devastatingly handsome with a navy button down that made his eyes glow.

"Good morning." She stepped back and let him enter.

"Morning. Meeting in your office today?" His eyes skimmed her up and down, a grin tipping his lips.

She closed the door behind him. She'd rather flirt with him than tell him what she was going to. "We have a few minutes before we join the others. I asked Danielle about what Gavin had said Friday." She repeated what Danielle had told her. "I can't shake the creepy feeling that Plan A was to get in my office. Why would he walk over here? He never does that."

Scott scanned her office, poked behind things, lifted a few items. He pointed to the lock on her cabinet. "Does he have a key to that?"

"No, only I do. And that's where the invoices are."

Scott shook his head. "This feels like something bigger going on here than some missing money and a spoiled kid."

"I know. I just wish I knew what. I called Carl Crocker, the board member that I have the best relationship with, on Monday. It was an unofficial call, just feeling him out for what the board might think and want to know. He was pretty interested in what I had to say and got me on the agenda for the next meeting."

"When's that?"

"Tomorrow. I feel like I should give Gavin a heads up. I'd hate to be blindsided in a meeting. But at the same time, that doesn't feel like the wise thing to do."

"Don't tip your hand. Information is powerful, and right now that's all you have going for you. Look what happened to you after the last time you tried to talk with him. Kyle told me yesterday he got confirmation about a drug gang working in the area that has ties to terrorism." He took ahold of her hand. "You have got to be careful. These guys don't play around."

She squeezed his hand. "I'm just going to the board. I'll let them decide what happens next. That's all I owe to this company." She glanced toward the door, thinking of her team. "I just hate to see it blow back on my team. They're the best, and they deserve to keep their jobs." She sighed. "Speaking of which, we'd better get in the conference room. I wouldn't want to keep you from the world's best bagels." She grinned.

THE MORNING FLEW BY. FOR THE FIRST TIME IN A LONG while, Scott felt in the groove, contributing and purposeful. Even his dull, nagging headache couldn't distract him. They were making progress, and it was because of his contributions. Melissa had given them a fifteen-minute break, and he used it to text Jessica. She was supposed to be in class at cosmetology school. It was the third or fourth thing she'd tried. He couldn't keep up. He'd always wanted to be a pilot, so he had little patience for her dithering around. Why couldn't she just settle down and be responsible?

He sent the text and then studied Melissa as she talked to some of her team. They respected her, and she was a good boss.

She listened to their concerns and kept everyone on track. She'd been a huge help yesterday with Jessica. No one outside Kyle, Joe, and Kim knew about Jessica's antics. He'd been reluctant to let Melissa in. But she kept surprising him with how much she understood his situation.

Now he had to help her with hers. There were a lot of pieces here that didn't make sense. And if he didn't have this nagging headache... He swallowed some Dr Pepper from the vending machine. It had been his first line of attack on the headache, hoping the caffeine and sugar would wash it away. Now he could only hope it would get him through lunch.

He left Melissa's problem for a moment and reviewed the avionics programming they'd been going through. Something didn't jive. But the answer floated just outside of his reach. He rubbed his eyes.

A warm hand on his shoulder made him look up. Melissa. She eased into the chair next to him. "Head hurt?"

He shrugged. "Not too bad. I'll be fine." He'd been through worse, and Melissa didn't need to worry about him.

She handed him a bottle of ibuprofen. "This should help. I can't tell you how invaluable your help has been to us. Your insight and perspective has cut through so much paperwork and the bureaucratic party line that we can finally make some progress. You're very good at this." She held his gaze for a minute, those beautiful brown eyes focused on him. For a moment, he forgot his head hurt.

"I know your plan is to go back to the Navy. And I'm sure you're an amazing pilot." She smiled. "You're so good at every-thing you do." She pressed her lips together. "But if that isn't an option for you at some point, or you want to do something different, I'd want you on my team in a heartbeat. You're an asset to any group."

His chest tightened, emotions warring. Anger, because of course he was going back to flying. There was no question about that. But also pride that she saw how good he was and wanted him on her team. For a moment he held that image of them working together, a thousand mornings just like this one. Them working together to solve problems and do great things that impacted so many people. Just like that summer he and Kyle and Joe had run that camp for those underprivileged kids.

It could never be. It was a beautiful dream, but their paths were too different. He reached for her hand. "Thanks. That means a lot coming from you. You have a great team here. It's a pleasure being here and being useful."

She held his gaze a second longer then nodded. Standing, she moved to the front of the room. "Okay, let's get settled back in and pick up where we left off."

He popped open the bottle and swallowed two pills, washing them down with the soda.

The rest of the team found their seats, and they began. Scott engaged, but his mind was somewhere else. If the ibuprofen would kick in, he'd be able to think. But the pain was becoming more of a distraction. He rubbed his eyes, trying to get them to focus.

Melissa glanced his way a few times, and he saw the brief furrow of her brow. He didn't want her to worry about him. He just needed to make it to lunch.

When Melissa finally called a break for lunch, he let out a sigh. His shirt stuck to his back from sweat, even though the room was cool. He hoped no one would notice. Maybe he could go lie down in his car. A few minutes with his eyes closed...

Melissa's hand landed on his shoulder. He knew her touch, could smell her faint vanilla perfume.

"I have a lunch date with Allie. Family drama." She rolled her eyes. "But Danielle can order something in for you, and you are welcome to lie down on my office couch if you'd like. Or you can take the afternoon off if you need to."

He started to shake his head but winced at the pain. He wasn't quitting, and he definitely didn't want Melissa to think he was weak. "I'm fine. Lying down sounds good. I'm sure if I close my eyes for a few minutes, I'll be fine." He got to his feet and followed Melissa to her office.

"Lunch order?"

"Same thing we had last week—minus the bonus side salad —would be fine." He gave her a wobbly grin.

She gave his order to Danielle then motioned to the couch. "It's all yours. I've taken more than a few naps on it in my time. It's surprisingly comfortable. Do you want an ice pack?"

He eased onto the couch and then laid back. Getting horizontal helped. "This is good. Thanks."

She was quiet then turned off the lights. The room dimmed, light filtering in only through the tinted windows. "Danielle also has access to this office. She'll bring your lunch in."

He turned his head. "Thanks, Melissa. You're a lifesaver."

She winked. "Sweet dreams."

He settled in, closing his eyes. The air conditioning intake vent was just to the side of the couch, where his head was. The in-rush of air as it kicked on would probably keep him from sleeping. On the other hand, it was nothing compared to sleeping below the deck of an aircraft carrier when it was launching planes.

Something he sure hoped he'd experience again.

———

MELISSA SAT IN THE BOOTH ACROSS FROM ALLIE AND stirred the ice around in her glass with her straw. Was Scott okay? Hopefully his nap would help, but the tight lines around his mouth and the beads of sweat on his forehead said far more about his pain than he admitted. She needed his help, but not at his expense. Maybe she should tell him to go home and not come anymore. The toll on his body was getting to be too high.

She'd done a bit of research on traumatic brain injuries. She didn't know how severe his was, but obviously significant enough to keep him from work and give him continual headaches. Likely the headaches were because he was helping her with the avionics testing. It was too much too soon. But he wanted to. He needed to clear his name. And she knew there was no way she could dissuade him. She just hoped it didn't make things worse and delay his return to duty. As much as she enjoyed spending time with him, she knew his true love was flying.

"So it is true." Allie's voice finally broke through Melissa's thought.

"What is?"

Her little sister grinned at her. "That you're in love with that cute pilot. You haven't heard a word I said."

Her face heated, and she took a bite of her Mexican chicken salad, shaking her head. "No, we're friends, helping each other. I am worried about him, though. But tell me about your trip to see Mom."

"She's working at an art gallery now. Seems to like it. Now is the big tourist season, so she's keeping busy. And Matthew and Brittany seem to like living out there. Daniel's got a girlfriend who's really sweet."

"I should go visit. As soon as this avionics testing is wrapped up." Guilt flooded her. She didn't visit their mom as often as she should. Didn't talk to her on the phone even as much as she should. They lived such different lives. Polar opposites. It seemed like Allie served as the ambassador between their two worlds. But there was always so much to be done, and Melissa had carried the load for far too long that her mother should have. Not a subject she wanted to revisit.

"I think she's going to remarry."

"What?" Melissa dropped her fork.

"She's been pretty serious with this guy for a while. Longer than any of her other boyfriends."

"I haven't even met him."

"That's why I'm going to go visit. You should too."

"You can bring me back the reconnaissance report." She

didn't want to think about it. "Speaking of which, talk to me about Steve. Is that *the* Steve from high school?" Allie had had a crush on Steve all throughout their school years, but Steve only seemed to treat her as a friend.

The pink in Allie's cheeks told Melissa all she needed to know.

"He's Kyle's partner. You're helping Kyle's sister. Seems like it was bound to happen. Maybe you two can make up for lost time."

"I was completely caught off guard. I don't think Kim ever mentioned his name, and why would she? I'm just happy she likes the cute condo we found for her. It's just perfect. She's happy; Kyle's happy. I wonder if he and Heather will get married now." Allie went back to eating her enchilada.

"Way to change the subject." Melissa grinned. "Still, now that he knows you're around, maybe you guys can reconnect."

"Not holding my breath on that one. He probably already has a girlfriend."

Silence fell over them. It was mostly companionable, but they both clearly had a lot on their minds. They finished up their lunches. She needed to get back to the office and check on Scott. Plus, she hoped they could narrow down the problem further. The plane hadn't responded the way it should. She believed Scott, and that report was consistent with a smattering of other gripe reports they'd gotten, none as severe as his. But what was causing that?

Allie's shoulder bumped her as they exited the restaurant. "I'll let you know when I firm up the dates with Mom, okay? But think about coming. Even just over the weekend."

"I will try. But with this big project at work, I can't promise anything." The avionics, Gavin, her creepy stalker. So many things she couldn't talk about.

"It's always work." Allie softened her words with a grin.

But Melissa was still turning them over in her head when she pulled into the parking lot at work.

"Scott? Scott." Someone was shaking his shoulder, making his head rattle. A vanilla scent floated over him. Melissa. He pried open his eyes. The lights were still off in the office, but a bag and a drink sat on the table. How had they gotten there?

"Hey." Melissa knelt on the floor next to the couch. "Sorry to wake you. Danielle said you didn't stir when she brought in lunch. Do you want to head home?"

He started to shake his head, but the stabbing made that a bad idea. Plus, if he was still, the image floating in his brain just out of reach might come to him. He'd had nightmares during his nap, but they were different, like another piece of the puzzle was sliding in from the side, but just out of visual range.

It was no use. He eased up. And immediately lurched to the trash can. He hadn't eaten anything since breakfast, but his stomach heaved up the Dr Pepper.

Melissa left the room. He didn't blame her. Some knight in shining armor he was turning out to be.

A minute later she reappeared, a wet towel in her hand. "Here. This will help. As soon as you're ready, I'm taking you home."

"No. You need to work with the team. Just give me a minute. I'll be fine." He wiped his mouth with the wet cloth. There was something just out of reach, something they were discussing earlier today that showed up in his dream. It felt like it was the answer. But with this pain, he couldn't think straight.

"I already gave them their assignments for the rest of the afternoon. We've got plenty to work on. We're in the ballpark. We know it has something to do with the air data inertial reference unit. Jeremy will be analyzing code all afternoon." She slid her purse strap over her shoulder. "Ready to make it downstairs?"

"Yeah." He levered himself up from the couch. "Any word from Gavin?"

"No. I don't expect there to be. We'll see what happens tomorrow at the board meeting." Her hand rested on his arm. Her touch was surprisingly comforting, but something he shouldn't need.

He slipped on his sunglasses before leaving the office. Sliding into her Audi, he reminded himself that they had done this before. Except last time he was a jerk. This time he was just weak. Neither of which would help them solve their respective problems. In this condition, he couldn't protect her against Gavin or his hired help.

Leaning his head back against the headrest, he closed his eyes until they got to Joe's. He hadn't had a headache this bad since the early days of his recovery. It must have been the fall he'd taken last night playing basketball.

He couldn't do anything anymore. Not his job, not play basketball, not help his friend. Not even remember what happened in the accident and clear his name.

Defeat hung on him like a cape, and it looked nothing like Superman's.

Chapter Thirteen

Melissa ran through the files and information on her computer one more time. She was ready to present her findings to the board. No recommendations, however. Just a hope that they would take everything she told them under advisement and possibly do more research into the situation on their own. Mostly she hoped that Gavin would admit to what was going on, and that they could find a solution that worked for all of them.

She glanced down at her broken desk drawer. When she'd come in this morning, it was skewed open. Someone had wedged a thin blade against the drawer and the desk frame and pried open the drawer. The very drawer that held the invoices. Which were now gone.

Security had no card swipes registering on her door from the time she had entered at lunch and then left again to take Scott home. But oddly enough, security footage of her team's work area had ended after seven p.m. and had not resumed until four a.m. Deliberate tampering, but by who? And eerily close to what happened around the fire alarm CCTVs.

She'd talked to Kyle, mostly to bounce ideas off of him. It was essentially an internal matter, unless she could prove otherwise. But she wanted someone outside this building to know what was going on. Just in case. In case of what, she wasn't sure. But too much was going on. Once she made her presentation to the board, though, more people would know. More eyes on the situation might turn something up. Or at least put a stop to it.

Sighing, she closed her laptop, made sure she had her purse, and headed to the boardroom. During the day, Danielle was usually out front in her office and someone would have to get past her to get to Melissa's office. But it was after hours, so no one should be around this part of the building. Still, she didn't trust leaving anything in her office, especially if no one was around.

She pulled out her phone to double check it was set to vibrate. How was Scott doing? She'd texted him a few times and only gotten a terse response. Joe had been at work when she dropped Scott off yesterday. Maybe she shouldn't have left him alone, even though he insisted he was fine.

She'd texted Joe what had happened, feeling a bit like she was going behind Scott's back. Joe had reassured her that he'd check in on him and thanked her for keeping him in the loop.

Slipping her phone back in her purse, she tried to push Scott out of her mind and focus on her task at hand. After the board meeting, she'd check in with Scott under the excuse of updating him on what happened. Though she wished she could see him in person, talk to him. See for herself how he was doing.

And yet, what exactly would happen when he went back on duty? She couldn't keep running to him. He was convenient because she could talk to him about the avionics issue and the problems at work. But more that, she was attracted and intrigued by his depth, beyond his charming flyboy exterior. If she didn't watch herself, she'd fall hard for him. That just couldn't happen.

She made her way to the boardroom, where many of the board members gathered around getting drinks and snacks before the meeting began. She greeted the ones she knew, grabbed a bottle of water, and found her seat. Printed agendas were at every place, and Shari bustled around the room, making sure everyone had everything they needed. She smiled at Melissa and said hi, but the strain around her eyes warned Melissa that Gavin knew something was up and wasn't happy about it.

Carl came over and patted her on the shoulder. "I've talked to a few others, and there's a real concern here. They're looking forward to what you have to say." He glanced around. "You should know that I did give Gavin a heads-up about today."

Her eyes widened, and her mouth parted. Acid swirled in her stomach.

"Now, don't worry. I didn't tell him everything, just that there were some concerns about the finances, some irregularities you had uncovered and wanted to bring to the board's attention so we could make a decision on it. If he had relevant info, he should be prepared to share it."

"But what if—" Her mind went to her destroyed desk and the missing invoices.

"The man has a right to defend himself and to not get sand-bagged. I'd expect him to do the same for me."

She nodded, and Carl found his seat. The old boys' network was alive and well. She knew she'd be going up against some element of that coming to the board. But still, she thought they'd put the company's safety first. On the other hand, if a man was presenting the case, maybe they would. She pushed the thoughts from her mind. She'd dealt with this before, she could do it again.

She successfully kept from fidgeting through the other items on the agenda, scrolling through all the evidence in her mind, the possible objections or other explanations for it. Bottom line, she didn't have to convince anyone. That wasn't her job. She just wanted to warn them. After that, she could wash her hands of the whole thing. She and her team would get the avionics working right, and they could all move on.

Though her relationship with Gavin was beyond repair, it hurt. It was painful to see your heroes crumble.

Shari's voice penetrated her thoughts. "Next on the agenda, Vice President of Operations, Melissa Ellis."

Melissa pushed to her feet, her legs suddenly wobbly. She grabbed her laptop and carried it over to the podium and plugged it into the Ethernet cable and the external screen cable. All eyes were on her, and she concentrated on getting the information pulled up from where she had minimized it earlier. She watched the big screen as her computer connected.

"Thanks for letting me present today. I have run across some financial irregularities that I wanted to bring to your attention. First, a bit of background. Two weeks ago, Mr. Broadstone asked me to investigate the significant loss of money we had been experiencing, to track it down and fix whatever the problem was. This was not an unusual request. As Vice President of Operations, I've often tracked down problems and created solutions. This search led me to the discovery of this project headed up by Trent Broadstone."

She clicked on her computer to bring up the project management screen. The project was no longer there. Or her permissions had been removed. Heat rushed to her face. What was going on? She'd checked everything just for this reason. "Excuse me. I had this up just a moment ago. I'm not sure what's wrong."

She caught Gavin's eye as she turned back to her computer. His arms were crossed, and he smirked. This was deliberate. Hot anger surged through her. But it wouldn't do to lose her calm. That would play right into his hands. She clicked a few more places but couldn't do troubleshooting on the fly with a restless audience. "I'm not sure what the problem is, but let me just tell you what I discovered. This project had no deliverables but an extensive amount of invoices charged against it. I received copies of those invoices and saw they had been countersigned by Ga— Mr. Broadstone since the amounts were large enough to require two signatures by senior staff. When I asked Mr. Broadstone about the invoices, he didn't have much to say about them and redirected the conversation to my department. I'm concerned that the money is being used for personal purposes and is putting the company on shaky financial footing."

Rumblings went around the table, and Shari called for order in a voice Melissa had never heard her use before. "If you would like the floor, please indicate so. Otherwise, keep side conversations down. I can't properly record when everyone is talking."

Melissa almost smiled.

Carl spoke up. "I think these are some serious allegations. We've all known Melissa long enough, and she's done a great good for our company. There's no reason to believe she's making this up." He turned to Gavin. "Do you have some explanation for her findings?"

Gavin looked around the table. "Part of what we love about Melissa is that she's so detail oriented. She is able to find every little problem and run it down." He gave a condescending laugh. "But we all know we have to spend money to make money. Trent has some unusual projects he's pursuing that could pay big dividends. But I don't think anything I've seen warrants the kind of panic Melissa is bringing in here. Which is what I tried to tell her when she came to me. She needs to focus on the avionics program for the Navy. If that falls apart, then we've got big problems. Possibly the stress is getting to her, or she feels like she's in over her head and is looking for excuses for her potential failure." He looked at Melissa. "If that's what's really going on here, then you owe it to your company, your team, and yourself to step down and let someone competent handle it before you ruin it for everyone."

So many words surged to Melissa's brain she couldn't even pick where to begin. The very nerve of him. He was slick. She'd seen him do this to competitors. She never thought he'd do it to her. Now who had been sandbagged?

"The avionics program has its challenges, but we are making

good progress. That's really beside the point and has nothing to do with the missing money. I'd like to suggest that I meet with finance and we bring more detailed information to the next meeting." She glanced at Carl who nodded. "If I'm wrong, we've only wasted a bit of time. But if I'm right, the company is in serious danger." She returned to her seat. There was nothing else she could do.

Carl spoke again. "I motion to table the financial discussion until the next meeting when Ms. Ellis can meet with finance and provide us with more details."

"I second that." Board member Joseph Nelson raised his hand.

Melissa nodded, relief making her weak. She gathered her things and slipped out of the boardroom. In the hallway, she leaned against the wall and steadied her breathing. She'd been set up. But how to prove it? And how could she keep the company from failing?

She headed down using the stairs, wanting to bleed off the adrenaline. Her phone buzzed, and she glanced at her watch to see the alert.

A text from Scott. **How did it go?**

A spark of pleasure lit in her chest. He remembered. But the answer would require a phone call. She could make it from the car. Security would walk her out. There was no telling what could happen next. Especially since she hadn't heeded the warning to stay out of it. She didn't think a broken desk drawer was all that the person warning her had in mind.

Down in the marble-lined lobby, she strode toward the security desk. "Hey, George. How's it going tonight?"

His smile lit up his face. He always had such a peace about him. "Hey, Ms. Ellis. It's been a nice, quiet evening. Just the way I like it."

"Good to hear. Has Trent Broadstone left for the day, or is he still here by chance? I just left the boardroom, and I wondered if he was waiting for his dad." *Or sabotaging my car or office.*

George punched in keys at his terminal. "Looks like he left around four this afternoon. Early day."

So he wasn't here when her computer files were tampered with. Though he could have gotten in on the VPN, the virtual private network, and done it remotely. Or Gavin could have done it easily.

"Thanks. Would you mind walking me to my car or have someone do it? Just feeling a little jittery." She gave a weak smile. In all her years here, she'd never asked for an escort to her car. Even when George offered after she'd stayed until two a.m. Which was why he'd presented her with the brochure on a self-defense class.

"Sure thing." He put a call in on his radio. "As soon as Doug is here, I'll walk you myself." If her request surprised him, he didn't show it.

"I'd appreciate that." She sent Scott a quick text. **I'll call you from the car. Leaving in a few minutes.**

Have security walk you out. Came back the quick reply.

Already asked. Way ahead of you, flyboy.

Doug entered the lobby, and George came around the desk. They headed outside where he switched his Maglite on, even though the parking lot was well lit. Once they reached her car, he shined the light all around it and inside. "Looks like you're good to go."

"Thanks, George. You have a good night."

"You too." He stood next to her car until she pulled out of the lot. Relief washed over her when she was able to get on Bake Parkway without incident. She thought about George's peace. *Lord, I need some of that. I know I've been relying on my own strength far too much. Please give me direction on what to do. And please heal Scott. I know he loves flying more than anything. Help me be a good friend to him and keep my emotions in check.*

Then she voice-dialed Scott.

SCOTT HUNG UP THE PHONE AND STARED AT IT FOR A minute before placing a pizza order via the app. Inviting Melissa over didn't fall under his plan to keep her at a safe distance. He'd successfully not texted her all day except a couple of quick replies to her inquiries. But he had to know how her presentation to the board went. And then… he just couldn't let her go home to an empty house after what had happened. That's what friends did, right?

Plus, as much as he didn't want to admit it to himself, he could use her company. He'd gone to the eye doctor today to have his vision checked, thinking that could be what was triggering his migraines. But now he was going to have to wear glasses. Hopefully just temporarily to help with the headaches. If his eyes didn't have to strain, then it should reduce the trigger.

Because he couldn't be a pilot if his eyesight was less than perfect.

Melissa's words had been floating in his head all day. *I know your plan is to go back to the Navy. And I'm sure you're an amazing pilot. You're so good at everything you do. But if that isn't an option for you at some point, or you want to do something different, I'd offer you a job in a heartbeat. You're an asset to any team.*

It'd been a long time since anyone had so honestly acknowledged his talents, and it felt good. Especially coming from Melissa. The vision of them working together intruded in his thoughts throughout the day. Someday, maybe after he retired…

Another vision floated on the heels of this one. One of Kyle, Joe, and him treating a bunch of sweaty, underprivileged kids to Popsicles after football camp. The grins on their faces, the sense of satisfaction and teamwork. It'd been a long time since he'd felt something like that. Until he started helping Melissa.

Why did life have to be so complicated?

The doorbell rang, and he opened it to Melissa looking every inch the polished professional in her skirt and heels. But her troubled eyes told a different story. And he was grateful he knew her well enough to see it.

Without thinking, he pulled her into his arms. Her arms immediately went around his waist. Vanilla floated up to his nose, and for a moment everything felt right.

But this was a bad idea. What was he thinking? She needed this, he reasoned. She'd had a bad day. And so had he. So for a moment, he'd enjoy the warmth of her pressed against him. This he could do for her.

She pulled back and gave him a wobbly grin. "Thanks. Been a rough day." She moved over to the couch and plopped down just as the doorbell rang again. Pizza.

Scott got the pizza and took it to the kitchen, getting out plates, drinks. The normalcy of this helped steady him, getting him back on his feet. Because he had not wanted to let Melissa go. Ever. The thought was like a punch to the gut, and he worked to make sure it didn't show.

He handed her a slice of pizza and a bottle of water. He sat in the recliner across from her. A safe distance. "Sorry you had such a rough day. I'd hoped to be there to offer you moral support at least."

She swallowed her bite of pizza and waved his comment away. "It's fine. You've got a lot going on yourself." She put down the rest of her pizza and pushed it away. "You know, I don't mind going up against the board and not really being trusted. I'm used to that. What bothers me is that every time that's happened in the past, Gavin had been there supporting me. Today, he was against me, and Carl was supporting me. The fact that Gavin threw me under the bus has been hard to swallow. I thought before that it was just Trent clouding his judgment. But I never thought he'd turn on me. It feels a lot like I've lost a father figure."

She rubbed her hands over her face, hiding tears he heard in her voice. His heart twisted, and it took everything he had to stay in his chair. He leaned forward and touched her knee.

"Hey. You're one of the strongest people I know. You'll get through this. Even Carl can see it. You will survive and come out stronger on the other side. I know it." He believed in her, even if she couldn't believe in herself in this moment.

She looked up, watery eyes meeting his. Her hand covered his where it rested on her knee. "Thanks. That means a lot. I think you of all people can understand what it's like to go through a huge roadblock in your career." She gave him a soft smile.

His chest twisted again, and all he wanted to do was leap over to the couch and kiss her senseless until she forgot all her problems. And he forgot his. But that would only make both of their problems worse.

He leaned back in his chair. "We need to do something fun this weekend."

"Aren't we helping Kim move?"

He frowned. "I said something fun. Kim has like three boxes. It won't take any time at all."

"Have you seen her closet?"

"How many clothes can one person have?"

Melissa laughed. "You clearly don't spend much time in women's closets."

"Um, no." He pointed to her plate. "You finished?"

"Yeah." She stood just as he did, bringing her face level with his chin. She looked up at him, and for a moment all he could think about was having this night every night. The two of them eating dinner, talking about their day.

She wet her lips, and he about groaned, the image of their previous kiss flashing through his mind. It had been a mistake, but it sure hadn't felt like it.

Swallowing, he turned and went to the kitchen.

Chapter Fourteen

Melissa pulled up to Kyle's house, checking to see if Scott's 'vette was here. Not yet. Good. She swiped her hands down her jeans. The sun was playing tag with the clouds, but it was supposed to be mid-sixties today, a great day to move. She grabbed a bag of bagels from the seat next to her and hurried inside. She got here early to meet Heather on the pretense of getting Kim's clothes moved to her condo before the actual moving took place.

In reality, she wanted to avoid Scott. They'd worked together the rest of the week, friendly, but professional. After she'd practically thrown herself at him Wednesday night, no wonder he was keeping his distance. They were just friends.

She rang the doorbell, and Heather opened it. "Hey, thanks for helping us get a head start on things."

Melissa lifted the bag. "Sure. And I brought sustenance. I hope you have coffee."

"Even got your favorite creme brûlée creamer."

Melissa gave her a side hug. "You're a good friend."

They went into the kitchen and began fixing bagels and coffee. Heather eyed her. "Sounds like you need a friend, especially these days?"

Melissa looked around.

"Don't worry. Kim's doing a few last-minute things at her condo with Allie, and Kyle is out getting boxes."

Melissa blew on her coffee and took a sip. "Things aren't going well at work. I went to give a presentation to the board, and all my data was missing. My boss deliberately threw me under the bus. And Scott and I—"

Heather raised her eyebrows.

"Well, he's been helping me, which is great. But I think the work is making his head injury worse. He's been having bad migraines and had to order glasses to help."

Heather winced.

"Yeah."

"None of those guys take any perceived weakness well. But Scott hasn't shut you out, has he?"

Melissa shook her head. "Yes, no. I don't know. I went over there Wednesday after my presentation, and I was upset. He was comforting and encouraging. I think I scared him off."

Heather laughed. "Scared is not a word that goes with Scott Blake. I've seen how he looks at you. But the two of you do have an interesting situation. I can see him being afraid of getting too involved with you, because once he goes back on duty, he's stationed three hours from here." She touched Melissa's shoulder. "But if you two truly have something special, every obstacle can be overcome. Careers come and go, but matters of the heart are forever."

Melissa started to sip on her coffee then stopped. Maybe there was a solution that she couldn't see. "I never thought Gavin would turn on me. If you'd asked me a month ago, I'd have said you were crazy." She dumped the rest of the coffee in the sink. "I like plans. I like to know what's going to happen. Letting things hang loosely and seeing what develops is hard for me."

Heather nodded. "I know. I so admire your planning skills. And I know how I felt when my life was turned upside down earlier this year. My advice is to trust God. Cling to him. He knows what the future holds, and no matter how it looks at any particular moment, it is for your good."

Melissa leaned over and gave Heather a hug. "Thanks. I needed that. Now, let's tackle Kim's closet before the guys get here and start making comments about her wardrobe resembling a department store."

"I've found her extensive collection of clothes and accessories quite helpful to borrow from." Heather sighed. "I'm going to miss having such easy access."

"It's a good thing you and Kim get along so well."

Heather slid open Kim's closet. "She reminds me of my sisters, who I don't get to see often enough."

They spent the next hour loading Kim's closet into both of their cars, laying the clothes stacked high across the backseats. They got most of her closet into the two cars, and Melissa followed Heather over to Kim's house, leaving just as Joe and Scott pulled up in Joe's truck. Melissa waved.

Scott rolled down his window. "Leaving so soon?"

She stuck her thumb toward the back seat. "Taking a load over already. We've been working hard while you guys were sleeping in. Bagels are on the kitchen counter." She grinned and followed Heather down the street.

In just a few minutes, they pulled up to a condo complex. It was small, but it was well maintained with a greenbelt between buildings and a walking path. Grabbing a load of clothes from the back seat, she followed a similarly laden Heather upstairs to the second floor.

"Good thing we don't have to get much furniture up here." Melissa panted as they reached the open door.

"*We* don't have to do anything. That's what the guys are for."

"Hey, ladies, come on in." Kim practically bounced as she held the door. "Follow me." Across an empty, wood-laminate floor which must be the living area, Kim showed them a short hallway and pointed to the right. "This room is my dressing room."

They deposited the clothes on the closet rack, managing to not lose too many hangers. Outside the room and down the hallway was a second bedroom. Both had attached baths. Off the living area was a small eat-in kitchen. There was a balcony with just enough room for a bistro set, and the surrounding mature trees made it feel a bit like a tree house.

"Once you get your touches in here, it will be so cute!" Heather surveyed the space. "Allie, you did a great job."

Melissa, arms now free, stepped over to hug her sister. "Good job, sis."

"My pleasure. This place really is perfect for Kim." She nudged Kim. "And it helped that Kyle had saved up the Kim Fund so she had a good down payment."

"Ah yes, the Kim Fund. Which almost had to be used to fund my protection." Heather shivered. "So glad, for multiple reasons, that that didn't have to happen. Your big brother is a pretty cool guy."

"I know. He told me he was saving all the rent I was paying him so I could have a down payment, but I didn't really believe him." Kim grabbed Heather's arm. "You can help paint, like you did Kyle's house. It'll be great. I'll help bring up the next load of clothes. Did the guys see?"

Melissa smiled at the energy bouncing off of Kim as she jumped from topic to topic. "Scott and Joe pulled up as we were leaving. They saw clothes in the back, but I don't think anything registered but the bagels I mentioned."

"Sounds about right." Kim skipped down the stairs ahead of them. They made one more trip each, and the cars were empty.

"I'll stay here to direct the guys when they come. You know what they should bring, right?" Kim looked at Heather.

"Everything in your room."

"Yep. The fridge is getting delivered today." She clapped her hands. "I'm so excited to have my own place."

When Melissa returned to her car, she was still smiling. She picked up her phone to see if she had any calls or messages while she was inside. There was one, a text from an unknown number. She clicked on it.

And her stomach dropped to her feet.

SCOTT WAS SHOVING A BOX IN THE BACK OF JOE'S TRUCK when Melissa drove up. She climbed out of her car, scanned the area, and hurried over to him, arms wrapped around herself. What could have happened?

He met her on the lawn. "What's wrong?"

She pushed her phone at him. A series of pictures greeted him, which at first didn't make sense. He frowned. Melissa leaving the office, entering her townhome, entering Joe's condo. Her and Scott sitting in her car. A photo of them eating lunch at the lake.

The coffee he had earlier turned to acid in his stomach. He'd hoped the board meeting was the end of it. Gavin won. Melissa's fears had been discounted and dismissed. In a way, he'd been glad there was nothing to show the board, no proof. It should have all gone away.

"Where'd this come from?" He caught Kyle's eye and waved him over.

"A text. But I don't know who sent it."

Kyle came over, and Scott handed him the phone. "Melissa got these today via text. Just now?"

She nodded.

He slid his arm around her shoulders and pulled her close, shutting down the part of his brain that told him this was a bad idea. He was in this now. His picture was there with hers, so whoever was after her knew about him too. Was it his imagination or did she melt into him?

"There's something else you should know." She looked up at

him. "I talked to Danielle about the missing files for my presentation. She has everything—screenshots and all—on a jump drive. I could go back to the board. I'm supposed to—"

Scott shook his head. "No, Melissa. I think you just need to drop it. Look where it's getting you. Escalating threats and warnings. Next time, whoever this is, is going to act. If Gavin wants to run his company into the ground, let him." He turned her to face him, holding onto her shoulders, running his hands up and down her arms. "Remember what you told me, that I had other options? You do too. It's not worth it."

Tears welled in her eyes. "If it were just me, I could walk away. But what about my team? They're relying on me. They need their jobs. Danielle is supporting her mom after her dad died. Marla is a single mom. Jeremy—no one would appreciate his genius and his quirkiness. I could go on and on. These were a group of misfits that had no one to believe in them until they became my team. I can't let them down." Tears spilled out of her lashes, and she swiped them away.

He sighed and pulled her close. "We'll think of something. But for now, let's let them think they've won. Make it look like you've given up. We've got plenty on our plate with the avionics testing."

She nodded, her head rubbing against his jaw.

A car door shut behind them. He looked, cursing himself for standing out here on the lawn with her. But it was just Steve Collins, Kyle's partner. Interesting that he showed up to help, considering how little Kim had to move. Scott pulled away from Melissa.

Kyle handed her phone back to her. "Don't do anything on that phone. We'll talk later." He strode across the lawn to shake Steve's hand, and the two of them headed inside.

"Stash your phone in the glovebox of your car and lock it up. Let's try to put it out of your mind right now. Nothing can be done anyway."

She nodded and did what he said.

Scott planned the next maneuver. He needed to talk to Kyle, but this was not the place. Besides, Melissa needed to get her mind off this, or she would stew about it all weekend. "Let's get finished up here then do something fun."

She raised her eyebrows but said nothing. They finished moving everything out of Kim's room, including the fancy chandelier light fixture. It all fit in the back of Joe's and Kyle's trucks. The room was completely empty.

Kyle slapped him on the shoulder. "Kim promised us all pizza, even though it's barely lunch time."

"Good. Because I have an idea."

Chapter Fifteen

Melissa looked around as all nine of them stood in Kim's empty living area eating pizza. It could barely be considered lunch time, and Kim had to wait a few minutes for the pizza place to open before she could even place their order. But how wonderful she had so many friends to help out.

"So, Kim," Scott started. "Since we all cleared our schedules for the day to help you move and were so efficient that we're already done, I propose that we spend the rest of the day doing something fun."

Kim crossed her arms and smirked. "You forget, Scott Blake, that I have tagged along on what you three considered fun." She pointed at him, Joe, and Kyle in turn. "We have different definitions. Besides, I have a fridge being delivered today."

"Okay, fine. You can miss out on the fun, but everybody else is going to like this. How about a trip to Holcomb Valley? It's a beautiful day to be up in the mountains. No snow yet. Kyle's dad used to take us up there to camp, but there's some cool old relics left from the gold rush era. It's a great day trip."

His words were to everyone, but his gaze landed on Melissa. He was doing this for her, to get her mind off things. She'd never done too much hiking around in the mountains, but it sounded like fun. And Scott needed a win too.

"I'm in. Sounds great." She made eye contact with Allie. "Come on. You too, Allie."

Allie glanced at Kim. "Is there anything else you need me to help with? I hate to leave you here all alone."

Kim raised her hands and shrugged. "What else can you do? You already shelf papered the kitchen and unpacked the boxes. I'm just going to sit here and sketch ideas and look for furniture on my phone until the fridge comes."

Steve's eyes never left Allie's face as he stood slightly behind her. "I'm in too."

Interesting. Maybe the old flame was fanning to life, despite Allie's insistence it wouldn't. Okay then. Should be fun to watch.

Everyone else agreed, and soon they were all piling into the trucks. Kyle's had him and Heather, with Steve and Allie in the extended cab. That was Heather's doing, pulling Allie along with her before she could protest. Melissa gave her a wink for that one.

She and Scott rode with Joe and Sarah. She didn't know Sarah that well. She was quieter than Heather and always went along with what the group decided. But Joe was absolutely devoted to her.

The two-and-a-half-hour ride went quickly as they chatted about various topics. Sarah's architectural firm, where she was managing partner, nearly went under a few months ago. But she was rebuilding it with a core team of staff and clients. Melissa asked her a few questions about her experience, thinking about worst-case scenarios. Could she take her team and start over somewhere? She forcefully cleared her mind. This was one day to not think about work.

Scott and Joe were sharing memories and talking about things they used to do as kids. She focused on their conversation instead. It was great to see Scott relaxed and in his element, equally at home here as he was with her company solving complex problems. He was a unique man. One she was going to hate to see leave when it was time. But she wanted him to be able to live out his dreams.

They wound through the mountains, the meandering road edged precariously near the drop-offs at points. They climbed higher, the valley falling away below them. And then the view opened up to the beautiful Big Bear Lake. They drove a bit along the shore, then followed Kyle as they pulled into a small market in the town of Fawnskin. They all got out, stretched their legs, and went inside to grab drinks and snacks. Pizza felt like a long time ago. The tiny market got crowded fast with all of them in there. Steve was practically glued to Allie's side, so Melissa couldn't pull her aside to hear how their car ride up had been.

Scott grabbed four bottles of Gatorade. Considering there were no bathroom facilities, was that wise? On the other hand, he was a guy and there were plenty of trees. She'd go a bit easier on the water.

The mountain air was crisp and pine tinged, energizing and cleansing. The wind blowing through the trees sounded like a giant waterfall just around the corner. She couldn't wait to get out and explore. She needed to get up here more often.

Kyle stood outside his truck. "We'll head to the Discovery Center first and get a trail map. Plus, all the newbies might find it interesting to look around there."

"I'll follow you." Joe climbed in his truck.

Everyone else piled back in. A short drive around the lakefront ended at the Discovery Center. A giant statue of a grizzly on its hind legs atop a pile of boulders stood out front, greeting visitors.

"Group selfie!" Heather shouted. She directed everyone around the bear and onto the rocks. Scott slipped his arm around Melissa and pulled her close just before Heather snapped the shot. Yes, she'd have one photo of her and Scott together to remember this day by.

She reached for her phone, just to remember it was locked

back in her car. Too bad. She'd have liked to take some pictures. Well, she'd get them from Heather later.

Once inside, Kyle headed for the info desk. Scott grabbed her hand and pulled her around to look at the displays. Stuffed versions of local wild animals such as eagles, bobcats, and coyotes were arranged in lifelike dioramas. Another display gave a bit of history about the local area. But mostly her attention was captured by the feel of Scott's big, warm hand wrapped around hers.

Kyle appeared and handed her a trail guide. "This shows where we're going and explains the history behind each stop."

"Thanks!" She loved maps. When things had been particularly bad at home, she would gather Allie, Daniel, Matthew, and Brittany and they'd spread a big map of the United States across the living room floor. She turned to Scott. "Have you ever taken a Great American Road Trip? Like where you drive across a significant part of the US and see the sights along the way? I've always wanted to do that."

"I drove to Pensacola, Florida for my naval aviator training. But I didn't do too much sightseeing on the way. Was in too big of a hurry. But I've always wanted to."

"Me too. My siblings and I used to dream about it all the time. We'd pick a destination and figure out a route there from home and talk about all the places we'd see along the way." She tapped the map. "Maps always remind me of that dream."

He met her gaze. "It's a good dream. You should seriously plan that, get it on the calendar. Life does unexpected things." A shadow passed across his eyes. Yeah, he knew about the unexpected. So did she.

He tucked a strand of her hair behind her ear. "We'd better go before Joe leaves us."

They headed back down the road the way they came before turning off onto a dirt forest service road. The close-to-the-road trees shaded them as they bumped along the rutted track. A green-and-white sign with a crossed pickax and shovel indicated the trail and the stops. There were remnants of mining equipment, hills left over from the mine tailings, an old cabin, and even a hanging tree. The map gave bits of history around each piece.

Scott looked out over pieces of old rusted metal. "Man, this used to be in much better shape when we were kids. You could actually see what some of this was used for. Now people have shot it up and torn it down."

Joe stood next to him. "I can't believe that Belleville cabin is still standing. Surprised someone hasn't burned it by now."

"Always thinking about fire." Scott clapped him on the shoulder then grabbed Melissa's hand. "Let's check it out. Do you think you could have lived in something like this?" He ducked through the doorway, and she followed.

"Dirt floor. Hole up there where the cookstove pipe must have been. Plenty of ventilation." Melissa leaned out the window hewn between the logs. "You sure can't beat the view." The cabin sat in a meadow surrounded by mountains soaring up around the edges.

Scott leaned over her. "My ancestors were from around here. Part of the gold rush. They were the smart ones though. They started a sawmill off the creek that turns into a river from the snow melt. They supplied the timbers for the mines. Then once things played out, they headed to Oregon to run a stagecoach line."

She turned, limited by his arms on either side of her. "So that's where your adventurous spirit comes from. It's in your DNA."

He nodded, holding her gaze. "Yeah." His voice softened. "Can't escape it." He ran his fingers through her hair, and she closed her eyes, enjoying his touch and being with him just for this moment, even if they didn't have a future together. His movement stopped, and she opened her eyes.

Scott winced, and she noticed the fine lines around his mouth. His headache was back. Was it the altitude?

"Did you finish all that Gatorade?"

"I've got one left. Why? Thirsty?"

"No. I have ibuprofen in my purse for your headache. I figured you'd need something to take it with."

He squeezed her to himself briefly. "It's the altitude. Over seven thousand feet shouldn't be a big deal. My plane's pressurized to over that. But this stupid TBI is making everything worse. I got all that Gatorade, thinking being hydrated would stave it off."

She pulled back. "Let's get back to the truck and get you something."

Everyone else was milling around the trucks, waiting for them. She climbed in, slipped Scott the pills as they headed down the road.

Joe's eyes in the rearview mirror flicked back to them. He likely had seen Scott was suffering too.

Joe leaned over to Sarah. "How's the ankle doing with all the walking?"

"It feels great. No trouble at all." Last summer, Sarah and Joe had fallen into the basement of one of her buildings that had been sabotaged. She'd broken her ankle. But since the cast had come off, Melissa hadn't noticed Sarah limp at all.

At the next couple of stops, Scott didn't wander too far from the truck. But at the Metzger mine, he perked up. "This is always the best part. Hey, Joe. Do you have a flashlight?"

Joe just raised his eyebrows and reached into the console, pulling out a heavy flashlight and handing it to Scott.

"Of course he does." Scott grabbed it with a grin.

"Why do we need a flashlight?" Melissa did not want to go into any dark caves or mines.

"You'll see."

They hadn't seen too many people while they'd been taking the gold mine tour. A truck here and there but usually far ahead of them. But here at the mine, a Honda Accord sat off to the side. Must have been a rough journey over the bumpy road in anything other than a truck.

Scott tugged her hand as they started down a path through the woods. It grew steeper, cut into a hillside with an increasingly sharp drop off to one side. They came around a curve and bigger boulders were strewn on either side of the path, like a giant had carelessly tossed them out of his way. A dark opening appeared among the boulders. Not a very big one, only about three feet high and with sharp rocks protruding from the top and bottom.

"That's the mine? They must have been awfully short." Melissa bent down to peer beyond the rocks.

"Some of it's caved in." He flipped on the flashlight and shone it into the opening. A pair of flip-flops lay on the rocks just inside the mouth.

Joe came up behind him shaking his head. "Excellent choice of footwear for scrambling over rocks. But bare feet will get cut up on those sharp edges. Wonder where the owner is and how he got out of here with no shoes." He glanced back at Sarah. "Watch your step. You don't want to re-injure your ankle."

She nodded.

"Hey! Anybody out there!" A voice came from the cave. Sounded like a young guy, but with the bit of echo it was hard to hear for sure.

Joe took the light from Scott, bent over, and entered the cave. "Yeah. Are you okay?"

"Not really." The strain in the voice was evident now.

"What happened?" Joe disappeared from view completely.

The response was mumbled, and Joe reappeared a moment later. "Looks like some sort of leg injury. We'll have to go in and get him. He's not very far in. Just past that first bend." He turned to Scott and Kyle. "Can you two go get him while I run back to the truck for my first aid kit? We've got zero cell service up here so we'll take him down to Big Bear with us."

Melissa wanted to protest on Scott's behalf. This might have been his favorite part of the trip, but the ibuprofen wasn't doing much good. Still, she might have as well asked the ocean to stop making waves.

Kyle grabbed the flashlight. "Got it." He bent his tall frame in half, barely avoiding scraping his back on the rock that protruded like a tooth from the entrance.

Scott gave Melissa a flashy grin. "We've been back in this cave a little ways as kids. It's not far. We'll be fine." Then he disappeared behind the rocks.

Steve stepped up. "It's a tight fit here around the mouth of the mine. How about I stay here to give them a hand and the rest of you move back toward the trail?"

Melissa's knee-jerk reaction was to object but then realized it was ridiculous. This wasn't a guys-versus-girls thing. This was what they all did for a living, and she and the other women needed to get out of the way. She caught Heather's gaze. "Maybe we should head back to the trucks."

Sarah nodded and started down the trail, Heather following her. But Allie piped up. "I'll stay here in case Steve needs me to run back and forth with a message or something."

Melissa kept her face impassive at Allie's faintly pink one. Okay then. "Sure. Good idea."

Heather had turned around. She was the runner of the group. It would make the most sense for her to stay. But she just shrugged and headed back down the trail.

The road back was much easier since the incline was in their favor. "Let's pray while we walk. Lord, thank you for your beautiful creation and this fun day we've all had to spend together. But we pray for the man stuck in the cave. Please keep him calm and help his injury not to be severe. Please be with the guys as they tend to him that they will be able to get him to safety without injury to themselves." She sent up a silent prayer for Scott, sure that he wouldn't want everyone else to know about his altitude headache.

Heather and Sarah added their prayers.

Joe met them running up the trail with his first aid kit. They stepped off the trail to let him pass. He winked at Sarah, tossed her his keys, and then was gone.

Melissa didn't know how he ran up that considering she had been panting just walking it. But it was probably a cake walk for him, considering how much gear he carried as a firefighter.

They reached the trucks. The Honda was still there. It probably belonged to the guy in the cave.

Sarah nodded at it. "One of us should drive that to the hospital for him. He's a lucky guy that we were here. He did everything wrong. Came up here alone without the proper footwear at the very least. And then he went into the cave." She shook her head.

The trucks were coated in dust from the dirt road, so Heather lowered the tailgate on Kyle's truck, and they hopped up there to wait. Sarah pulled out some granola bars and water bottles from Joe's truck and passed them out. The silence was peaceful.

Melissa laid back in the truck bed and looked up. The wind pushed through the trees on occasion, but in the silence, just the sounds of birds floated through the air. No cars, no traffic. Just sky above and trees around. She needed more peace in her life. More days like this. In fact, all of the restful and relaxing days she'd had recently were a direct result of Scott. He was good for her, helped her take breaks and not take life so seriously. How would she continue to sustain that once he was back on duty?

Voices from the trail floated to them. The guys were coming. She sat up and climbed out of the truck. Heather and Sarah were already on the ground.

All four men had a guy in his early twenties slung between them. His lower leg was bandaged, but blood had seeped through. His face was pale and his eyes closed. Allie trailed behind carrying the first-aid kit.

"Lay the passenger seat back on my truck." Sarah scrambled

around the truck and did what Joe asked then got out of the way. The guys got the injured man situated.

"I'll follow in his car." Scott glanced at Melissa. "Come with me?"

"Sure."

Joe handed Scott the man's keys. "Bear Valley Community Hospital."

And within seconds, they were all on the road with Kyle in the lead, heading down the mountain past the ruins of an old mining derrick and a beautiful view of valleys on both sides of the mountains.

"Kyle will be calling this in the moment we get into cell phone range so they'll be expecting us." Scott drove far behind the two trucks, having to go much slower in the Honda as well as trying to avoid the dust the trucks kicked up. "The guy had climbed back into the cave wearing flip-flops. He soon figured out that wasn't going to work so his brilliant idea was to take them off and go barefoot. But he slipped and gashed his leg open on a rock and busted his ankle. No telling what would have happened to him if we hadn't come along."

Melissa squeezed his hand. "Your great idea paid a lot of dividends today."

He pulled the Honda to a stop, opened the door, leaned out, and threw up.

Chapter Sixteen

Scott glanced at the GPS on his phone while he sped down the highway. Should he call Jordan's wife, Ashley, before showing up? He'd gone back and forth on it, wondering what the right thing was to do. In the end, he decided to just show up. She could slam the door in his face, but at least he could get out an apology. Then there was the chance she might not be home. Round and round it went in circles in his brain.

He wanted to call Melissa and ask for her advice, but he forced himself to keep his distance. Saturday had been great, even with his altitude headache. He loved spending time with her, talking about what they used to do as kids, hanging out in the mountains. Up until the end, it was nearly a perfect day. And while he vaguely remembered leaning over on her while he dozed, he at first thought it was part of his dream. It felt so good he didn't want to stop. And she didn't seem to mind.

GPS told him the next exit was his. He moved over and took it.

But other than church on Sunday, he had chosen to keep his distance from her. And since this was a light work week for her with Thanksgiving, it was a good excuse to create some space between them. But he kept replaying Saturday over in his mind. It was a good memory.

Having to wear glasses and the headaches just reinforced to him that maybe helping her discover the avionics bug wasn't his best plan. All it seemed to be doing was making his TBI worse.

He didn't know what he expected from Ashley. Probably not absolution of his guilt. But he did need to do something. He'd talked to her only once since the accident. He'd missed Jordan's funeral because he'd still been in the hospital. He'd called Ashley as soon as he was able, but she was short and distant. He couldn't blame her.

But now, it was time. Past time. He needed to see her in person, apologize and offer his condolences. Question was, would it be enough? No, of course not. Nothing would be.

He wound his way through the suburban neighborhood in the high desert town of Ridgecrest, where NAWS China Lake was situated. He'd been to their home many times for dinner. Their two kids felt like the niece and nephew he didn't have. Jordan had a life that was like the other side of the mirror. Wife, kids, a home. All things Scott didn't have and figured he'd have time for later.

Now they didn't have Jordan. Was it his fault? Somehow it was. As pilot in command, he was responsible for everything that happened to his plane. And the Board of Inquiry seemed to think there was enough evidence that Scott was responsible. Even though his gut told him he had done everything right, that niggling of his conscious asked him if that was quite true. Had Superman failed when it was most important?

He pulled up to the curb, the place he always parked his Corvette. The minivan sat in the driveway, so they were home. The house looked the same. He might as well be coming over for a barbecue. Funny how things could look the same on the outside but be so different on the inside. Something he knew far too well.

He climbed out and headed up the front porch steps, then

knocked at the door. Feet scampered behind the door, voices drifted out. Then the door opened.

Ashley stared at him.

"Hey. Sorry I came by without calling. I just… I know a conversation with you is long overdue."

Ashley crossed her arms over her chest. "What do you want, Scott?"

This was not going well. He'd figured she'd at least invite him in, offer him a glass of iced tea. It would be awkward, but they had a history of friendship behind them. Surely that would help carry them through this. "Um, I guess I just wanted to tell you how sorry I am. Jordan was the best there was, and he should have had a long career and time to see his kids grow up. I still can't wrap my mind around it."

She didn't say anything, but she didn't shut the door so he plunged on. "I don't have much memory of the accident. Bits and pieces mostly that come to me during my nightmares. But I am working to figure out what happened. I want justice for Jordan and to make sure that it doesn't happen to anyone else." So yeah, guess he would have to keep working with Melissa to figure out what happened. Not just for his sake, but for Jordan's.

Her eyes narrowed, hard and flat. "Justice? Justice won't bring him back. Justice won't read his kids their bedtime story or warm my bed. Believe me, Scott. I'm interested in justice, but not the way you think. I thought you were Jordan's friend, but you got him killed. Superman. Ha! Hotshot is more like it. Thinking you were better than everyone else, that you could handle anything and didn't need any help. I heard the stories. And I know it's your fault Jordan was killed. And I intend to make you pay." With one last venomous look, she slammed the door in his face.

Stunned, he couldn't move. Couldn't believe what he heard from Ashley. Even in his nightmares, he hadn't expected that.

He turned and headed down the porch steps to the sounds of heartbreaking sobs.

MELISSA SAT AT HER DESK EATING HER ROAST BEEF ON multigrain. It was cool and cloudy out, so no matter what lessons she'd learned from Scott about taking a break, she wasn't going outside. And knowing that someone might still be watching her creeped her out and kept her looking over her shoulder, not that she could spot anyone. Cameras were so small they could be anywhere. Maybe even in her office.

Given that Thanksgiving was Thursday, this was a light week with only two and a half work days. Many of her team were out of town early for the holiday.

Kyle had taken her phone Saturday when they'd gotten back from the mountains. The trip down the mountains had been pretty silent, everyone worn out by the events of the day. Scott had fallen asleep on her shoulder after they'd gotten the injured guy admitted into Bear Valley Community. It had been nice to feel his weight on her and to let her mind wander, imagining what a life might look like where days like that day were a regular occurrence.

They'd all shown up for church Sunday, but there had been no talk of going out to lunch after. Maybe a bit too much togetherness. She'd spent that afternoon getting a new phone, since the LVPD techs were going over hers. Who knew when she'd get it back? And today she'd avoided everyone but Danielle. Melissa's very presence could put her team in danger.

She dropped her sandwich and put her head in her hands. Maybe Scott was right. She should drop the whole Gavin/Trent/missing money thing. Someone was making it pretty clear that something bad would happen to her if she didn't. She'd done her duty and told the board. Did she really have an obligation to do anything else?

Plus, as she needed to remind herself more often, going after Gavin caused her to rely on Scott more. And he wouldn't be around to support her much longer. Yes, he still had headaches and vision problems, but as soon as those were cleared up, he was going back to the Navy to do what he loved. She didn't want him to give up his dreams.

The more she became emotionally dependent on him, the more she would be wrecked when he left. Probably had already passed that point.

Of course, if she lost her job, that would make her free to go somewhere else, maybe somewhere near Scott. Possibly China Lake could have a spot for her. But her life was here. Her siblings who relied on her, her friends. And what about her team? She couldn't just up and leave them. They needed her.

And most of all, what about justice? What about doing what was right? What if this whole thing was a lot more than just Gavin giving Trent money? What if Kyle was right and there could be links to terrorism?

There was a lot at stake here.

She moved over to her couch and bent her head. *Lord, help me do the right thing here. You know what's happening and what's going on. You know all of the details. Please guide me so I can do the right thing. You know I want to protect my team, and I'd really like to not look foolish. But I will do whatever it takes to do what you want me to. Please show me the way.*

She sat in silence for she didn't know how long. Her watch buzzed. A text from Kyle asking her to come over after work. She simply replied **okay**, knowing the less she said the better. Kyle obviously didn't want to say much over text or with her in her office. Goosebumps lifted over her arms. Something much bigger was going on here. The question was, what was it?

She needed to take Danielle for a walk and warn her. The other team members could be ignorant, but Danielle had seen the same evidence Melissa had, and she needed to know she might be in danger.

THIS WAS ONE TIME SCOTT WISHED JOE WAS HOME AND not working. The empty house mocked him, and Ashley's words hadn't left his head the whole drive home. He needed to get out of his own head. And he wasn't going to call Melissa.

After nearly wearing a hole in the carpet, he picked up his phone and called Kyle. "Any chance you're available to go for a run or shoot some hoops?"

Kyle must have heard the desperation in his voice. "Let me tie something up here and then meet me at my house in an hour. We'll run the hills. I'm sure you're ready for a challenge."

Sounded exactly like what he needed. Something to push him physically so he wouldn't be able to think so much.

He did an extra round of PT exercises to kill time and then grabbed his running shoes and headed to Kyle's. Kyle met him outside his front door, and they headed up his street into the hills.

"I drove out to Ridgecrest today to visit Ashley, Jordan's widow. It didn't go well." He told Kyle what she had said. "Melissa and I are working to determine what really happened, and we're close to figuring it out. But what if Ashley's right? What if it was pilot error and I've just been deluding myself this whole time?"

Kyle shook his head. "If you take this one incident out of your career, you have an excellent record. You've been able to pull out of tough situations before with your quick thinking and way-above-average skills. Plus, you said it yourself. There is something with the avionics that you and Melissa are close to tracking down. I get that Ashley's words have shaken you. They would anybody. But think of it from her perspective. She needs a target for her grief and anger. Her life has been turned upside down. You're the best target there is. You're Superman."

Sweat poured down Scott's face. "Not feeling much like Superman lately." He panted the words out, breathing hard, turning Kyle's words over in his head for a while.

"That guy we rescued Saturday up in Holcomb Valley called

the police station and thanked me today. He's got a cast on his ankle, but other than that, he'll be fine. He said he knew the minute he ducked in that cave that it was a bad idea. He just thought he'd take a quick look and get back out."

"Best laid plans, huh?"

"Yep. Looks like he learned his lesson. And Joe got to rescue someone, which we all know he loves to do."

They laughed. Kyle tilted his head. "And you seemed to be having a good time with Melissa. Seemed like more than friends to me."

Scott shook his head. "Yeah. If things were different... Honestly, I've been trying to keep my distance. We just don't have a future together. I'm in China Lake, she's down here running a defense contracting firm and doing a dang good job of it. I can't ask her to give that up to follow me around."

"What if she wants to? More and more people work remotely now. She could come back for meetings. There are solutions if you look for them. If the two of you put your minds together, you could conquer all the world's problems." Kyle grinned. Then he sobered up. "Seriously. If there's anything you should take away from your conversation with Ashley, it's that life doesn't go according to plan. Don't wait if there's something —or someone—you really want."

They finished their run. Scott suspected Kyle took it easy on him and cut it shorter than he usually ran. They headed back to the house.

Kyle tossed him a towel and a bottle of water. "I'm going to hop in the shower. Let Melissa in when she gets here?"

"Melissa?" Elation and wariness chased each other through him.

"I uncovered some things that I didn't want to tell her over the phone or at her office." Kyle met his gaze. "She needs you, Scott. Things could go very bad. I don't want to scare her—and I can't prove anything—but my gut tells me I'm right. And the guys behind this are very bad players. I've reached out to my contacts at the FBI, and we've been quietly putting out feelers. No hard evidence of anything yet. Just a lot of nasty coincidences."

Scott toweled the sweat off him while chugging the water. He didn't exactly want Melissa to see him all sweaty, but if she was going to be in his life, then she needed to see the good and the bad. Actually, she'd seen a lot of the bad already with his headaches and throwing up around her. So a little sweat might be a step up.

A knock at the door propelled him off the couch.

Melissa's eyes widened when he opened the door. "Wait. I'm at the right house. Why are you here instead of Kyle?"

"We went for a run. He hopped in the shower and left me here to wait for you." He stepped aside so she could come in and closed the door behind her. "Water?"

"Sure." She headed toward the living room.

He grabbed a bottle from the fridge and handed it to her where she sat on the couch. He took Kyle's recliner, not wanting to be too close to her before he got a shower.

Kyle came out from the hall, freshly showered, hair still damp. "Thanks for coming over, Melissa. I have some concerns that your office might be bugged. Can you ask security to sweep it? Will they do that without asking too many questions?" He sat on the other end of the couch.

"I think so. I'm friendly with one of the senior guards. I think he can do it without escalating it to the head of security. I just don't want word to get back to Gavin or Trent."

"Agreed. I didn't find anything conclusive on the text that sent you those surveillance photos. It was bounced around a bunch of places so we can't determine where it originated. About what we suspected. I have a gut feeling about this. If it were simply about money, then Trent and Gavin won when there was no evidence for the board to take your complaint seriously. Gavin's excuses were flimsy but reasonable. But given the kind of money you're talking about, Trent's playing with the big dogs.

And the top ones are tied to terrorism and have been making inroads in this area. We've got a couple of guys following Trent to see if we can turn up his associates. I'm putting out some feelers and hoping we can head this off without getting you involved." His gaze narrowed. "You need to be very careful. If I'm right, these guys don't mess around. Just stay out of Gavin and Trent's way, and let them think they've won."

Melissa nodded. "What about my team? Are they in danger?"

"If they don't pose a threat to Trent, if they don't have any information that could prove harmful to him, then likely not."

"My admin, Danielle, she saw all the evidence I did and kept it on a jump drive. I did take her for a walk away from the building yesterday and told her about my threats and to keep that jump drive locked up. We're going to pretend it doesn't exist for now."

"Good idea. I need to get that jump drive. Since it's not unusual for Scott to be at your office, you can give it to him to give to me. The best thing you can do is keep doing your job and make it look like business as usual. If you stumble across anything, just let me know, and we'll take it from there."

"Okay." She paused. "Here's something that bothers me. We don't do just any ordinary work. We do classified work that provides systems for the nation's defense. You say Trent might be dealing with terrorists who are running drugs to raise money. What if they want his connection to Broadstone Technologies? He has access to nearly everything. And what he doesn't have access to, Gavin does. It would explain the pulled fire alarm, the missing CCTV video, the unrecorded swipes in my office. Especially if he's got someone in security working with him."

A cold stone formed in Scott's stomach. He'd made the connection but didn't know that Melissa had. He should have known. She was smart and observant. She put things together and came up with patterns. And she had a strong sense of justice. If she thought Trent would try to sabotage any of their technology, she'd do everything in her power to stop him. And that terrified him.

Kyle's voice was calm but threaded with steel. Scott knew it was his not-messing-around tone. "That's why I've contacted the FBI."

Melissa straightened her shoulders, and she looked at Scott. "We'll figure this out and not let on to Trent. He's not a super bright guy, more of a manipulator. He'll get caught, and we'll be watching."

"I'm going to be at the office every day, then. I'm not letting you be there alone and potentially in danger."

He'd made his decision.

She was worth fighting for.

Scott walked Melissa to her car, checking out the neighborhood and her safety, she was sure. And she appreciated it. Kyle had confirmed all her worst fears, ones she had desperately hoped she was wrong about.

"Why don't I swing by in the morning and pick you up? I'd feel better if we rode into work together." Scott leaned on her open car door, his gaze intense.

Her first instinct was to brush off his concern. But after what Kyle had said… She nodded. "Okay, thanks. That's probably a good idea. Are you sure being at the office all day with me won't be a problem for your physical therapy or appointments?" She slid into the driver's seat.

"I'll make it work. Don't worry about me." He gave her his dazzling grin, one she realized was meant to distract her from whatever she was worrying about.

"Okay. See you in the morning." She shut the door and waved before pulling out of Kyle's driveway. Scott stood there, watching her.

Her phone rang. Allie. She used voice controls to answer it. "What's up?"

"Just checking to see if you're going to Mom's with me for Thanksgiving. If so, we need to make plans. And, yes, you need to come."

Melissa groaned. "This is not a good time. There's so much going on at work."

"It's never a good time for you. And your team is not going to be working on Thanksgiving. You're not a slave driver. We can fly there on Wednesday and fly back on Saturday. Unless you'd rather drive. But I've already bought you a ticket."

"Oh, Allie, you're good." She laughed. "No, I don't want to spend six hours in the car each way. As much as I love you. Did you happen to get us a motel too?"

"Already done. Mom doesn't have enough room for all of us, and I don't want to sleep on an air mattress with you any more than you want to spend six hours in the car with me."

She let out a breath. "Is the food already arranged?"

"Done. Daniel and Matthew have planned the menu and are helping Mom with the cooking. Brittany's bringing desserts. We just need to show up."

"This is why you're so good at your job. Nice work on Kim's place, by the way."

"Aw, thanks. That was easy."

She wanted to bug her little sister about Steve but figured she had the whole plane trip to do that. She was pulling into her complex now. "I'm home, so I'm going to go."

They hung up, and Melissa pulled into her garage, watching her surroundings carefully and making sure the door closed securely behind her. The silence of the garage enveloped her. She wished she'd been able to just spend the rest of the evening hanging out with Scott and Kyle, eating pizza and not worrying if her actions or lack thereof would create a national security crisis.

She rubbed her neck then got out of her car and into her

house. Dropping purse and keys on the console table, she headed for the fridge to find something to eat.

Her phone buzzed. Scott. **Get home safely?**

Yes. Just now. Figuring out dinner.

There was a long pause. Would he offer to bring over dinner? No, he was at Kyle's. They probably had something planned. Besides, she was supposed to be keeping her distance from him. It was bad enough that he had appointed himself her bodyguard, and she would be spending all day with him tomorrow. Inviting him over for dinner would be a bad idea.

Three dots appeared on her screen. He was typing.

She hurriedly tapped before his message came through. **Just going to have leftovers and call it an early night.**

The dots disappeared, and the screen was blank. Then, **Have a good night. See you tomorrow**.

Was that what he was really going to say? No way to know. She pulled out some leftover Chinese food and put it in the microwave. She clicked the TV onto Netflix. A few hours of brainless movie watching sounded good.

But an hour later, the Chinese food was gone, and she couldn't remember what she'd watched. Between thoughts of Scott and heading to Mom's for Thanksgiving, she hadn't had any mindless time at all.

Chapter Seventeen

They pulled into Broadstone Technologies' parking lot early. Melissa had barely gotten ready when Scott had knocked on the door of her townhome. A pleasant surprise. The earlier they got in, the fewer people they were likely to run into.

"I don't know who's working security today. Hopefully, one of the guards that likes me and won't ask questions."

Scott nodded. "I'll follow your lead."

They strode across the parking lot and into the building. Melissa headed to the security desk. "George! I'm surprised to see you here. Normally you have the second shift."

"Morning, Ms. Ellis. I switched with Max for the next month. His wife's schedule changed, and they have little kids at home. Our kids have all flown the nest, and sometimes I think my wife is happier when I'm not around." He chuckled. "What can I do for you?"

She pulled Scott forward. "He needs a badge for today and tomorrow." She scanned the lobby while George punched in some buttons. It was early enough that only a few people were around, all employees who hustled straight to the elevators.

She leaned further over the counter. "I also have a favor. Any way I can get my office swept without making any waves?"

George handed Scott his badge. "Let's see here." He looked at his display. "Seems to me like you're overdue for a sweep. Should have been done after the fire alarm. I'll get someone up there this morning."

"Thanks, George. I appreciate it."

They headed up in the elevator. She glanced at Scott and let out a sigh, raising her crossed fingers where he could see them.

Upstairs, she stopped at Danielle's desk and said good morning then scribbled her a note about security coming to sweep. She didn't want to give anyone listening a heads up. She and Scott headed for coffee. She turned to him while their cups were filling. "I think we should start by checking with Jeremy and see what he's come up with. Most everyone else is off this week. I have reports to review, which will be extremely boring for you. But maybe there's something you can help Jeremy with."

He spread his arms. "At your service."

They stopped by Jeremy's cubicle on their way back. He was just settling in for the day. She updated him on the plan.

"Cool. I actually have a few things I wanted to ask you about. Give me five minutes."

They headed over to her office and went inside. Considering she didn't want to say anything important, silence hung awkwardly around them.

"What are your plans for Thanksgiving?" She gestured to the couch, where they both sat.

"I'll be at my folks' with Jessica. Joe's working. Kyle and Heather are heading up to her folks' place in the Valley. I think Sarah's tagging along with them. What are you doing?"

"Allie and I are going to Phoenix to visit our mom and siblings. We're flying out tomorrow and back on Saturday. I haven't seen Mom's new place yet. Or met her new boyfriend."

Scott nodded and widened his eyes, propping his elbow on his knee, over exaggerating his interest. She giggled.

A knock sounded on her door. She jumped up and opened it.

George and two other security guys stood there. "Okay if we start here?"

"That will be great. We'll get out of your way. I'll be somewhere in the team area. Just come find me when you're done." She and Scott slid by them out the door. "Jeremy's probably ready for us anyway."

Jeremy had booted his computer and was settling into his chair. It wasn't a big enough cube for more than one chair, so she and Scott hovered over Jeremy's shoulders.

"Okay, you told me that there was a problem with the plane not responding to your controls. We found something odd with the main computer." Lines of code scrolled by too fast to read. "So I concentrated on that. My theory was there could be bad sensor input somewhere, so I started through all the sensor data. And I found this." He pointed to several lines of code on the screen.

"What is it?" Melissa bent to get a closer look.

"This is the code that is supposed to be giving sensor readings on the angle of attack, basically the angle of the airflow relative to the plane's wing. But it's labeled altitude data."

The wrong data input would certainly make the plane act in an erratic and unpredictable matter without any way for the pilot to correct it. Very much like what Scott had described happening.

She glanced at Scott. His face was intent, eyes narrowed but shifted off to the side, arms crossed. She knew he was comparing Jeremy's findings with his experience, probably trying to grab some of those elusive memories. She said nothing, just let him process the information.

"Ms. Ellis?" George stood outside the cubicle. "May I have a word with you?"

She stepped out and followed George back to her office. "We found something in here. A camera in your desk lamp. Likely has audio too. The techs are going to look at that. We're sweeping the team area now, as well as the conference room." He lifted his tablet. "The thing is, I pulled up the records of the entry swipes of security badges to your office going back to the fire. Nothing but you and Ms. Reid." His gaze was steady on her.

She nodded. "About what I suspected. Just like when someone broke into my desk. Probably planted the bug then."

"Could be. That was the only missing time record. I'm going to review CCTV footage and see if I can come up with something. However, this kind of security breech has to get escalated."

"I understand." How long did she have before the head of security, Adam Martinez, reported it to Gavin? "If you come up with anything, would you let me know?"

"Will do." George moved off.

Melissa headed back to Jeremy's cubicle. Scott was bending over Jeremy's screen, and they were discussing something. She put her hand on Scott's shoulder and whispered, "Kyle was right."

He turned, putting their faces inches apart. He reached for her hand and squeezed it. She squeezed back then moved slightly away. "So anything else you guys discovered? As soon as security is done with their sweep, we can take this to the conference room where we'll have more space."

Scott turned to Melissa. "Can we take a walk? I need to clear my head." He rubbed his eyes. His glasses that were supposed to help with the computer work weren't coming in until tomorrow.

It was cloudy and cool out. "Let me grab my jacket."

A moment later, they were outside walking away from the building. The business park they were part of had a nice path along the greenbelt between the buildings. It was where she and

Danielle had walked the other day. She headed for that, letting Scott lead the conversation.

"Where did they find the bug?"

"In my desk lamp. I think it was planted when whoever broke into my office and stole the invoices. The entry card swipes were erased. Only a few people have the access to do that. Trent could be paying off someone in security to do it for him. He's the owner's son, so no one would expect anything nefarious from him. He could have made an excuse like he left his phone in my office and didn't want his dad on his case about him being careless. He's really good at getting people to do what he wants."

Scott pulled out his phone. "I'll text Kyle. Then he can get in touch with security."

She sighed. "I don't see how he can investigate without this blowing back on me and my team."

He rubbed her arm. "Kyle will do everything to keep you out of danger. So will I."

She stuffed her hands deep in her coat pockets. What if that wasn't enough? But she didn't want to be more of a burden to Scott. "What did you think of Jeremy's discovery?"

"It helps verify my account. If the plane's computer thought the angle of attack was actually the altitude, then it would explain the stall warning and the computer simultaneously trying to push the nose up. Two incompatible things. Bits and pieces float back to me. So much of the plane is now controlled by the computer, that even if I could shut the computer off, I'd have no engines and no controls. But it raises the question: How did that code get in there? And what other planes are being affected by it? And why didn't that show up earlier in the flight?"

She touched his arm. "All things we can ask Jeremy. He'll figure it out, if anyone can." Mixed emotions swirled through her stomach. Scott had proof that could vindicate him. But she had proof that her company had provided faulty military equipment. One that had likely cost one pilot his life. And someone inside the company was working against her. Was this somehow part of the plot Kyle suggested could be happening? Her head hurt with all the potential problems.

"Hey." Scott stopped walking and turned to her, lifting her chin with his finger. "It's going to work out. Let's just solve the next problem, okay? I can see your mind whirling with all the possibilities and all the ways you're blaming yourself."

Her eyes widened at his mind-reading abilities. He knew her well.

"First problem. Figure out how the code got there. And then how to fix it." He slid his hand behind her neck, sending fire down her spine. All she wanted to do was throw herself in his arms and pretend it all didn't exist.

But she couldn't. She stepped back. "You're right. Let's get back to the office and talk to Jeremy. See what his ideas are."

She turned and headed back to the office, taking several steps before Scott caught up to her.

SCOTT WATCHED MELISSA WALK AWAY AND CURSED HIMSELF for wanting to pull her into his arms. His emotions were all over the place. Images from the crash bombarded him then faded away before he could fully grasp them. Joy at being proven right in his account of what had happened, when even he was beginning to doubt it.

Then the desire to protect Melissa from all of it. His victory was a blow against her. Something he hated. Surely there was a better option here. There had to be. For now, his job was to support and protect her.

He jogged a few steps to catch up with her. They headed back to the office in silence. At a stop to deposit her coat in the office, George caught up with her.

"Scott, why don't you let Jeremy know we can move to the conference room? I'll meet you guys there."

She turned back to George, and Scott headed to Jeremy's

cubicle and gave him the message. He and Jeremy arrived in the conference room, and Melissa joined them a few minutes later, her face unreadable.

While Jeremy connected to the big screen TV, Melissa leaned over to Scott. "The rest of the team area and the conference room are clean. He'll let me know if he discovers anything else."

Scott nodded, mentally putting that issue on the back burner. One problem at a time, and right now it was this buggy code.

Jeremy pulled up on the big screen TV the same code that they had seen in his office.

"First question." Scott pointed at the screen. "How did it get there?"

"Good question." Jeremy typed something in and a secondary screen popped up to the side of the code with user names, dates, and times. "According to the source control log, this code has been here from the beginning. The date and time are the same as the code around it and the user name is the generic one that came with the source code."

Melissa leaned forward. "But we know that's not true. We've been running this basic code for several years and have had no problems like this. Like Scott said, the problem likely came from the most recent update we pushed out to his plane and a few others."

Jeremy pulled up another screen of scrolling code. "The latest update had nothing to do with either the angle of attack, altitude, or sensor controls. It was more of a graphical user interface update, making it easier to use."

Scott sighed. "Which we already discussed in our previous meetings."

"Is it possible the code was lying dormant before the latest update? What would make that code activate?"

Jeremy stilled his fingers and sat back. "There could be a subroutine that triggered it or an outside source. It'll take some digging. But that assumes a deliberate sabotage of the code, not a bug."

Melissa met his gaze. "Yes, it does."

A sick feeling filled Scott's stomach. Not only had the accident not been his fault, someone had deliberately sabotaged his plane, deliberately trying to kill him and Jordan. Anger welled up, and he pushed out of his chair. "I have to get some air." He tossed his comment over his shoulder as he left the conference room, the concern on Melissa's face etched in his mind.

———

"JEREMY, I'LL BE RIGHT BACK." MELISSA FOLLOWED SCOTT out of the room. He couldn't walk around unescorted as a visitor. She touched Scott's arm. "Why don't you hang out in my office for a bit?"

Scott stared right through her but finally nodded. She let him into her office and shut the door behind him. It took all her willpower to let him be by himself. He needed to sort through his emotions, and she knew him well enough to know he wouldn't want an audience while he did it.

"Danielle, bring Scott back to the conference room when he's ready. Thanks."

Danielle nodded, and Melissa went back to the conference room, closing the door behind her and taking her seat.

She turned to Jeremy. "Okay, so currently our theory is that somehow this bad code got put in at some point. We can't determine when or by whom. And then it was somehow triggered to go off in Scott's plane."

Jeremy nodded. "Sounds about right." He stared at Melissa. "We're defense contractors. If someone is messing with the code in our systems, that's sabotage, and it's a national security threat."

"Yes. There are other things going on too, but I don't know how all the pieces fit together. People are looking into it, but please don't share your thoughts or conclusions with anyone but me."

"We need to figure this out. People are going to get hurt." He paused, clearly thinking of Scott's EWO, Jordan. "People already have."

"I know. And we have to figure out how to stop that. But I also have an obligation to this company. If this gets out before we can figure out what happened and how to fix it, our credibility will tank and we'll lose all of our government contracts. Then we're all out of work."

Jeremy nodded. "It seems like our first job is to figure out how that code got there and how it was triggered. I can work on that."

"One question for you. And we're assuming sabotage here. I don't have any doubt about that, though I couldn't really prove it. Who could put that code there? Who would have the skills to make it look like it was there from the beginning?"

He stared off for a minute then looked at her. "I can't think of anyone here. Other than me."

Chapter Eighteen

As Melissa and Scott entered the building's lobby the next morning, it was as empty as if it were the weekend already. She waved at George as they headed to the elevator.

"You're not going to stay too late, are you, Ms. Ellis?"

"No, my sister is coming to pick me up and take me to the airport after lunch, so I'll have no excuse to stay late."

"Well that's a good plan. You have a good Thanksgiving."

"You too."

Scott punched the button on the elevator, and they waited for it. He'd been quiet the rest of the day yesterday. She'd sent Jeremy to figure out what he could while she finished up reports in her office. Scott dozed on her couch. She had remembered to get the jump drive and give it to him to give to Kyle.

When they got upstairs, Danielle was already at her desk.

"You're here early."

"I'm planning on leaving at noon. I have a long drive to my folks' house, and I don't want to sit in the inevitable traffic more than I have to." She pointed at Melissa. "And you'd better be close on my heels." She turned to Scott. "Can you make sure she leaves early today?"

"Allie's coming to get me at three to take me to the airport, so I'll have to get out of here."

Danielle gave her a mock frown. "I suppose that will have to do."

With coffees in hand, Melissa and Scott retired to her office. She was dying to go over to Jeremy's cube to see if he'd discovered anything, but she knew he'd tell her if he had anything to report. With the long weekend, she had to resign herself to not getting any answers until next week. In the meantime, she had performance reports to finish up. And poor Scott, he had to be bored out of his mind.

He'd settled into the couch and was doing some stretching. He caught her staring at him. "Trying to make good use of my time." He smiled and then it faded. "But if you have a moment, I do have a question for you."

"Sure."

"When can I get some of this information to the JAG Manual so I can get my case dismissed?" He swallowed. "I'd also like to be able to tell Jordan's widow what happened too. She still blames me."

Her shoulders slumped. "I want to help you clear your name. But we don't have anything other than conjecture at this point."

"That line of code."

She nodded. "Yes, we do have that. And it proves your case. But it's proprietary and under high security clearance. I can't release it." She tilted her head. "But you could probably talk to your JAG lawyer and tell him we have proof that there was a problem with the software. Then the court can subpoena it, and we can let the higher ups sort it all out. You just can't be specific about the software problems. And if he doesn't believe you, I can talk to him."

Though letting anyone outside of this building know about the problems was just asking for trouble. Gavin would likely fire her for it. Because if word leaked anywhere about Broadstone

Technologies creating a flawed product that killed a serviceman, they'd all be in big trouble. She let out a breath. "It's the right thing to do."

Scott moved over next to her and leaned against her desk. "I know what this is costing you."

"This is more than just Gavin bailing out Trent or missing money. If something really is rotten in our company, it needs to be rooted out and dealt with."

Scott took her hand and kissed the back of it. "You're a good woman, Melissa. I'm proud to call you my friend. No matter what happens, I'm sticking with you."

For a moment, she let his words wash over her bruised heart. She lost herself in his endless-blue-sky eyes. Maybe this was the most important thing in life: having someone who saw the best in you and believed in you.

A knock sounded at the door then it opened. Danielle.

Scott unhurriedly pushed away from the desk.

"You didn't stick this in Diana's cube for any reason, did you?" She held up a shipping box.

Melissa frowned. "No. Diana's been out all week. Is there anything in it?"

"Just a bunch of wadded up packing paper. It's one of those double-walled boxes like they use when you get food shipped to you. The walls usually have dry ice in them, but this just looks like Styrofoam. Kinda heavy, though."

"No name on it?"

"Nope. The label's been ripped off. I think someone just ditched it in her office because they didn't want to deal with taking it to the Dumpster." She shook her head. "People are so lazy. I'll take it there on my way out." She glanced at her watch. "Which is now."

Melissa looked at her computer. Lunch time already. "Okay, scoot. Have a great Thanksgiving, and I'll see you on Monday." She stood and hugged Danielle.

Danielle looked at Scott. "Don't let her stay too late."

"No, ma'am. I'm dragging her off to lunch right now."

Melissa raised her eyebrows. "Okay then." She shut down her computer as Danielle left. She grabbed her coat and purse. "Let's stop by Jeremy's cube on the way out and see if he's still there."

He was. He turned around in his chair. "I was just going to stop by your office before I left. I don't have any proof of this, but I thought about what I might do if I were going to create this situation. The code could have been introduced through some external program. Best way to do it without a trace would be via a jump drive. Some smart person outside the building could have gotten someone in the building to do it for them. If they followed directions, they wouldn't have to know anything about coding, just have access somehow."

Melissa nodded. "Okay, good. I can think through who might have that kind of access."

Jeremy grinned. "Here's the kicker, the really outside-the-box idea. A drone could remotely activate the program. Just the same way your phone can tell your house to turn on your lights when you cross the geofence. Fly the drone through the geofence and boom, the program is activated."

"Wait." Scott spoke up. "Drones aren't supposed to be anywhere near aircraft."

"Aren't supposed to be, but are. Maybe you can see if there were any reports of drones in the area the day of your crash."

Scott nodded. "I can look into that."

Jeremy powered down his computer. "I'll keep thinking about it over the weekend, play around on my home computer to see if I can replicate it. Monday, I'll see if I can find any trace of my ideas."

Melissa squeezed his shoulder. "Thanks for all your hard work. Enjoy your Thanksgiving."

She and Scott headed toward the stairs. They passed Diana's cube, where the light was on. Odd. Maybe Danielle left it on when she removed the box. Diana's chair was pulled out too. She shut the light off and pushed the chair back in, then they took the stairs down to the lobby. She waved to George at the security desk.

"You leaving for the day, Ms. Ellis?"

"Not yet, just lunch."

"Have a good one."

Once they were in Scott's Corvette and headed out of the parking lot he said, "I have a stop to make first. My glasses are in. And there's a great taco place next door."

"Sounds good." She mulled over what Jeremy had told them. "His ideas seem pretty out there. But they do fit what we know so far. We just don't know who."

"If it's terrorists like Kyle suspects, they'd likely have some pretty advanced programmers on their side. Either by ideology or by bribes."

"But it also means someone on the inside had to have access to put that bug into the computer. I don't know if Trent has that access. Gavin does because he started this company as a programmer, and he chimes in on projects now and then. But I don't see Gavin going that low, even for Trent. Money, yes. National security, no."

Scott reached over and squeezed her knee. "Put it out of your mind. There's nothing you can do about it now anyway."

She nodded, feeling the fire up her leg from his touch. Yep, he made it easy to forget work.

They arrived at the optometrist's, and the woman behind the counter greeted Scott with a big smile that dimmed slightly when she spotted Melissa. She brought out a pair of dark, angular frames that made his blue eyes pop. She spent a bit more time than necessary making sure they fit him correctly. "Be sure to come back in if you have any problems or need any adjustments."

Melissa suppressed a giggle.

They went next door to the taco place and stood in line to place their order. "Those glasses look great on you. They make your eyes look really blue. Great customer service too." She grinned.

Scott shook his head. "She was just being helpful. She knew I didn't want to wear glasses."

"Uh huh."

Scott turned to her. "What?"

"She was totally flirting with you. And she was not happy to see me with you."

They moved up to the front of the line and placed their orders. Once they were seated at their table, Scott studied her. "Do you think she thought you were my girlfriend?"

Melissa shrugged, her face heating. For a moment, it was nice to pretend that she was. Even if it was just to annoy a saleswoman.

Scott leaned over the small table. "Maybe you should be."

"Number twelve?" A server appeared with their orders and set them on the table, causing Scott to sit back. "Can I get you anything else?"

"No thanks."

Which was just as well. She surely hadn't heard what she thought she did. Did she?

Scott just studied her, a grin playing around his lips while he bit into his taco.

THEY RODE BACK TO THE OFFICE IN SILENCE. NOT awkward but still expectant with Scott's comment. Should he have said it? He hadn't planned on it, just blurted it out. So unlike him. But so what? He wanted Melissa as his girlfriend. Kyle was right. They could figure things out. Somehow.

He glanced over at her. She chewed her bottom lip as she stared out the windshield. He reached for her hand. "I meant what I said. I know there are a lot of complications between us, but we're both smart, determined people. We can make this work. I want to at least try. Life's too short." He swallowed, thinking about Jordan and Ashley.

She nodded but didn't say anything.

He pulled into the nearly empty parking lot at Broadstone Technologies. "Melissa." He waited until she met his gaze. "We make a good team. Somehow, I think we can make this work. Are you willing to try?"

She nodded again, this time more confidently. "Yes. It scares me a little."

"Aw, if it's not a little scary, it's not worth doing." He leaned over and brushed his lips across hers, lingering, enjoying her closeness.

He held her hand across the parking lot. "What time is Allie coming to get you?"

"Three. We've got an hour and a half. That should give me time to finish up those reports. Then I won't have that hanging over me for the weekend."

"How often do you get to see your mom?"

"Not too often. It's not super convenient and—" she shrugged—"there's a history there. It's complicated."

They entered the lobby, and she slid her hand away. George waved at them. "You're not staying too long now, are you?"

"Just another hour and a half. Most everyone is already gone, right?" Melissa punched the elevator button.

"Pretty much. Trent and Mr. Broadstone are still here."

Something flickered across Melissa's face.

The elevator dinged, and they stepped inside.

Chapter Nineteen

Melissa's watch buzzed as they stepped out of the elevator. "Danielle forgot to toss her lunch leftovers from the fridge. She asked if I could do it so they wouldn't be disgusting come Monday."

"Well, we wouldn't want that. Lead on." Scott slipped his hand around hers again, grinning. He was having too much fun with this.

She'd like to enjoy it more, but she was at work and that took priority. Too bad she wouldn't see him until Sunday. It would be nice to spend time with him away from work and all the stress. It was supposed to rain Sunday. Maybe they could watch a movie.

She tossed Danielle's leftovers in the trash. As they headed back to the team area, she heard voices and stopped. "Someone's still here."

Scott nodded. "George said Trent and Gavin were. Sounds like they're arguing."

Trent's screaming voice floated to them. "More than arguing." Goosebumps lifted on her arms.

Scott tilted his head. "Is there a way we can get closer? Something said in anger might be helpful."

Fear nearly rooted her to the spot. But Scott was right. They needed to learn whatever they could.

She eased them along the hall to where it intersected with the one to Gavin's office. She peeked around the corner. Shari was gone. She could see Trent and Gavin in his office. The door was open. She slipped back.

Scott tugged her behind him and took her place at the corner.

"Where is it, Dad? We are so screwed." The panic in Trent's voice almost made him sound like a teenager.

"Trent. I can't keep bailing you out. You've got to get a grip on this, or we'll both end up losing our security clearances, and the whole company will come down." Gavin's voice was laced with exasperation.

It was about time. Finally, he realized what a liability Trent was to the company. Maybe he'd fire him.

"Dad. You don't get it. This is more than drugs. A lot more. That shipment that I can't find? That's only the tip of the iceberg. I'm into them deep."

Gavin sighed. "Where did you leave it? And why on earth did you bring it here anyway?"

"It's in the operations team area. One of the empty cubes. I figured it'd be safe there with everyone out for Thanksgiving, and if it was found, it'd blow back on Melissa."

She clapped her hand to her mouth to keep from gasping. It was one thing to think that Trent was setting her up. Another to actually hear it.

Scott wrapped his hand around hers.

Wait. What was he talking about? He hid drugs in one of her team's empty cubes?

Gavin spoke again. "And you're sure it's not there? Someone didn't just move it?"

"It's not there. I checked everywhere."

Diana's cube. The light and the chair. The box that Danielle had thrown out. Maybe that hadn't been Styrofoam. Her stomach sank to her shoes.

Scott glanced at her. He'd made the same connection.

"I'll get you into rehab."

"Dad, I'm not doing another rehab. This is way beyond rehab. Do you know what they'll do when I don't bring them their drugs? Do you know what they've been asking me to do? So far, it's just been a little glitch here and there. Next time, who knows what could happen?"

A glitch? Could this "glitch" be the problem with the avionics? Could Trent be the one that planted the bad code? He didn't have access. But Gavin did. Her tacos threatened to come up. She couldn't believe it of him.

Gavin's voice cut low. "You'll destroy us both."

Trent gave a harsh laugh. "You're in it as deep as I am. I've been using your computer and logging in under your credentials. Now, we're doing this my way."

Scott pulled on her hand and tugged her back the way they came. She raised her eyebrows and then heard footsteps.

Scott pulled her along faster, and she broke into a run, glad she had ballet flats and pants on today.

"Hey! Wait!" Trent's voice.

She didn't turn around to look. He'd spotted them. This was not good at all.

"Let's head to your office." Scott pulled her around a corner and into the team area. They flew past Danielle's desk.

She grabbed her badge, swiped it at the door.

Scott yanked the door open, and she fled inside.

He pulled the door shut behind them. "How long before he can get access?"

"I don't know. He shouldn't have access at all. Not to my office, not to Gavin's computer. Doesn't seem like any of that has stopped him."

Scott pulled over one of the conference table chairs and jammed it under the doorknob and pushed his weight against it, leaning away from the view through the sidelight window. She ducked around the credenza.

Pounding on the door. "Melissa! I just want to talk. I think there's a misunderstanding."

Scott shook his head, finger to his lips.

Her purse slipped off her shoulder and landed at her feet. She'd forgotten it had been with her this whole time. She picked up her phone and showed it to Scott mouthing, "Kyle?"

He nodded.

The pounding and pleading continued.

She tapped out a quick text to Kyle saying they found info but were trapped in her office and needed help.

"Melissa! Come on. Let's just talk." Silence. "Okay, fine. Be that way. You'll regret it." His footsteps receded.

She waited a moment, then whispered, "Do you think he's gone?"

Scott leaned against the door, listening. Then he peered around the sidelight before easing away, making sure the chair was securely under the knob. "Let's put some paper over the sidelight. He knows we're in here, but the less he can see, the better."

She dug around in her desk and pulled out an old report and a tape dispenser. He waved her to the couch while he taped over the window. When he was done, he joined Melissa on the couch.

"What did Kyle say?" His voice was low.

She glanced at her phone. A red exclamation point showed the text hadn't sent. The upper left corner of her phone said No Service.

———

Scott checked his phone. Same thing. No Service. He nodded to the phone on her desk. "Call security."

Melissa slid over to the phone and lifted the handset to her ear. She pressed the receiver a few times then shook her head. "No dial tone."

What kind of access did Trent have that he could disable all the comms?

She moved back to the couch, and Scott slid his arm around her shoulders, pulling her close. He kept his voice low. "Allie will be here in a bit. When she can't get ahold of you, she'll call Kyle."

Melissa nodded. "True. She is a worst-case scenario thinker."

He scanned the room looking for tools or weapons. He had a small pocket knife on his keychain. Likely they just needed to wait Trent out. He was a spoiled kid throwing a temper tantrum. Though how he got the comms shut off was an interesting question. He must have an inside man in security.

"Trent's used to getting what he wants. He's not going to like that he can't get to us." Melissa laid her head on Scott's shoulder.

It felt right to have it there, and for a moment he just enjoyed the moment and didn't think about where they were or what might happen.

"What's Thanksgiving like at your house?"

"It's just me and my folks and Jessica, but my mom usually lays out a spread that takes us days to finish. Dad will watch as much football as humanly possible." He let out a sigh. "Hopefully Jessica will behave herself. My folks pretend not to notice, and then I end up picking up the pieces. I feel like her parent more than her big brother."

"What's the age difference?"

"She's ten years younger. She should be in college figuring out what she wants to do with her life, but she keeps dropping out when classes get challenging. Right now she's tending bar and heading to Vegas on the weekends with her friends. Not a great life plan."

"You mentioned your older brother, Christopher, before. So now it's only you and Jessica?"

He nodded but was silent for a long moment. "His death is

why Jessica's drinking and her job bug me so much. She was born after Christopher died, but there are pictures of him everywhere at our house and even at the high school we all went to. There's a tree planted in his honor there and a plaque with his name on it. In the trophy case there's a display about him. I used to walk past it every day. He was this big football hero at the high school."

"Was that why you went into football?"

"I think so. My folks were so sad. I was only seven. I'd seen my dad throw the football around with Christopher, and sometimes they'd include me. It seemed to be the only thing that made my dad happy. When I scored my first touchdown in Pop Warner football, it was the first time I'd seen him smile since Christopher's death. Seemed like I had to keep doing that to make him happy."

He shifted on the couch. "Then I met Joe and Kyle two years later, and we all played together. We became the dream team, man." He chuckled. "When my parents had Jessica, football was the only thing that made me feel important, like I was good at something, that someone noticed me. My friends became more of my family because I felt almost invisible at home living in the shadow of Christopher and the needs of a baby sister."

Melissa nodded. "Yeah, I know a bit about feeling invisible."

"Jessica started getting into trouble in high school, staying out late, partying. I was in the Navy and gone a lot. But Joe and Kyle took my place and picked her up puking from parties, kept my parents from having to do it. I just didn't want them to lose another child due to her stupidity and selfishness."

Melissa sat up and touched his face. "That's why you're Superman. You want to take all the hits so no one else has to."

Considering they were trapped in a room with no way to reach anyone, he didn't feel much like Superman.

Melissa dropped her hand. "Thank you for sharing that with me. It means a lot. You don't talk about it much, do you?"

He shook his head. "Kyle and Joe know it all, and there's never been anyone I wanted to share it with. Until now." He ran a knuckle down her cheek. "I want you to know the real me. That's the only way we're going to make this work."

Tingles followed in the wake of his touch, and she briefly closed her eyes. Despite the crazy situation they were in, sitting here with Scott was good and grounding. Beyond all the flash and flyboy flare, he had a lot of the same growing-up issues she did.

He dropped his hand. "Your turn."

She checked her watch. "It won't be too long before Allie is here, but it'll take her awhile before she realizes there's a problem and I'm not just late. And I'm never late. Then she'll realize something is wrong."

"You're stalling." He grinned at her.

"I'm not. Just trying to decide which level of detail to tell based on the time we have."

"Always the planner. Tell me about your childhood. You've mentioned that there's a bit of a strain in your relationship with your mom."

She nodded. "Yeah. My mom's an artist. Our house was pretty chaotic growing up. My dad left us when I was ten, just after Brittany's birth. Mom would vacillate between being emotional or going on an artistic jag. Either way, she'd be so far off into some other land that there would be no food in the house or any clean laundry. Allie's two years younger than me, so she and I took care of Daniel, Matthew, and Brittany, making dinners and lunches, getting groceries, doing laundry, making sure they got their homework done."

She let out a breath. Those were such dark days. Sometimes she wondered how she survived. "My mom wasn't very good with money, so I got to the point where I'd tell her I needed a lot more than I did so I could make sure there was enough for food and the utilities. I rode my bike all over town taking care of things. I remember once running into my friend's mom at the water department. She was shocked that I was there paying a bill. Up until that moment, I didn't realize that it wasn't normal. Then I started noticing I was the only kid doing actual shopping at the grocery store."

"Did your mom notice or get upset?"

"Sometimes she noticed, but she was happy about it. She'd say, 'I don't have to worry. You're my good little girl.' Then she'd go back to painting or whatever project captured her fancy that week. It was up to me to create order for the younger ones, to make sure they got their homework done and got to bed on time."

"It's why you're so good at it."

"It's my natural habitat. I'm not sure if it's out of talent or necessity. Either way, it's ingrained in my DNA." She let out a breath, not liking the memories that surfaced, but Scott had been open and vulnerable. She needed to validate that by reciprocating. And she thought he might actually understand.

"One night, the littlest ones had been sick and home from school. I was cleaning up after them, making dinner and lunches, and getting everyone to bed. I sat down at the dining room table to finish a presentation due the next day. With all I had to do, I hadn't been able to get to it before then. I fell asleep, and I didn't finish it. When I was at class the next day, all I could do was tell the teacher I didn't have it done. She berated me in front of the whole class for not planning properly or being diligent in my work. It was humiliating. But the truth was worse." Tears pricked her eyes even now, but anger welled up too.

Scott laced his fingers through hers. "I see why your relationship with her would be strained even now. I'm sorry you had to go through all that. But I get why you are so prepared and organized for everything."

"It's too scary not to be." She sniffed back tears. The air

smelled a little like smoke. Her mind was playing tricks on her. She picked up her phone. Still no service. "Allie will be here any minute." She moved to the window and looked out. The reflective coating allowed her to look out but no one—and no prying electronic devices—could see in. "Allie's car is in the parking lot, parked next to yours."

Scott stood behind her. "Then this should all be over soon. I'm going to see if Trent has left us alone. Maybe we can just sneak down the stairs. It's been long enough. He probably got bored and left."

He eased the paper off the edge of the sidelight so he could peer out. Then he moved the chair from under the knob. He grabbed the knob and turned, then pulled. The door wiggled in the frame but didn't open.

He pulled the paper farther from the edge and looked around.

He turned to Melissa. "He's trapped us in here."

Chapter Twenty

"Hand me your coat." Scott reached out his hand.

Melissa handed it to him. "Why?"

"Not only has he slid a bar through the handle, he's started some sort of fire in front of your door." He shoved her coat along the bottom of the door. "The sidelight is impregnated with wire, so even if I could break it, I wouldn't be able to reach through to dislodge the bar."

Melissa looked out the window again. "She's so close but no help to us. And these windows are unbreakable."

He wrapped his arms around her. "Let's just wait. We've got some time. A door does a remarkably good job of blocking smoke. The fire department will be here soon, and we'll be rescued." As if in response to his words, the fire alarm sounded, and the light in her office strobed.

"Except last time the fire alarm went off, it was a false alarm. I wonder how seriously they'll take this one on a holiday weekend with no one in the building." She turned, facing him. "Maybe that was a trial run for Trent? He had some sort of plan to burn the building down if someone got too close to what he was doing?"

Which meant either someone was feeding Trent instructions

or he was smarter than Scott had given him credit for. "Nothing we can do about that now." He looked over her shoulder to the parking lot that was empty except for his car and Allie's. "She can probably hear the fire alarm. When the fire department shows up, she'll tell them we're still inside." He hoped so. He wasn't sure how long he could handle the flashing light or the high-pitched ringing before he got a migraine. And that was the last thing he needed. He was going to have to be on the top of his game to get them out of here.

Melissa nodded.

"Good. We just need to wait. Let's sit on the floor." Faint tendrils of smoke curled in through the top of the door. They put their backs to the couch, and he spotted the AC intake grate that had kept him awake when he'd tried to nap on the couch one day. "Hey, let's move this couch." He lifted the end and swung it around, giving them access to the grate. He pulled out his pocketknife and flipped open the screwdriver blade. "We can always get out through here." He went to work, but the pocketknife's poor leverage made it hard to turn the paint-caked screws. "Where do you think this goes, based on the building's layout?"

"There's an open work space, then the conference room, then the hallway to the break room."

The noise and lights caused the pressure to build in his head, and the stupid screws were moving far too slowly. His inclination was to just kick the grate, which wouldn't help things from this angle at all, just dent it inward. "That should take us parallel to the fire. Which isn't my favorite choice. But it's better than being in the path of the fire, which we are now. But hopefully we won't have to use this option at all."

The second screw came loose. He inched his fingers under the edge of the grate and wiggled it back and forth loosening the other screws. He went back to work on the remaining two screws.

With a loud pop, the sidelight shattered, gobbling up the paper instantly and filling the room with smoke.

"Get on the floor, belly down!"

Melissa did as told, slinging her purse across her body. Both fear and trust filled her gaze, something he'd seen in the men he'd led before. If there was ever a time to be Superman, this was it.

Third screw fell out, and he twisted the grate, pivoting it around the remaining screw. "I'm going in first. I don't know what we're going to encounter. You follow me. Hold on to me."

She nodded, and he slipped into the metal tunnel, her hand cold on his ankle.

MELISSA HATED TIGHT, DARK SPACES. BUT SHE DIDN'T WANT to be burned alive or die of smoke inhalation, so this was the lesser of two evils. Scott's ankle in her death grip and the light of his phone bouncing ahead of them brought her comfort.

The fire alarm was slightly muted in here. Each placement of elbow or knee in the inch-deep dust reverberated. The blessing was that the fire system shut down the AC unit, so the dust wasn't blowing around them.

"You okay?" Scott looked back over his shoulder as much as he could in the confined space.

"Yep. Keep going. The sooner we're out of here, the better." She was not going to think of the walls closing in on her, or the air growing more stale. *Focus on Scott.*

He stopped. His light moved around the tunnel.

"What's the problem?"

"We're at a T. Just trying to match up what I see here with your office layout. I don't want to go in the wrong direction."

"I don't think we want to go left. That's the rest of the executive suite, finance and such. They are all gone, and I don't have permissions for that area, so my card can't swipe us out of there.

I know there's a fire exit for every security zone, but I don't know where it is in that department. We could be trapped."

"To the right it is." His body snaked around the corner, and she almost lost her grip on his ankle as he made the turn. "Hang on, sweetheart. We're on the home stretch."

"I hope so." Her elbows hurt from digging into the metal with each crawl. Her clothes were ruined, which was no great loss if she got out of here alive. Her purse, slung crosswise over her body and pushed to her back, bumped along with every movement. Yes, it was all replaceable, but not having her phone and keys would make things extremely inconvenient to even get in her house, let alone get on a plane. *I can do all things through Christ who strengthens me. Get us out of here, God. Please. I don't want to die like a roasted chicken.* She wasn't going to think about death. Just the strength she had in Jesus. She would focus on that. She put her gaze on the top of Scott's head and used it to measure their forward progress.

Was it her imagination or did the tunnel seem like it was getting lighter up ahead?

"Good call, Ops. I think we're close to something."

"Ops?"

"Yeah, operations. You're VP of Operations. I've decided that's your call sign. Ops."

She laughed. "All right then, Superman. Where are we?"

He paused and his head moved from side to side. Light striped the walls of the vent. Must be another grate. "Cupboards, tables. Looks like the break room."

"Thank you, Jesus."

"Scoot back a bit. I'm going to have to pound on this grate to get it loose. Screws are on the other side." He reared back and slammed his hands into the grate several times then stopped, breathing heavily.

No. They weren't going to come this far just to get stuck here. The walls seemed to be moving in, and sweat poured off her forehead. Focus. Was there anything she could do to help?

Anything in her purse?

"It'd be easier if I could turn around and kick the thing. But we're in here too tight." He banged on it some more. "It's getting looser. I think. I just don't have enough leverage from this angle."

Melissa swallowed. She could probably get turned around feet first. But then, she'd have to wiggle past him. There was room. Maybe. Or they might just get wedged in like sardines.

They didn't have a choice. "I think I can do it. I'm smaller than you." She rolled to her side and slid her purse off, pushing it in front of her. She pulled one knee to her chest, then the other. It hit the side wall and stuck. She let out a breath and tugged till it came free. Curling her shoulders, she pushed her torso back into the dark while inching her feet forward. Pressing hard, she popped free and was now feet first.

"Okay, I did it." She was breathing hard and could only see metal above her.

"I'm going to roll to my side. You slide past me."

Scott's feet moved closer to her as he pushed himself back the way they had come.

She used her arms like a modified side crawl to push herself forward. Her head was past his knees now. Her shoulder was burning with the effort. As their waists drew closer, their clothes dragged across each other. "I hope we don't get stuck this way. Like two wedges."

"Suck it in, Ops."

She wanted to laugh, but he was right. As he came even with her, he pushed against the far wall, levering himself past. He dropped a quick kiss on her nose. "You've got this."

Her feet touched the grate. She levered herself up on her elbows. Was that voices she heard? She couldn't tell over the blaring alarm. Drawing her knees in as tightly as she could, she exploded them outward with as much force as she could muster.

The grate flexed and bent, the screws had more play.

One more. She took a deep breath as she pulled her legs in

and forced it all out with her legs. Her feet flailed out the empty opening.

She did it!

THE SMOKE-TINGED AIR OF THE BREAK ROOM GREETED them. Melissa shoved a table and chairs out of the way as she and Scott shimmied out of the vent.

A gloved hand reached down to help her up. Firefighters. Relief weakened her knees, and she was glad for the help.

"Anyone else in the building?" the firefighter asked.

"Not in my area. Trent and Gavin were both here earlier. But the fire started by my office." She pointed them in the direction.

"Security told us only you were in the building."

She pointed. "Gavin's office is that way. So is Trent's."

He said something into his mic, and the other firefighter came over. "Let's get you two out of here."

They hustled down the backstairs, just like they had for the drill. Except this time there was no drill. When they burst through the outside door, the cool, fresh air was a relief. She took a deep breath and coughed.

Behind the fire apparatus, she spied Allie, Kyle, and Steve talking with the incident commander.

The moment Allie spotted her, she began bouncing on her toes. Only the fact that Steve had his hand on her arm was keeping her in her place.

Melissa ran over and wrapped her in a tight embrace. "I'm okay. Everything turned out okay."

Allie pulled back. "I was so worried. You're never late, and Scott's car was here, but neither of you answered your phones. Or your office phone. I called Kyle. Then I heard the fire alarms and called 911."

Melissa gave her another squeeze. "You did the right thing."

Scott came up behind them and conferred with Kyle and

Steve. He could give them the update. She was exhausted, and the last thing she wanted to do was relive the whole thing.

One of the firefighter/paramedics came over. "Hey, why don't you let me check you out. Any pain anywhere? Any trouble breathing?"

Melissa allowed herself to be led over to the engine bumper. "No, I don't think so." The adrenaline drained from her, and she was grateful to be able to sit. Her elbows and knees were sore from crawling.

He took her vitals and listened to her heart and lungs. "Everything checks out. But don't hesitate to go to the emergency room if you start feeling funny."

"Okay." Not going to happen, but whatever. She escaped a burning building. Anything after that was gravy.

He checked out Scott too, and Kyle called her over. Steve was on the phone, but his eyes kept straying to Allie. Scott had told them about the drugs in the Dumpster, and Kyle already had an officer on it.

She gave him her statement, but as she did it sunk in. Trent had tried to kill them. Deliberately.

Kyle studied her. "We can't find Trent anywhere. Steve talked to Gavin, who's on his way back here to see the damage to the building. He admitted that he and Trent argued but said Trent stomped off mad, and Gavin assumed he'd left the building."

"I'd really like to get out of here before Gavin gets here. I just can't face him right now."

Kyle nodded. "Understood. I don't need anything else from you right now. I can reach you if I need to."

"I'll be at my mom's in Phoenix, but I'll be answering my cell."

A woman rushed across the parking lot, beelining toward Kyle.

He turned away and grimaced. "Monica West, reporter for the *South County Times*. Now would be a good time for you guys to get out of here before she starts hassling you. I'll hold her off."

"Have a good Thanksgiving, Kyle." Melissa gave him a slight wave. "And thanks for answering Allie's call."

He glanced over his shoulder at Steve and gave her a grin. "Sure."

Scott finished with the paramedic and put his arm around her, guiding her toward his car. "Good job, Ops. I'd say that was a successful ex-fil."

She gave him a wry smile and shook her head. "You're an adrenaline junkie." She leaned into him. "I'm just glad I had you with me. Now, I need to get my bag out of your car so I can get on the road with my antsy sister."

Allie popped up beside her. "We've missed our flight, so now we have a six-hour drive."

"One more thing to blame Trent for." Scott unlocked his trunk and pulled Melissa's bag out. He handed it to Allie who headed for her car. Steve wandered over and said something to her.

Scott pulled Melissa into a tight hug. "I'm glad we made it out. Please let me know when you get to Phoenix. I want to know you're safe." He kissed her cheek and then let her go.

A minute later, she and Allie were driving out of the parking lot, Scott and Steve waving.

As the smoking building got smaller in the side mirror, Melissa wondered what real firestorm she'd return to on Monday.

Chapter Twenty-One

Scott walked through the front door of his folks' house to the smell of good memories. Pie, rolls, veggies, and a roasting turkey made a cornucopia of delight. After yesterday, he was ready for the comforts of home and some good food. What was Melissa doing today? Probably the same thing he was. He was glad she'd shared her family dynamics with him yesterday. He prayed things would go well with her family this weekend. She deserved a break after everything she'd been through. She'd been amazing yesterday, not freaking out and keeping her wits about her while they worked together to solve the problem and rescue themselves. There weren't too many people he could say that about.

His stomach growled. He couldn't wait to eat. It had been slow going this morning. Too many nightmares last night.

In the den, his dad sat in his recliner watching a football game. "Hey, Dad."

Dad turned his head. "Hey, Scott. Grab a seat and come watch the game with me."

"I'll go say hi to Mom first. See if she needs anything." Scott pivoted and headed to the kitchen, where Mom stood at the counter with a mixer in her hand, making mashed potatoes.

"Smells amazing."

She turned. "Hi, Scott. You're just in time. Ooh, I like your new glasses. Very sharp. Can you get the turkey out of the oven for me? I'll whip up some gravy while it's resting, and then we can eat."

"Sure." He grabbed hot mitts from the counter and pulled the bird out, setting it on top of the stove. The center island was laden with side dishes and two pies sat off on a side counter. "Did you do all this yourself? Where's Jessica?"

His mother waved him away. "It was nothing. I'm sure she'll be here soon. Now, can you put the turkey on the platter? Then I can drain the drippings into the saucepan."

He did as instructed, but he couldn't believe that his mom had done all this work. There was enough food for an army. And where was his sister? He sent her a quick text.

Mom whisked her slurry of milk and flour into the drippings and stirred. "How was your week, hon?"

"It was fine. Not too busy." No way was he telling her about the fire at Broadstone. She'd just worry. And with Dad's heart, they didn't need any more stress. He snatched a bit of crispy skin off the turkey.

"I can see you. Stop picking at the food."

He laughed. "Still have eyes in the back of your head, I see."

"Always."

He sneaked a peek at his phone. No answer from Jessica. He punched her number. It went straight to voicemail. Great. Either her phone was off or dead. Why couldn't she be responsible for once?

Mom poured the contents of the saucepan into a gravy boat. "We're ready. Go call your dad, and we'll ask the blessing."

Scott headed back to the den. "Dad? We're ready to eat." He had to raise his voice to be heard over the blaring TV.

"What? Time to eat? I'm starving. Is your sister here?" Dad pushed out of his recliner and stood, wobbled a bit.

Scott rushed over and grabbed his arm. "You okay?"

"I'm fine. Just stood up too fast. Nothing a good meal won't fix."

Scott raised his eyebrows but said nothing, just kept an eye on Dad as they moved to the kitchen.

Mom had taken off her apron, revealing a brown sweater with fall leaves embroidered on it. "Should we wait for Jessica?"

"Nope. I tried getting ahold of her. Her phone must be off. She'll be here when she gets here." Scott held out his hands to his parents. "Dad, do the honors, please."

They bowed their heads. "Father, thank you for the blessings you give us every day and for the abundance you provide. Help us to remember that more than just one day a year. Thank you for this food, and bless the hands that prepared it. Amen."

Scott squeezed his parents' hands. Yes, he had a lot to be thankful for. It had been a rough year, and yesterday had been a rough day that could have ended a lot differently. *Thank you, God, for watching out for us.*

They had just finished the first round of eating, and Scott was seriously contemplating seconds when the front door opened. He pushed back his chair and headed for the entryway.

Jessica stood there. "Hey, Scott. Happy Thanksgiving."

He lowered his voice and stepped closer. "Where have you been? I tried texting and calling."

"Oh." She reached for her purse and stumbled a bit. Alcohol fumes wafted off her.

He reached out and grabbed her arm. "I can't believe you. Why'd you come here like that?"

"What? It's Thanksgiving, and I just had a little bit to celebrate."

He wanted to shake some sense into her. But he didn't think even that would do any good.

"Scott? Who's there?" His mom's voice floated from the dining room.

"Jessica's here." He made his voice much more cheerful than

it was. He glared at his sister. "Get in there and behave. And I hope they don't smell any alcohol on you."

She gave him a too-cheerful smile. "Of course, big brother." She patted him on the cheek as she passed him on her way to the dining room. He heard his parents greet her with joy and relief. He leaned against the wall, half listening to them while he got his anger under control. What he really wanted to do was call Melissa, but he wasn't going to ruin her holiday too.

He headed back into the dining room. "Mom, want me to start some coffee for the pies?" He sent Jessica a glare. She had loaded her plate and was digging in, but some coffee would help too. He couldn't believe she drove over here like that. Though, it wasn't the first time. He had no idea how often she drove that way and was sure he didn't want to know. It made him sick.

He busied himself with the coffee so he didn't have to sit around the dining room table and make nice with his sister. He listened to his parents ask about her plans. She always had great plans. Terrible follow through, but great plans.

His phone buzzed in his pocket. Melissa. **In a turkey coma yet?**

He grinned. **Nah. Just starting on coffee and pie. You?**

Still too much adrenaline from yesterday I think. How did you sleep?

He didn't want to worry her, but he also knew he could be honest with her. **Not that great. You?**

Same.

He wanted to hear her voice. **Can I call you later?**

Looking forward to it.

He pulled four coffee mugs out of the cupboard. Being away from Melissa had left him feeling lost, unmoored. Especially after yesterday. He got the tray down from above the fridge, loaded the cups, the cream and sugar set, and the coffee carafe on it and carried it into the dining room.

"Oh, thank you, Scott." Mom made room on the table. "Jessica was just telling us about her classes next semester."

"Interesting." He had no interest in whatever lies Jessica was spewing. He didn't understand why his parents never called her on it. They always seemed so excited. "I'm taking orders for pie." If he kept busy, he wouldn't stew about his reckless sister.

And maybe it'd make the time go faster until he could talk to Melissa.

Melissa stood in the kitchen loading the dishwasher with Allie, while her brother Matthew brought dirty dishes from the table. Daniel and his girlfriend, Nikki, sat at the table with Mom and her boyfriend, Larry, while Brittany was getting coffee and pie for everyone.

It hadn't exactly been a traditional Thanksgiving. She and Allie had gotten into town about ten o'clock last night. The six-hour drive had been long enough for Melissa to probe Allie about her relationship with Steve and what had happened during the Big Bear trip. Allie had said they'd chatted, but she didn't think Steve wanted to be anything more than friends. And she was okay with that. Melissa wasn't sure she was buying that, but she had been too exhausted to probe further.

She'd given Allie a high-level view of her day, leaving out that she'd been particularly targeted by Trent, just stating that there'd been a fire in the building that had trapped them in her office. Which was terrifying enough.

After a shower to wash off the dust and smoke, she fell into the motel bed and slept until the nightmares took over.

That morning they'd hit the motel's breakfast bar for fruit and yogurt before heading over to Mom's. Matthew had assured Allie that he had the turkey covered, that Daniel and his girl-friend were bringing the side dishes, and that Brittany was taking care of dessert. Allie and Melissa didn't need to do anything but show up.

Except that Matthew didn't know that turkeys had to be

thawed. So they had no turkey. Poor Matthew felt terrible, shoving his hands in his pockets. "Sorry, Lis. I didn't know, and I didn't want to call you guys. I wanted to do it on my own."

Allie looked at Melissa. "I think Fry's is open for a few hours this morning. Maybe Basha's."

Mom floated in, her batik-dyed peasant dress billowing behind her. She slipped her arms around her girls. "Why are you two frowning and stressing about this? It'll all work out. It always does."

Melissa clenched her jaw. It always worked out because she made it work out. But today, she was too tired to care. They could have pizza, and it'd be fine with her. If there was a pizza place open on Thanksgiving.

Daniel and Nikki had saved the day bringing scalloped potatoes, green bean casserole, and a fruit-and-Jello dish. So that was their Thanksgiving feast. And the conversation around the table was pleasant. Larry told a good story and seemed to be a nice, solid guy. Her little brothers had grown up, something she'd also missed by not getting back here as often as she should.

And given what had happened at work yesterday, it seemed like she'd be having more free time on her hands soon. She didn't think Broadstone was going to survive, and for once, there was nothing she could do to stop it from happening. She'd turned over every possible angle in her mind last night during the drive. She'd sent a message to her naval liaison to pull the latest software update and go back to the previous version. They hadn't been using the newer version after Scott's accident anyway, but this would ensure it was wiped out. That was one thing she could do to hopefully prevent any other accidents.

Melissa loaded the last dish then closed the dishwasher and joined everyone else at the dining room table for coffee and pie. Brittany had brought chocolate and lemon pies. Brittany's favorites, if not exactly seasonal.

Matthew told a few stories on Daniel to Nikki. Despite their difficult childhood, there had been some good memories, some bright moments. And she was grateful to Matthew for reminding her of that.

Brittany got up and came back with something that she spread out on the table. It was the battered old map of the US that they used to plan their dream trips on.

"I can't believe you still have that." Melissa leaned over and traced one of the pencil marks with her finger. It was their great southwest trip, with stops at the Grand Canyon, Monument Valley, Arches, Zion, and Bryce Canyon. It would take at least two weeks to see everything, and that was just one corner of the United States. They had several other trips mapped out too.

"Are you kidding? I think about this all the time. We really need to plan one of these trips." Brittany touched the crease of the map where it wore thin.

Matthew leaned over, and Daniel turned to Nikki. "Melissa would bribe us with this. If we did all our chores and got ready for bed, we could get the map out and plan a trip."

Mom glanced over from the end of the table. "I don't remember that."

Melissa slid her gaze around the table, watching as her siblings did likewise. No one wanted to say what they were all thinking: They got the map out when she wasn't around. "Someone else told me recently that we should get a road trip on the calendar. So let's start talking dates." After yesterday, she was acutely aware that life could be cut short.

Her siblings began a discussion of the pros and cons of different dates. She would go with whatever they decided. Her phone buzzed. Scott. She stepped out onto the back patio to answer. It was a lovely seventy-five degrees in the Valley of the Sun.

"Hey, Ops. How was your Thanksgiving?" Scott's voice was like warm honey over her heart.

She slid into the patio chair and closed her eyes. "Well, I'm not in a turkey coma." But a bit of unexpected contentment seeped through her bones.

Chapter Twenty-Two

Melissa dropped her bag inside her front door. Allie had dropped her off. Leaving Arizona had been bittersweet. She and Allie had stayed a day longer than originally planned, coming home on Sunday. All of them had hiked South Mountain Park—and the oppositely named Fat Man's Pass on the Mormon Trail—and visited the Desert Botanical Gardens. The kids had invited Mom and Larry, but they declined the extra physical activity. Her little brothers and sisters had grown up into adults she enjoyed spending time with. She needed to do it more often.

And it looked like she would, since they'd picked the Great Southwest Trip as their road trip and planned on late spring next year. She'd achieved a lot of goals in her professional life, but making this one particular dream come true brought tears to her eyes. The map had been a way to dream about something beyond their rather dismal childhood, but she'd never seriously thought it would come true. Well, now it would.

She texted Scott. **I'm home.**

She had received two calls from Gavin while she was in Arizona. Neither of which she had responded to. The first one, he wanted to just talk to her. Given the strain in his voice, she suspected he wanted to know what she knew, what she had told the police. So she wasn't going to talk to him until she'd talked to Kyle.

The other call was to let her know that the office would be closed Monday and Tuesday due to the smoke damage. They'd see if they could reconfigure things to get everyone back to work once the building was deemed safe. She'd sent a group text letting her team know. They wouldn't complain about getting an extra-long holiday.

Her phone rang. Scott. Interesting.

"You're home."

She grinned. "I just texted you that."

"So you did. I have a proposal for you."

Her heart hitched at the word *proposal* and then settled down. "Really?"

"Since you can't work tomorrow, I thought we'd play hooky. Get away from this mess and have a good day spending some time together."

She slid into a chair. "I like how you think. What did you have in mind?" She'd had more fun days in the past month than she'd had all year. She'd had more stressful ones too.

"I'll pick you up in the morning. We'll grab breakfast, and then I'll take you to an unknown location. Wear boots, jeans, and a jacket."

"So I don't get to know where we're going?"

"Do you trust me?" His voice cut low.

"Yeah, I do." And she did.

After what they'd been through, trust was not a question.

SCOTT RANG MELISSA'S DOORBELL, AND THE DOOR OPENED almost immediately. She smiled at him, wearing jeans, hiking boots, and a medium-weight jacket over a printed T-shirt.

"Good morning." She picked up a small backpack. "I'm ready and starving."

He stepped in and pulled her into a hug. It felt so good to hold her after being away from her for several days. Today, it would be just the two of them without any interruptions or work worries. "I missed you."

"I missed you too." Her voice reverberated through his chest. She pulled back. "You know, there's not too many people I'd trust to take me somewhere unknown. I must really like you." She poked his chest.

Warmth curled through his chest at her words. "I really like you too." He dropped a kiss on her forehead. "Which is why I'm not telling you where we're going." His gaze skimmed her up and down. "You're dressed just fine. And I'm starving also. Let's go."

They ended up at Mimi's Cafe for breakfast. "Eat a big breakfast," he told her. "We're going to be burning a lot of calories today."

The server slid french toast stuffed with cream cheese and berries in front of Melissa.

Scott had cinnamon roll french toast. They split a side of bacon and drank several cups of coffee.

"Good thing we'll have a lot to do today." Melissa patted her stomach as they left the restaurant. "It'll have to be a lot to work off that breakfast."

He glanced at her, enjoyed the smile that played around her lips, the relaxed set to her shoulders. She was carefree, a look he didn't often see on her. He wanted them to have more meals like this together, a lazy breakfast with the whole day to themselves stretched out before them.

They headed out of town, inland. Melissa didn't ask questions about their destination, and they shared about their complicated Thanksgivings. Maybe next year, things would be different. Maybe they'd be together.

"It's weird thinking about next Thanksgiving. Neither one of us has any idea what life will look like then." Scott glanced over to gauge her reaction.

"True. If Broadstone survives what is now a police investigation, which likely will trigger a Defense Department investigation, it'll look a lot different. I'm not sure how Gavin will be able to maintain his position as CEO." She stared out the window at the brown coastal hills that flanked the freeway but was as relaxed as he'd ever seen her.

"What happens if he steps down?"

"The board will bring in a new CEO, and things will change. How much they will change is the question." She turned to him. "What do you think will happen with you this time next year?"

He reached for her hand. "No idea. I have to get back to duty status first. But whatever happens, I want it to be with you." He kissed her fingers.

The coastal hills flattened out into the Inland Empire then narrowed again as the I-10 freeway moved through the Banning Pass. Hundreds of wind turbines dotted the landscape on both sides before the San Bernardino mountain range rose up behind them to the north and Mount San Jacinto to the south. The coolness of the coast and valley gave way to the warmer temps in the desert.

Melissa tilted her head. "Palm Springs?"

"Maybe. You'll see." He took the exit for Highway 111, which hugged the base of the mountain. After a while, he turned right.

Melissa grinned. "The tram! I've always wanted to do this but never have. It's a perfect day for it."

Scott grinned. Good, he'd gotten it right and pleased her. Something glowed in his chest. "Sunny and low sixties up at the top. Great hiking weather. And a little bit of adventure with a tram that rotates and takes us up two and a half miles from the desert floor to the top of the mountain. A six-thousand-foot elevation gain."

She shivered. "Okay. Not a fan of heights, but this is going to be worth it. And you'll be with me."

"I'll be with you. Every step of the way."

AFTER DRIVING DEEPER INTO THE CANYON, THEY PARKED and hiked up to the tram station. Scott bought the tickets while Melissa looked around.

Her stomach got a bit wobbly as she studied the tram car and the towers that supported it. They were so high, and the wires looked so thin.

Scott wrapped his hand around hers. "I've got you. And we're just in time. The next tram leaves in a few minutes."

When it was their turn, they stepped into the surprisingly spacious tram. Scott guided her over to the side. Windows wrapped around the circumference of the tram, nearly floor to ceiling. He locked his arms around her waist. A few more people filed in behind them and then the tram doors closed. She braced herself against him as the tram began to ascend and slowly turn. They were surrounded by craggy rocks as they continued up the canyon. Then as the tram turned, the Coachella Valley slowly came into view, growing smaller and smaller as they rose up the steep terrain. It was terrifying and breathtaking.

The tram rumbled over the tower supports, causing it to shake. Melissa squeezed Scott's arm. It felt like they were going to shake right off the wires.

"We're fine." His whispered words slid past her ears and caused shivers down her back. She let out a breath and enjoyed the scenery, bracing herself as another tower approached. They bumped over it. This time it wasn't quite as terrifying, but still a little unnerving.

The ten-minute ride to the top ended when they exited the tram at Mountain Station. A building greeted them at the 8,500-foot elevation. They stepped inside and wandered through the displays about the area and the history. They even watched a short documentary.

Finally, Scott tugged her outside to the observation deck. "Let's experience it all instead of just learning about it." He led her to one of the telescopes on the deck that gave her a closer view of the valley far below them. She swiveled it around to see rocky peaks on either side.

"It's just amazing." There was so much to take in, it was nearly overwhelming.

"One day, we'll hike to the top of Mount San Jacinto. It's about five and a half miles from here. On a clear day you can see the ocean, all the way to Catalina Island and the glow from Las Vegas at night. One year, Kyle's dad took Kyle, Joe, and me hiking up the backside from Idyllwild, and we camped out."

They rounded the building and looked down on a switch-backing concrete path that led steeply away from the building and wound through the trees. Scott held out his hand. "Let's go."

Melissa looked down then took his hand. "Let's go. After the tram ride, I'm feeling rather confident."

"You do realize you have to ride the tram back down."

"I'll deal with that when we get there. One problem at a time, right?"

He laughed. "Right."

They bent their knees to slow their pace as they marched down to the mountain meadow, passing those going far more slowly heading up. At the bottom, the meadow was surrounded by trees that soared into the sky and granite boulders that had been tossed down from the peaks.

They looped around the meadow on a fairly flat trail that had signs along the way pointing out the native flora and fauna. A tree had fallen across the trail at some point and had been cut to let the path go right through it. The dappled shade gave an occasional break from the bright sun, and the slight chill to the breeze made her glad for her jacket.

"Ready for something with a bit more of a challenge and some fantastic views?"

"We're not heading to Mount San Jacinto, are we?"

"Not this time. This is only about a mile and a half."

"Lead on."

This hike had a few more strenuous parts to it, but it lifted out of the meadow basin and up around the ridge. The view was spectacular in any direction. Rocky peaks rising out of the flat, desert valley floor crisscrossed by roads and fields. They scrambled over some rocks to find a few flat ones that sat back a bit from a precipitous drop-off but overlooked a panoramic view of the desert. Giant rocks rose around them, and a few pines provided shade. The rocks were warm from the sun, and sitting was a welcome relief.

"Hungry?" Scott slid off his backpack.

"I could eat. And I didn't think I'd say that after that breakfast we had."

He handed her a water bottle and then kept pulling out cheese, salami, crackers, olives, and apples.

She raised her eyebrows. "I'm impressed. That's quite a spread."

"You learn a few things when you've done this as much as I have. You never think you'll be hungry, but then you get up here climbing around and you're starving. The guys and I only made one trip without bringing a snack. We were starving when we got back. Never made that mistake again."

They ate in silence for a minute, the wind through the trees and the birds providing a better serenade than any orchestra. The whole weight of the past month slipped from her shoulders. It was peaceful here.

"Let's grab a selfie so you can prove you were up here." Scott pulled out his phone and swiveled around so his back was to the valley spread out below. He motioned for Melissa to do the same. Once she was turned, he snugged close to her, leaning his head to touch hers. Her body went on high alert at his nearness as she relaxed into him.

Positioning the phone so it captured their faces and the valley behind them, he took a couple shots then lowered the phone. "I'll text them to you."

"Thanks." A tangible memory of this day would be perfect.

Scott leaned over and grabbed an apple. "Did you ever get away to nature as a kid? Even though you had all your brothers and sisters to take care of?"

"I got to go to summer science camp one year. I got a scholarship and went all the way to the piney woods of Texas. It was one of my best memories. I made two great friends, Gracelyn and Halley, that I still stay in touch with. For once, I had no one to be responsible for but myself. I got to be a kid with other kids who love science and STEM before it was called that. We solved problems together as a team. I didn't have the burden of figuring it out all alone and being responsible for the outcome."

He nudged her shoulder. "Kinda like what we do together."

She grinned, leaning into him. "Yeah, kinda like that. What about you? You said Kyle's dad took you guys camping."

"Yeah, he did. I have a lot of good memories of getting out to places like this. We camped all over the San Bernardino mountains. I think he figured it was the best way to deal with three overly energetic boys."

"Sounds like you guys did everything together."

"Yeah, we even ran a football camp for underprivileged kids together one summer. It was the best. We had just come off our championship season and had gotten all this press. There was a lot of pressure on us from all directions. But these kids didn't know who we were. They just loved that we were out there hanging with them and playing football." He looked off over the valley. "That's what I love about the Navy. Working as a team, solving problems. It's never about any one of us." He turned to her. "What do you want for the future?"

She shrugged. "I don't know for sure. For a long time I

thought Broadstone was my future. But now..." She sighed. "Something like this. More of this. More of helping people without all the pressure and limelight. Just doing what needs to be done and doing it with the people I care about."

He leaned close, bracing his arm behind her. "That seems like a really nice future."

"Yeah." Her heart beat faster at his nearness. He smelled like the mountains and a scent that was uniquely him.

His gaze darted to her lips before he bent his head and touched his mouth to hers. He wrapped his free hand around her neck, pulling her closer. Deepening his kiss.

She fisted his shirt, hanging on to the emotions that threatened to undo her control, but finally let herself be carried away by the moment, by Scott and being in his arms.

WHILE THE HIKE BACK UP THE CONCRETE SWITCHBACK TO the main level was possibly the most strenuous part of their hike, Scott felt lighter than he had since before his accident. His head didn't hurt even though they were about a thousand feet higher in altitude than in Holcomb Valley, and having Melissa by his side made him feel like everything would be okay.

The shadows were lengthening by the time they reached the top. The short winter days were playing a part in the final bit of his surprise day for her.

At the top, he refilled their water bottles and let her look around the gift shop. They had a little bit of time to kill. When she went to the bathroom, he sneaked back into the gift shop and made a purchase, tucking it into his backpack.

When she came out, she took his hand and smiled. "Thanks for an amazing day. It was just the best."

He led her in a different direction. "It's not over yet."

"Well, I know we have a long drive back..."

He shook his head and grinned. They walked over to Peaks

Restaurant, which sat cantilevered over the edge of the mountain giving a spectacular view of the valley below where lights were beginning to twinkle on. He gave the hostess his name for the reservation, and she seated them by the window where he'd requested, so they'd have the best view.

Melissa's mouth dropped open in surprise. He was quite pleased with himself.

She still seemed stunned as she perused the menu. "What an incredible view to dine with."

"I'm glad you like it."

After the hiking, he was hungry. He ordered the filet of beef, and she had the lemon salmon. And they shared Godiva double-chocolate cheesecake for dessert. They talked a bit about their favorite memories and future dreams, entranced by the good food and the sparkling blanket below them. It almost seemed like anything was possible.

With Melissa by his side, he might actually believe that.

Pleasantly full after dinner, they watched the city lights below while they waited for the tram to return them to the valley. They were the only passengers, and he tucked her in front of him as they began the descent. As the tram turned, they traded the valley's lights for the mountain's solid black bulk. Then they slowly spun back around. They rode in silence, her breath moving her back and shoulders solidly into his chest. She tensed when they went over the towers, but that was the only thing that rippled across their perfect, companionable silence.

As the valley grew bigger and then disappeared behind the ridge as the Valley Station grew closer, it was as if they could feel the magic spell of the mountain was about to be broken.

Interruptions were waiting to pounce, and he wanted to beg for just a few minutes longer alone with the woman who had his heart.

MELISSA LEANED AGAINST THE SEAT HEADREST AND watched Scott. He had given her an amazing day. Perfect in ways she didn't even know she wanted. She couldn't remember the last time she'd been this content. It'd been a long time.

They turned onto the highway, the mountains that they had been on top of earlier looming over them once again. Her backpack at her feet buzzed, reminding her that she hadn't checked her phone once all day. They'd been out of cell service most of the day, and she hadn't wanted anything to intrude when they weren't. She hadn't even worn her Apple Watch. She couldn't remember the last time that happened.

She reached for her backpack and then put it back. The day had been too perfect. She didn't want it to end. And once she stepped through her front door, the real world would come crashing back around her soon enough.

She must have dozed, because they were pulling up in front of her townhome before she knew it.

"Hey, Sleepyhead. Glad you got some rest." Scott's gaze was soft on her.

"Yeah, me too. I'll sleep good tonight after all that hiking, fresh air, and good food."

Scott walked her to her door, made sure she was able to get it open. "Call me in the morning. We'll figure out the next steps."

She sighed. "Yeah, back to reality." She touched his cheek, roughened by end-of-the-day stubble. "Thank you. Today was magical."

"You deserve more of that." He kissed her cheek and stepped back. "Tomorrow, Ops."

"Tomorrow." She stepped inside and closed the door, dropping her backpack at her feet. Tomorrow. She'd look at her phone then. But right now she wanted to crawl into bed and hope that her dreams were a continuation of today.

Chapter Twenty-Three

S he slept hard, woke up, and was shocked how late it was. But she felt good, for the first time in a long while. She reached for her phone next to her bed and immediately remembered where she had left it.

"Ugh. Coffee first." She padded downstairs and started the coffee before rummaging around in her backpack for her phone. As soon as she unlocked the screen, she saw all the texts and calls she had missed. Gavin. Jeremy. And some numbers she didn't know.

She scrolled through things and listened to messages while she had coffee and a bagel. Jeremy had had some success from home. They'd need to find someplace to talk about that. It was too cold to go to the park, and the office was closed.

Gavin insisted that she call him as soon as possible. She would talk to Kyle first, see what he'd discovered.

And then there was a message from Monica West, that reporter from the *South County Times*. Kyle had mentioned her at the fire. She wanted an interview. Not happening.

Melissa scrolled through her news feed. And froze. Looked like Monica West had run a story without Melissa's interview. Or maybe she wanted a follow-up. But given what all she had included in the article, there wasn't much Melissa could add. Monica wrote about the fire at Broadstone, the discovery of drugs there by the LVPD, the possible connection to naval aviation accidents due to their product, and the disappearance of Trent. She'd definitely done her homework. And talked to someone on the inside. Melissa desperately hoped it wasn't anyone on her team.

She dropped her head in her hands. Everything that she'd been trying to hide and manage had just blown open. There was nothing she could do. Events were now spinning out of her control on their own trajectory.

And only God knew where they would land. But one thing she did know: Nothing would be the same again.

She texted Scott the article then called Kyle.

Scott got Melissa's text while he was on a run with Shadow and Joe. He'd click on the link when he got back.

Joe glanced over at him. "Problem?"

"Yeah, I think so. Looks like Monica West ran a story on Broadstone Technologies. I haven't read it. Melissa sent me the link. But it's not going to be good. There's going to be an investigation, and her whole department or even the company could be shut down."

"That's too bad. She's good at what she does." Joe shrugged. "Does it mean that it makes it easier for the two of you to be together?"

"Everything's up in the air. I don't even know what I'm doing. I got an email from my JAG attorney asking for more information on the avionics bug so he can work on getting my case dismissed. I just hate to ask Melissa for that while she's dealing with everything else. I don't even know what she can access with the computers down."

They ran in silence, looping back around to Joe's complex.

He also had a call from the naval hospital in Balboa reminding him of his appointment with his neurologist. The one that would determine if he was back on track to return to duty or not. His PT appointments had been going well, but he still struggled with the balance challenges, and the fact that he had to wear glasses would be a problem for flying. Though they would find something else for him to do. But he didn't want to do anything else.

God, why does this have to be so hard? None of this had been his fault, and yet he felt like he was being punished.

Melissa might be feeling a bit the same way.

MELISSA WAITED FOR SCOTT TO PICK HER UP, PACING IN the entryway. She'd talked to Kyle, and they were on their way to meet with Jeremy at the Jitter Bug, a retro coffee place that had amazing desserts. And where Heather had almost been killed in a gang-initiation shooting. It had since been renovated and recently reopened.

The Corvette pulled up in front of her townhome, and she dashed outside.

"Hey, Ops."

"Morning."

Once she was settled in her seat, Scott leaned over and kissed her. "Sleep okay?"

"Like a rock. There's something to all that fresh air and physical activity." She winked at him. "And the company too."

They headed out, and she updated him on her call with Kyle. "He said because Trent was being watched, they were aware he had associations with known terrorists. It's pretty much in the FBI's hands now." She sighed. "Broadstone's going to come down. There's no way it can survive something like this."

Scott rubbed her knee. "What are you going to do?"

"I don't know. I feel like I need to ensure the investigators have all the access and information they need. Kyle's putting them in touch with me. And then I have to get my team settled well at other places. After that, I might have some brain space to think about what I should do. But you taught me something yesterday."

"What's that?"

"The importance of getting away and taking a break. I'm going to do that before I start on the next thing. Whatever the next thing is."

"Might I remind you—" he grinned—"that the company was a key part of that ingredient."

"Oh really? I'll have to keep that in mind." She smiled back.

They arrived at the Jitter Bug. She had Scott grab a table toward the back while she stood in line to place their orders. She had just gotten to the front of the line when Jeremy walked in. "Give me your order. This is going on the expense account while we still have it."

Jeremy grinned and ordered a caramel macchiato and then joined Scott at the table. She gave the barista their orders and picked out several pastries from the case. This place had the best sweets.

She returned to their table. Jeremy and Scott were talking. She slid in next to Scott.

"I was telling Scott that I was able to do it. Recreate the problem at home. I created a sandbox program and entered the code. I was able to trigger that code in a simulation with an external program that could be run with any device: phone, drone, et cetera. So it is possible."

The barista approached with their orders. They fell silent and leaned back as he set the drinks and pastries on the table. They waited until he left before speaking again.

"Great job, Jeremy. I was talking to Kyle this morning. He said the FBI has all but taken over the investigation. So I think they'll be interested in what you've come up with." She took a sip of her drink, but the yummy pastries had no appeal given what she had to say next. "Broadstone is done. Did you see the article?"

Jeremy swallowed and nodded, pastry half in his mouth.

"The reporter was right about a lot of things. Not sure how she knew, but she did. It's just the tip of the iceberg. With the FBI now involved, I don't think Broadstone will survive the scandal. And as much as it was staffed with good people doing good things, the leadership ruined it for everyone. So please begin looking for work. I'm going to make a list of the companies I have contacts at and start hitting them up to hire my people." Her voice caught. "I'll write you a glowing recommendation." She patted his hand. "I hate to lose you. And I hope you land some place that appreciates your genius. I know I benefitted from it all these years."

Scott's arm slipped around her shoulders. She drew strength from its comfort and was surprised. She was used to doing it all alone. It felt strangely good to have someone in her corner.

Now she had to talk to the rest of the team.

Chapter Twenty-Four

I t felt odd to Scott to be making the drive to Ridgecrest and nearby NAWS China Lake with Melissa. He normally made this trip alone, but his JAG attorney wanted her to give him a statement. She had spent the previous day talking to her team and working on places to find them jobs. Today she was setting all that aside to help him.

They pulled up in front of his attorney's office and got out. Scott wrapped his hand around Melissa's as they headed inside. A strange mix of emotions swirled through him. He was hopeful that what Melissa would say in her statement would release him from the investigation that had been hanging over his head. At the same time, it meant that their future was murkier. If he went back on duty, what would she do?

On the drive up, he tried to look around Ridgecrest through her eyes. He would be taking her away from her friends, her church, her sister. Was that fair?

He squeezed her hand, and she looked up at him with a wavering smile. This was costing her big time, and she was doing it for him. His chest warmed at the idea that someone would sacrifice a part of themselves for him.

The secretary ushered them into a conference room and

brought them coffee, but Melissa set hers to the side without drinking it. She pulled out some documents from her portfolio.

When the attorney entered, he greeted them, but he was a no-nonsense type of guy, and they got right down to business. "I hear you have more information about Lieutenant Commander Blake's accident that is pertinent to the investigation."

"Yes." Melissa handed him the documents and explained their significance. She also explained Jeremy's findings, and their theory about how the bad code was triggered. "I believe when the FBI has completed their investigation, they'll determine that this was an act of sabotage motivated by terrorism and had nothing to do with Lieutenant Commander Blake's piloting skills. In fact, given what I've seen, I'm amazed they had enough time to eject."

"You may have to come testify before the board under oath."

"I understand."

The attorney stood and shook both their hands. "This has been quite convincing. I'll let you know how it turns out." He looked at Scott. "How are your injuries coming along? You're wearing glasses now."

"Yes, sir. I'm progressing just fine. I have an appointment with my neurologist this week, and I expect to be cleared to return to some level of duty."

"That's good to hear. I don't foresee this event having a negative impact on your career."

As they left his office, a weight slid off Scott's shoulders. He reached for Melissa's hand. It was like ice. "Do you want to get something to eat?"

"Sure."

He took her to his favorite dive, a hamburger joint that had the best onion rings and shakes. It was nothing special to look at. The decor had probably last been updated in the 70s and was covered with memorabilia from the naval air station. But the food was amazing.

Since it was late for lunch, they didn't have a wait. They

ordered, and then he met her gaze. "What's going on in there?" It was like she had retreated into a shell.

She put her head in her hands for a moment before looking up. "I just can't shake the feeling that I've failed somehow. I know I did everything I could. But what I did back there, Gavin would consider the ultimate betrayal."

"He doesn't have any room to talk. He put his son before you, his company, his employees, and his country." He reached for her hand. "You did the right thing."

"I know. It's just that doing the right thing doesn't always feel good."

"I know." He let the silence linger between them for a minute. "But you know what always helps? Onion rings."

She laughed, like he knew she would. For a moment, he could picture this being their place. They'd come here to eat then grab a movie. He was tempted to drive around and show her the area. But given how she was feeling, it might taint the trip. They could do it another time.

Their food came, and Melissa took a bite of her hamburger. Juice dripped on the plate, and she closed her eyes. After chewing she said, "I think you might be right. This is amazing."

He grinned.

After a few onion rings, she perked up. "Another bit of good news. My Navy contact said that they had pulled all the latest updates and reverted to the previous version. I'm going to send Jeremy up here tomorrow to run another round of diagnostics just to be sure. Now that we know what we're looking for. I'd hate for there to be another hidden trap in a previous update."

"Good. Crisis averted."

Her voice got quiet. "Not quite. You and Jordan paid a high price."

"Yeah." He thought of Ashley. How close her house was to where they were. How often they all had eaten here.

Melissa wasn't the only one who felt like a failure.

The ride home from China Lake had been mostly quiet. They'd talked a little about Christmas plans. Heather was throwing a friends' Christmas party at Kyle's house. At some point, Melissa should probably go to Phoenix to be with her family. Without Broadstone Technologies consuming so much of her life, she'd have time to go. In fact, she felt a bit adrift without a regular schedule.

She'd been to Naval Air Weapons Station China Lake before for some on-site testing, but this time she wondered what it would be like to live in the area. It was pretty far away from her usual life. The high desert was quite a different environment from the coastal area, with temps well above 100 in the summer and much drier. But her friends wouldn't be too far away. Only three hours. And she'd be with Scott.

How did people make these decisions anyway? Well, it wasn't one she had to make today.

"So you're heading to Balboa tomorrow to the naval hospital. Want some company? I have a pretty wide-open schedule unless the FBI wants me for something."

Scott stared out the windshield, and the silence drew out.

Heat filled her face. She'd overstepped. Should she take it back?

He touched her knee. "I appreciate the offer, but I think I'd better go alone."

There was something in his voice she hadn't heard before. Uncertainty. He wasn't as confident about his results as he had presented to his attorney.

But if he got bad news, wouldn't he want her there with him? On the other hand, their relationship was new. He'd been friends with Kyle and Joe almost his whole life, and she didn't see him inviting them along. He was proud and didn't like to show any weakness. Likely that was why he didn't want her along. If he got bad news, he'd want time to process it on his own.

At least she hoped that was the reason.

They pulled into her townhome complex. "Do you mind stopping by the mailboxes on the way in? I just don't feel like walking back here. I know, I'm lazy." She flashed him a grin.

"Sure." He pulled up in front of the cluster of metal boxes.

She fished out her key and hopped out, opening her box and removing the letters. She climbed back in the car and flipped through them. Probably all bills. Except for one with a return address of Broadstone Technologies.

"That's odd. What's this?"

She slit it open and pulled out the letter.

She'd been fired for divulging company secrets.

Chapter Twenty-Five

Melissa put her favorite mug under the Keurig and pressed the button. Today was going to be a retreat at home. Scott was gone to Balboa, and she was going to get some headspace and think about things. As much as she'd like to go somewhere other than her living room, it was chilly out. Too cold to go sit on the beach.

She grabbed her coffee, heavily dosed with creme brûlée creamer, scooped up a chocolate eclair, and then moved to the living room. She'd have to eat some protein or she'd come crashing down from the sugar high, but she felt she deserved to eat her feelings at least a little. One eclair would be indulgence enough.

After flipping the switch on her gas fireplace, she settled into her comfy chair with the ottoman. Her favorite journal and pen already sat on the side table. *Lord, please be with Scott today. I don't know what this appointment will mean for his future, but you do. Please remind him that no matter what happens, it is no surprise to you. And help me know how to support him and how to move forward with my own life.*

She sipped and ate, letting her mind wander. When was the last time she'd actually done this? A long time ago, when Broadstone Technologies was a startup and Gavin was still doing most of the programming, she would regularly find time to sit and let her mind spin out. It almost always resulted in some new break-through. But then as they grew, she'd gotten caught up into being more of a manager of the people with the ideas instead of the idea generator.

She thought back to her fire-destroyed office. There was really nothing there that couldn't be replaced. All of her awards and accolades didn't mean much, everything considering. But she did miss the photo of Halley, Gracelyn, and her at Camp Eureka. She jotted a note in her journal. She probably had another copy on her computer. She wanted to print it out again. It had been a touchstone of what had always been important to her: her team. How had Broadstone Technologies gotten so off track?

How had she?

She flipped back to the list she'd started of her team. She'd need to write letters of reference for each of them. Even though Gavin had fired her, she could still use her title, since that's what she had been as their boss.

His firing her for cause created some problems for her. Which was exactly why he did it, she was sure. She'd have no paycheck coming in. She had savings, so that would be okay. And she'd be able to get her profit sharing out at some point, if there was anything left after the government fined them. But it pointed to the fact that Gavin planned on making her the scape-goat, making it hard for her to get another job and possibly changing her security clearance. She'd seen the signs that he would try to blame this on her, but she was still shocked that he actually did.

But what did this now make possible? She'd heard someone say that one time. When you're in a disappointing situation, think about what is now possible that wasn't before. Now she had more free time. Now she could design a life she loved. She was good at taking care of her team, but she wasn't so good with boundaries. She didn't take care of herself, and work had become so all-consuming this last year that it was amazing that she had any friends at all. She had barely attended the Bible study group she started.

If she could create the perfect job for herself, what would it look like?

She started writing.

"YOU CAN HAVE A SEAT." THE NEUROLOGIST POINTED TO the regular chair in the room.

Scott slid off the examination table, the crinkling paper sounding his exit as he moved to the chair.

The neurologist sat on the wheeled stool and removed his glasses. "You've made good progress. You can do everything a normal person can do, reasonably well. The glasses seem to be helping with the migraines. You're sleeping better. I'd say it's generally a good report." He tapped his glasses on his knee. "However, naval aviators aren't normal people. Your brain is subjected to much greater forces, and there is no margin for error. I'm sorry, Commander, I can't recommend you return to flight duty. However, you can return to any other type of non-combative duty, such as instruction or administrative work. I'll put in my report, and I suggest you speak with your CO."

Scott nodded, barely noticing that the doctor left the room, leaving the door open. That was probably his signal to leave, but he couldn't make his legs move. Maybe if he didn't move, the news wouldn't be real. He was numb everywhere, and it was like the words the doctor had spoken were outside the wall of ice that encased him.

He dropped his head in his hands. His whole world just came crashing down around him, and he was supposed to walk out of here like everything was fine? How could anything ever be fine again?

A nurse poked her head around the doorway. "You can check out up front." She paused. "Everything okay?"

"Yeah. Fine." At some level, he had been expecting it. Maybe. He thought he'd have more time, be able to charm his way around it like he normally did. For once, he'd encountered an obstacle he couldn't get around.

He got to his feet, checked out, and headed to his car like he was sleepwalking. He pointed the Corvette up the highway and drove north.

On the seat, his phone buzzed. Melissa.

He ignored it.

MELISSA CLIMBED OUT OF HER COMFY CHAIR TO TURN ON A light. It had grown dark, and her hand hurt from writing so much. But she felt more at peace about work and her career than she had in a long time. She had a plan, and it was a good one.

She couldn't wait to share it with Scott and to hear how his appointment had gone.

She'd texted him twice and then called but had gotten no response. That wasn't like him. Worry snaked through her chest, and she tamped it down. She didn't want to be the hovering girl-friend. That was why he hadn't wanted her to come, right? She didn't want to prove his fears correct. There could be a whole host of reasons why he hadn't contacted her.

She could wait.

Once her stomach growled, she ran out for Chinese food. She'd hoped to share this meal with Scott, talking about the future. But after she'd eaten and cleared all the dishes away and done every puttering thing around the house she could think of, it was late. She had a legitimate reason to be worried.

She texted Kyle. **Have you heard from Scott today? He had a drs appt in Balboa and I haven't heard from him.**

Kyle's response came back a minute later. **No. Let me try.**

Okay. *Lord, please let nothing have happened to him like a car wreck. I'm sure it's just something about his phone being dead. But still, he should have been home by now. Help me not to worry. Protect him.*

It was a full thirty minutes before she heard back from Kyle. And it was a phone call not a text. Her heart beat triple time when Kyle's name came up on her screen.

"Hey, I don't want you to worry. Scott's fine. He just got some bad news, and he's going to be by himself for a few days. Melissa, this is what he does. He needs time alone to process. Try not to take it personally."

The kindness in Kyle's voice about undid her, and tears welled up. "Okay, thanks for letting me know. Do you know what the news was?" She so didn't want to be the clingy girl-friend in front of Scott's friends, but she also wasn't sure she could stand not knowing. She'd imagine the worst, like he had a terminal illness or something.

Kyle was silent for a moment. "He lost his flight status. He can't be a naval aviator."

Oh, Lord. Tears poured out of her eyes for real, and she could barely say goodbye to Kyle as she hung up. No wonder Scott was devastated. That was all he'd ever wanted to be. That was his identity. He'd never even considered any other option.

Had he? He always seemed so positive and self-assured. She knew there was more to him than that, but this had to rock his world.

She wished she could be there to work through this with him, but they just didn't have enough history together. Still, he'd been there for her through the worst time in her career. She wished she could return the favor.

And hopefully, they'd still have a future together. But if Scott couldn't do what he loved, what did that mean for him?

Or them?

Scott took the keycard from the manager and headed over to his little cottage. This Lone Oak Lodge was a series of cottages from the 1950s that had been made into a motel park. He had a small kitchen, bedroom, bath, and patio. It'd be perfect for holing up for a few days.

He should text Melissa and let her know he was okay. It wasn't fair to worry her. He unlocked the door, dumped on the couch the contents of a plastic bag from CVS that held the toiletries he'd bought, and flopped on the bed.

Somehow, though, he couldn't bring himself to pick up the phone. It wasn't too late. Yet. Though he suspected she'd welcome a safety check from him no matter what the time.

But Kyle had called, having located him on the Find Friends app, and had guessed about the bad news. He'd taken Kyle's call because they'd been friends long enough that there was no pretense. With Melissa, he still felt like he had to be the strong one. And he wasn't sure what that would look like now, or who he even was.

And until he could figure that out, he didn't want to drag her down with him. She didn't deserve that, especially with all that she'd been through lately.

He flipped off the light and tried to sleep. But his mind wouldn't settle down. He finally switched on the TV. His stomach growled. He'd missed lunch and dinner. But he didn't really feel like going anywhere.

He padded into the kitchenette and grabbed a water bottle and a candy bar that he'd also bought at CVS from the retro fridge. He settled back to watch an old western. His phone sat on the nightstand, charging. And mocking him.

Add being a lousy boyfriend to his list of failures.

Chapter Twenty-Six

Melissa kept herself busy. Her phone was nearby at all times. She didn't want to miss Scott in case he decided to call. But she tried to distract herself as much as possible. She had a marathon shopping trip with Sarah and Heather and her sisters. They interrupted their day with lunch and sketched out the plans for the Christmas party.

Which had reminded her that she should put up some decorations. She was usually too busy, but she was determined to do better. Besides, she didn't have a job now. So for the second part of their shopping day, she grabbed a fake tree, lights, and some decorations.

Sarah and Heather decided to come home with her, ostensibly to help put up the decorations, but she knew it was to keep her company. She appreciated their kindness. As much as she had enjoyed heading up their Bible study, many times she'd seen it as one more task on her list to check off. She was grateful they still wanted to be her friends.

They piled all the packages in Melissa's entryway. "Okay, where do you want the tree?" Heather stood with her hands on her hips, surveying the room. "You have a great spot in that corner between the fireplace and the front window. It's perfect for a tree. Can't believe you've never had one since you've lived here."

"That's a great spot." Melissa moved to the other end of the couch to scoot it down and make room for the tree. "It's only ever just me. I go to Allie's or Mom's for Christmas. It never seemed to be worth the bother."

"If we're going to put up Christmas decorations, we need music and Christmas cookies." Sarah waved a roll of slice-and-bake cookies she'd pulled from a bag. "I'll take care of the cookies if you can take care of the music."

Melissa went to a control panel on the wall. She had a whole-house speaker system she rarely used. She fiddled with it a bit and finally got a Christmas station selected and playing throughout the house.

"Much better." Heather had pulled the tree out of its box and was laying out the pieces. Between the two of them, they got it up and lit.

"When do the two of you begin your Christmas concert marathon?" Melissa opened a box of sparkly glass ball ornaments. "Or do you? Did Ryan ever say anything to you, Sarah?"

"Next week." Sarah slid a cookie sheet out of the oven. "Amazingly enough, he never did. Just acted like it never happened. But he's dating Ashley, and I think they're a much better match than we *never* were."

They all laughed. Ryan had manipulated Sarah and told everyone they were dating. And then when she broke off something she never really wanted to begin with, he got angry. But since someone was burning down all of her buildings, she had a few other things on her mind than Ryan. And of course, Joe was there to help her through it all.

"I'm glad it all ended well. For both of you." Melissa pointed to Sarah and Heather.

Heather came over and put an arm around Melissa's shoulders. "It will for you too. Just wait and see. God's got bigger plans at play than what we can see right now."

Melissa nodded. "My head knows that. My heart's struggling with it."

"That's why we're here." Sarah brought over a plate of sugar cookies, still warm, with Christmas-colored sprinkles on them.

"Wow. Clearly I need to hang out with you two more. You've got this whole celebrating thing down." Melissa grabbed a warm cookie and popped it in her mouth where it quickly melted on her tongue.

One more thing to add to her new life plan: spend more time with good friends. She glanced over to the photo of her and Scott from their day on Mount San Jacinto that she had placed on the fireplace mantel. Her heart twisted, but somehow, she'd survive.

One way or another.

SCOTT WANDERED DOWN FISHERMAN'S WHARF IN Monterey. It was cool, so not too many people were around, and much less crowded than it would be come summer. But the families and couples heading into the restaurants to eat and the shops to browse reminded him of Melissa. He missed her. More than he thought possible. His chest squeezed at the thought of her. A hundred times he'd picked up his phone. But anything he had to say seemed so empty and stupid.

At the very end of the wharf, he leaned over the railing and watched the sea otters play in the bay, the birds dipping and gliding just above the water. He thought back to his phone call with his CO two days ago.

He'd been cleared in the investigation. That news lightened his shoulders a bit, but not as much as he had thought it would. His CO had also given him a few options, depending on what Scott wanted to do. He could arrange for a medical discharge, an administrative position, or he could be an instructor.

His CO's words played through his mind. "I'd hate to lose

you, Scott. You have real leadership skills, and you're a sharp pilot. I know you've been dealt a huge blow. A lot of men don't come back from something like that. But I think you can. I don't think your days with the Navy are over. Take some time and think about it."

He'd always been Superman. And now he wasn't. He'd never be again.

But if he was honest with himself, there was a bit of relief in that. Being Superman had been a big load to carry. It came with a lot of expectations.

Melissa had seen behind the mask, and she hadn't gone running. In fact, even at his worst, she had been there, calmly by his side, solving the next problem. He and Melissa had made a great team. Maybe, just maybe, there was a life for him as simply Scott Blake.

He pushed off the railing and headed back toward shore. There was only one person he wanted to make this decision with.

A bit chilled, he arrived back at his motel to find Jessica sitting on the front porch step, coffee cradled in her hand.

"What are you doing here?"

"What took you so long?" She stood and handed him a second coffee he hadn't seen sitting next to her. "It's not my fault if it's cold."

He stepped past her and unlocked the door. "Come in. And then tell me how you knew where I was."

She plopped on the couch. "I have great detective skills."

"Kyle told you." He sat next to her.

"Yep."

He sipped his coffee. It was still hot, and it felt good going down, warming his chest. Sitting comfortably with the decision he'd made. "Why'd you come here?"

"To get you." Tears welled in her eyes. "Scott, I know I'm a big screwup. I get that. Mom and Dad try to be encouraging, but I see the disappointment in their eyes." She looked at her cup. "Last week, I woke up and thought it was Monday. But it was Wednesday. I couldn't remember Monday or Tuesday. And it scared me. I went to my first AA meeting that night, and I've done one every day since." She pulled out her phone. "So if I'm going to make the one I really like, we need to get going so I can get back in time."

Scott leaned over and put his hand on her knee. "Jess, I don't know what to say. I'm glad you're getting help finally. But why did you come up here? Just to tell me that?"

"For such a smart guy, you're kinda dumb. Melissa's the best thing that's ever happened to you. I don't want to see you screw it up. And I know screwups. It's kinda my specialty. Plus, I did want to tell you. You've always been there for me. You and Kyle and Joe. It was like having three big brothers. And I didn't really appreciate that before now."

He pulled her into a hug. "I'm proud of you for making the right decision."

She smacked him on the back and pulled away. "Good. Now get packed. We've got to hit the road."

"Yes, ma'am." He grinned. Probably best to let her think she was bringing him back and not let her know that he'd come back here ready to head out.

He had a couple of things to do back home.

MELISSA WAS SIPPING ON TEA AND WRITING IN HER journal in her comfy chair when her doorbell rang. Odd. She wasn't expecting anyone. She'd gone to church with her friends and then out to lunch afterward. Scott's absence was keenly felt, but they all did such a great job of making her feel at home. It was one more thing to be grateful for.

She went to the door and looked out the peephole. No one was there. But something was on the ground. She pulled open the door. A paper airplane rested at the base of her door. A new marketing technique? People weren't supposed to solicit in the complex, but they did, leaving flyers on her door. She scanned the area in front of her townhome. Nothing.

She picked up the paper airplane and came back inside, closing the door. It reminded her of the time she and Scott made paper airplanes with Jaxon when his grandpa had a heart attack. This one had writing on the top. OPEN ME. She unfolded the wings. There was writing inside. I THINK YOU'RE AMAZING.

She laughed. Was this her friends' way of cheering her up?

The doorbell rang again. This time, she yanked it open. Two paper airplanes sat on her steps. Again, she couldn't spot anyone. How in the world were they doing this?

These also said OPEN ME. Inside one read, YOU'RE BEAUTIFUL. The other read, YOU'RE INCREDIBLY SMART.

The doorbell rang again. Pulling it open, she said, "Okay, guys. Thanks. You can come out now."

But no one showed themselves. She was staying outside. She picked up two more paper airplanes and opened them. I WAS A JERK. CAN YOU FORGIVE ME?

Scott? Her knees went weak and her heart leaped in her chest, her mind whirling to make sense of it all. She opened the second one. I LOVE YOU.

Tears sprung to her eyes, and she ran out to the sidewalk in front of her townhome, scanning in both directions.

Scott came around the corner and jogged over to her, picking her up and spinning her around. "I'm so sorry I took off like that. Can you forgive me?" He set her on her feet and gazed into her eyes.

She cupped his cheeks with her hands. "Yes. Kyle explained. I just missed you so much."

"I missed you. And I promise you, I'll never take off like that on you again."

She nodded, unable to speak.

He touched his forehead to hers. "I love you, Ops. I realized how much when I didn't have you with me."

Her heart flipped in her chest. "I love you too, Superman."

He winced. "Not anymore. I'm hanging up that call sign."

She threaded her hands around his neck. "You'll always be my Superman."

He leaned down and kissed her, pulling her closer, deepening his kiss like a man starving.

Her heart felt like it was going to break free of her chest, every bit of his nearness, his words, penetrating her very soul.

He was home. And so was she.

Chapter Twenty-Seven

Melissa stood in the entryway of her townhome, peering out the window. She wore leggings and boots with a long-sleeved dress, her coat over her arm, her overnight bag at her feet. The guys had decided they wanted to do something special to surprise the women. Heather had protested that she was already planning a friends Christmas party. But Kyle insisted this was just for the six of them. So the guys had rented a cabin up in Big Bear, and were taking care of the food and everything. Melissa, Heather, and Sarah just had to show up.

Scott pulled up in front. She turned to check the mirror one last time, then opened the door.

Scott stood poised to knock, a bouquet of mixed flowers in his hand. "Eager, are we? These are for you." He handed her the flowers.

"Of course I'm eager. And thank you. They're lovely." She stepped aside to let him in, but he snagged her arm and gave her a lingering kiss.

When he let her go, she realized she was clutching the flowers in a vice-like grip. "I'll put them in water." She headed for the kitchen. She resisted the urge to ask him if the guys had thought of everything. She and Sarah had texted back and forth and figured out that Kyle was going to propose to Heather, and the rest was just a ruse to get her friends up there. So Sarah and Melissa wanted everything to be perfect for Heather. Sarah had hinted around to Joe, too, but the guys were stonewalling them, assuring that they had everything taken care of.

Scott grinned. "I can see the wheels turning in your head. Just relax and enjoy yourself. It'll be fun." He scanned her living area. "The house looks amazing all done up for Christmas. I'm glad you decorated."

"Me too. It was fun, and I like what it does to the place." She pulled down a vase and filled it with water then plunked the flowers in it.

He wandered over to the mantel, picking up the framed photo of them. "I love this picture of us. It was a great day with great memories."

She slipped up behind him, her hands around his waist. "Yes, it was."

He turned in her arms and kissed her forehead. "Here's to many more."

"I like that plan." She grinned.

Once in the car, they headed inland toward the mountains. Unlike last time, all the couples were driving separately, so that gave them time to talk. Scott asked, "Any other word from Gavin?"

"No, and the FBI doesn't want me to talk to him. Trent is in the wind, last I heard, but with the FBI trailing him, he won't be for long."

He reached for her hand. "So what do you want to do next? You told me you've been journaling and letting your imagination run wild."

The warmth from his hand made her believe that just about anything might be possible if they were doing it together. "This time, I want to run my own firm. A much smaller one, essentially just my team from Broadstone. With sane hours, like weekends and holidays off, generous vacation time, things like that." A sense of rightness settled over her as she talked about her plans. She could almost see it. "With Broadstone gone, there's a hole we can fill. But it'll be on my terms."

"I like how you think. You've changed through this process. Become more of yourself, I think."

"Yes." His words settled on her, the truth of them weaving their way into her soul. "Yes. I'd left myself behind somewhere, but you helped me find my way back."

The conversation moved to other things. Her shopping trip with the girls, his stay in Monterey.

"Next time I go there, I want it to be with you. It was lonely without you. But I did need to do some thinking." He told her about his conversation with his CO. "I think I'd like to become an instructor. But I wanted to see what you thought."

"You'd be great at it. I saw how you were with the team, a natural leader, helping bring out the best in them, keeping them on the right track."

"It would mean a change of station to NAS Whidbey Island in Washington state." He glanced at her and then back at the road again. "I know things are early with us, and neither one of us is in a position to ask the other to make a huge life change. But we do have something special, and I don't want to make this decision without considering how it will impact us."

For some reason, she had pictured him returning to NAWS China Lake. A drive, sure, but doable until they solidified what their future together would look like. "I have no illusions that as long as you have a career in the Navy that I won't have to follow you around. It's a given. I hadn't pictured Washington state, but there are planes that fly there from here. My company is going to be a remote company. We'll all work from home and conference in as need be. If we all need to be together, we can do that. But I wanted to create the flexibility to go where you are."

Scott's shoulders relaxed, and a smile played around his

mouth. "I should have known you'd have already thought of a solution, Ops."

———————

Scott followed the directions on his GPS to the address Kyle had given him. The sun had just gone behind the mountains, casting deep shadows as they pulled up to the cabin perched on the side of the hill. Two trucks sat in the parking area, leaving just enough room to squeeze the Corvette in.

This was going to be fun. He turned to Melissa, grinning. "We're here."

She laughed. "I can see that. This place looks great. A real log cabin surrounded by woods. What's not to love?"

They climbed out, and Scott pulled their bags out of the trunk. Clouds were piling up over the mountain tops, and the wind was brisk. "A storm's coming in. Maybe we'll get some snow."

"The forecast said there was a chance." Melissa shivered and pulled her coat tighter. "Let's get inside. I smell woodsmoke. Joe must have a fire going."

They entered the cabin directly into the two-story great room with exposed beams and a stone fireplace, which did indeed have a roaring fire. They hung up their coats on the hooks beside the door.

Sarah came over and gave Melissa a hug. "Grab your bag. I'll show you to your room. You too, Scott." Down the hall, Sarah pointed out the half bath and then the four bedrooms. "The girls are in these two rooms, the guys in the other two. We saved the big bed in the room by yourself for you. Heather and I are sharing the other room."

"Are you sure?"

"Positive." Sarah looked over at Scott. "Not sure if you guys decided on sleeping arrangements."

"We'll figure it out." He tossed his bag in the nearest room.

Something smelled good, and he was hungry. He reached for Melissa's hand and pulled her out to the kitchen, just off the great room. In the fading light, he could see a deck outside the french doors.

Kyle was setting out meat, cheese, and crackers on the breakfast bar. A cooler with ice and drinks sat on the floor below. His movements were a little more harried than usual. He was nervous. Would Heather notice?

She was parked in front of the fire with a mug of something, her back to the kitchen. Kyle had probably banished her. Good idea. Scott steered Melissa in that direction. "Go join Heather. You too, Sarah. I'll bring over snacks and drinks."

Joe moved around the room, lighting the candles that were scattered about. Twinkle lights draped off the beams overhead. Soft music filtered through the air. This should be perfect for Heather. The women should all be pleased.

He headed to the kitchen and caught Kyle's gaze, eyebrows raised. Kyle ignored him.

Scott turned his back to the living room and lowered his voice. "Everything ready? Need help with anything?"

"Lasagna's in the oven. It's got another thirty minutes."

That wasn't what Scott was asking, and Kyle knew it. He flashed Scott a tight grin but patted his pants pocket.

"Why don't you take the appetizer tray out to the ladies?"

Which would keep them from coming in the kitchen. He did, along with some drinks. Joe had joined Kyle getting salad and garlic bread ready. Scott peeked in the fridge and saw a cheesecake from the Jitter Bug and a few bottles of something bubbly. Definitely keep the women out of the fridge.

Finally, the lasagna was out of the oven and cool enough to cut. The guys served the women seated at the large trestle table set in front of the french doors.

They'd dug into the cheesy, tomatoe-y goodness when Melissa started telling them about Scott's paper airplanes. "I still don't understand how you could ring my doorbell and disappear so fast."

He laughed. "You didn't see? I had a Bluetooth speaker on your doorstep behind that plant pot. I played the sound of a doorbell through it from my phone. I wasn't actually ringing your doorbell."

She nudged his shoulder as the table laughed. "You think of everything."

He held her gaze. "I try."

They were still eating when the outdoor lights reflected a few flakes falling. He stood and peered out the window for a closer look. "It's snowing!" He opened the french doors, letting in a gust of cold air. Flakes swirled lazily in the air, covering the deck.

Melissa touched his shoulder then pushed past him onto the deck. She spun around, looking up at the sky, smiling. "Magical! It's like being in a snow globe." She moved to the railing and looked over. "Oh wow, there's nothing down there but a straight drop."

He peered over. The cabin was built on the side of the mountain, pilings holding up part of it, making it seem like a treehouse from out here. A steep set of stairs off to the side led down into the darkness.

The others had joined them outside, and he wrapped his arms around Melissa from behind as they all watched the snow fall. She shivered, and he rubbed her arms. "Let's get back inside. We can watch the snow while we finish eating."

They seated themselves back around the table, gazes glued to the increasing pace of snowfall.

"I wonder how much snow we're going to get. Getting the 'vette down the hill tomorrow might be a problem." The moment Scott said the words, he wished he could take them back, not wanting Melissa to worry.

Joe pointed his fork at him. "That's why you should drive a truck like we do."

Scott laughed. "Why do I need a truck when you have one?"

It was an old debate, which they continued as they cleared the table and took care of the food and dishes.

Dishes done, Scott slid onto the couch next to Melissa, draping his arm around her, pulling him to her. He glanced back at Kyle who was roaming the kitchen, ostensibly putting things away. If he didn't settle down, Heather would suspect. The plan was to wait until dessert, to put the ring on Heather's slice of cheesecake.

"Anyone ready for dessert?" This from Kyle. Clearly he was ready to get things moving.

"I'm still pretty full." Heather glanced over to Kyle then patted the leather couch next to her. "Come sit with me and enjoy the fire."

He hesitated. "Anyone else ready?"

"Nope," chorused around the room. Maybe a little too unified. Scott shot a glance at Heather, whose gaze was glued to Kyle as he approached her and sat on the couch. She didn't seem to suspect anything.

Comfortable silence descended, the soft music inside accompanied by the wind outside. The full stomach, warm fire, and Melissa next to him made Scott sleepy. Could anything be more perfect than this moment?

The lights went out, dousing the room in only candlelight, and the music shut off, leaving only the sound of the wind to fill the room.

"Storm might have knocked the power out." Joe rose. "I'll check the breaker box just to be sure. Any idea where it is?" He looked at Kyle.

"Not sure." He got his feet. "Let's go find it."

Scott patted the back of the couch. "I'll just stay right here. Make sure the ladies are safe."

Which brought a round of laughter from the women and guffaws from his friends. So they didn't have power. They had candlelight and firelight. If anything, it just got more romantic.

They could still figure out how to serve dessert by the light of their phones.

There was nothing to worry about. He leaned over and kissed Melissa's temple. It was still a great night.

MELISSA SNUGGLED AGAINST SCOTT FOR A MOMENT THEN looked around. It was still going to be a good night for a proposal. In fact, the power outage would just make for another fun story to tell. But they would need pictures.

Her phone. She was wearing leggings, and her skirt didn't have pockets. So it must be in her purse. She scooted to the edge of the couch to get up.

Scott put a hand on her knee. "What do you need?"

She lowered her voice. "My phone." She cut her eyes toward Heather.

Scott rose. "I'll get it. Where is it?"

"It should be in my purse. If not, I might have left it in your car. In fact, I think I did because I was charging it."

"Be right back."

She glanced out the patio. Without the lights on inside, the snowfall was more obvious. The deck was completely coated. Maybe they could make a snowman or snow angels. She stood and went to the french doors to get a closer look. She'd never been in a snow storm before. She opened the doors and stepped outside. Just for a minute. She wouldn't need her coat.

She walked over to the railing, the snow crunching under her feet. The trees off the deck looked frosted with the snow clinging to the branches. Snow pelted her face, sticking to her eyelashes. Beautiful but chilly. She turned to go back inside.

But there was another set of footprints on the deck, over by the stairway. Neither Joe nor Kyle would have climbed up those steep stairs from down below, would they? Didn't make any sense.

And then the deep shadows moved, a figure pulling away from the log wall.

Trent.

"Trent? What are you doing here?" Adrenaline shot through her; her legs shook. She glanced inside but Heather and Sarah couldn't see Trent from where they were sitting. And they weren't paying attention anyway.

He held a gun on her. "You made things really difficult for me, Melissa. I had a good thing going and you messed it up. If you had just minded your own business, none of this would be happening." His eyes were wild, darting around the deck. His face was sallow, his eyes sunken. He was probably on some sort of drugs.

"Look, Trent. I don't want any trouble. You can go on your way, and I won't even tell anyone I saw you."

"You're going to pay for this! I'm dead anyway, don't you know that? Those guys don't mess around. It was never about the drugs. It was always about my access to the technology. I don't know how I didn't see it at the time. Until it was too late."

Melissa struggled to keep her voice calm. "I'm sure if you tell the FBI that, they'll work out a deal. You probably have a lot of information that would be helpful to them."

"It's too late." His voice had the same strident tone it had the night she'd heard him arguing with his dad.

"It's never too late." She reached out her hand to touch his arm, but he jerked it away.

"They're going to kill me! Who do you think I've been running from? But if I'm going to end it, I'm taking you with me. It's your fault. You need to pay too."

Her heart pounded in her throat and she swallowed, trying to keep her wits about her. *Lord, give me wisdom. Help me know what to say to diffuse the situation. Just something, Lord. I can't believe this is my time.* The men would be back at some point, but if someone walked out here, they wouldn't know what was going on, and Trent would have another hostage.

She glanced into the cabin. Both Sarah and Heather were staring at her, probably wondering why she was just standing out here talking to herself. They couldn't see Trent from where they were. She backed up a step. If she could get Trent more visible on the deck, then maybe someone could get him from behind. He was between the stairs and the doors to the cabin, so that wasn't an option. Over the edge of the deck wasn't either.

He didn't seem to notice, so she took another step back.

"Stop. Stop moving!" His hand was shaking as much as his voice.

"Trent, we can work this out. Just put the gun down. You're only making things worse."

She saw movement inside the cabin. Heather and Sarah stood on either side of the french doors. They'd seen Trent. And across the room, Scott had just come through the front door, her phone in hand.

Trent must have seen her gaze, because he turned and looked inside the cabin. He grabbed for her.

"Oh!" She doubled over, grabbing her stomach.

His hand grazed her arm but didn't get a good grip.

She lunged forward, shoulder into his stomach, pushing her weight against him, knocking him off balance.

The french doors flew open. Scott came through in a low crouch.

She rolled to the side. Just to see Trent lose his balance on the wet snow. The gun went off, and she ducked. Trent fell backward down the stairs.

Scott followed, with Kyle and Joe at his heels, and they disappeared down the stairs into the dark.

Shaking, she sat on the deck, not sure her legs would hold her.

A moment later, Scott came up the stairs and wrapped her in his arms. "It's okay. He's not going to hurt you." He kissed her forehead. "He's not going to hurt anyone ever again."

Epilogue

Melissa sat with her hand firmly in Scott's as they sat on Kyle's couch. Heather had a big Christmas tree decorated in front of the window, and the whole house had touches of Christmas everywhere. It was perfect for the friends' Christmas party. They had finished eating, but far too many Christmas cookies sat on the kitchen counter, along with hot cider and hot chocolate with plenty of add-ins like marshmallows, whipped cream, chocolate chips, and candy canes. With the Christmas music wafting through the air, it was a perfect setting.

Different than the cabin in Big Bear two weeks ago, but just as warm and happy. She was glad they were all here to be able to enjoy it. Trent hadn't survived his fall down the stairs. But he was the only injury. The bullet had gone into the decking, and Kyle joked about not getting his deposit back. But by the time the police had finished taking their statements and Trent's body had been removed, the shine had gone off the night. It was definitely not a night to propose. That was not the kind of proposal story anyone would want to remember.

But the next morning, the sun was out, making the snow glisten like a winter wonderland. They made a small snowman and snow angels. And with the help of chains, Scott was even able to get the Corvette down the hill. And as far as she knew, Heather didn't know—or even suspect—that the plan that night had been for Kyle to propose. Sigh. Someday they could tell her.

"Okay, everyone, gather in the front room for the gift exchange." Heather was directing people to chairs.

"Want anything before we get locked in here and can't move?" Scott leaned over and whispered in her ear, sending shivers down her spine.

"Nope. I'm perfectly content." She smiled. And she was. She and Scott had spent days dreaming about what the future might look like and how they would manage. She was confident that they could handle what would come their way, even when he reported back for duty after the first of the year.

Heather passed around a bowl with pieces of paper folded up inside. Everyone took a paper with a number on it. Everyone was supposed to bring their favorite candy for the gift exchange. Melissa had brought a box of Almond Joys. Scott had brought a box of Twizzlers.

She drew number five. Scott showed her his. Number nine.

The game began. When it was your turn, you could open a new package or steal someone else's. It was Melissa's turn.

Scott leaned over. "How about I grab it for you?"

"Sure." She didn't really care what she got. If it was something really good, someone would just steal it anyway. It was what made it so much fun.

He stood and reached toward the back of the tree. There were a few twitters and giggles, but he grabbed a small box and handed it to her.

"Kind of small to be a box of candy." Melissa gave him a wry grin. Something was up.

He shrugged his shoulders and gave her his winning grin.

Oh something was definitely up. She slid the bow off and slit the tape, then lifted the lid off. Inside, nestled in soft batting was a small charm of the Palm Springs tram attached to a charm bracelet. It sat on top of a small paper airplane that had written on its wings, TO MORE ADVENTURES AHEAD.

"Oh, Scott. That's so beautiful! Thank you."

He lifted the bracelet out of the box and fastened it around her wrist. "It's a good way to keep track of our adventures."

She kissed him on the cheek, acutely aware of their audience. "I love it." She looked around the room. "And no one's stealing this!"

They laughed, and the game continued. Scott ended up with a giant tub of Red Vines, which he offered to share with Melissa. Ugh. She declined.

Heather had the last number, and there was one box left under the tree. A flat one, like a chocolate sampler. Melissa hadn't seen it back there before.

Kyle handed it to Heather. "The last one is yours."

She looked around the room before taking it from him. "I guess there's nothing out here that I'm dying to have."

Melissa thought Kyle paled a little, but he took a knee next to Heather as she unwrapped the box. It was an assorted chocolates box from See's Candy.

"Better open it to see what's really inside," Joe called out. "You never know with this group."

That brought a round of laughter.

Heather lifted the lid. The box was empty except for a smaller box inside. A ring box.

Her hand went to her mouth, and her gaze darted to Kyle.

He picked up the box and opened it, the Christmas lights glinting off the diamond inside. "Heather, you've trusted me with your life and your heart. And in front of our friends, I want to pledge to continue to do that for the rest of our lives. Will you marry me?"

Heather burst into tears and nodded.

Kyle slipped the ring on her finger. "Is that a yes?" He grinned.

"Yes!" She flung her arms around his neck, and the room burst into applause.

Melissa couldn't help but glance over at Joe and Sarah, snuggled on the other couch. And Cait and Grayson, who were already planning their wedding for the spring.

Scott squeezed her shoulder, and she leaned into him. Life was always bringing changes, even among their group of friends. But as long as she had Scott by her side, she thought she could weather whatever life brought her way.

Are you curious about Allie and Steve?

When will Joe and Sarah get engaged?

And what other adventures await Kyle and Heather, Joe and Sarah, and Scott and Melissa?

Find out by signing up for my latest news and updates here at www.jlcrosswhite.com and you'll get the prequel novella, *Promise Me*— Grayson and Cait's story.

You won't want to miss the spin-off series, In the Shadows. It follows the siblings of our Hometown Heroes: Allie, Jessica, and even Ryan and Macy will make an appearance. And of course all of our original cast will be there as well.

My bimonthly updates include upcoming books written by me and other authors you will enjoy, information on all my latest releases, sneak peeks of yet-to-be-released chapters, and exclusive giveaways. Your email address will never be shared, and you can unsubscribe at any time.

If you enjoyed this book, please leave a review. Reviews can be as simple as "I couldn't put it down. I can't wait for the next one" and help raise the author's visibility and lets other readers find her.

Keep reading for a sneak peek of *Off the Map: In the Shadow book 1.*

Acknowledgments

The expertise on all things aviation related came from my dad, David Crosswhite, my favorite pilot.

Thanks to Tracy Borgmeyer for letting me borrow Camp Eureka from her *Halley Harper: Science Girl Extraordinaire* series. If you have school-aged kids, pick up those books! You won't regret it.

A special thanks to my dear readers who helped me brainstorm names. Especially to Lisa Stillman, Joan DeLeon, and Camille Howard for coming up with Gavin. Jeannine Wickliffe for coming up with Broadstone. Katrina Dehart and Deborah Genard for Trent. Natalya Lakhno and Diane Stewart for Jaxon. You guys are the best!

This book would not be possible without the patience and willingness to read many, many drafts by Diana Brandmeyer, Liz Tolsma, Jenny Cary, and Danielle Reid. Special thanks to Sara Benner for her expert proofreading and Danielle Reid for her eagle eyes! Many thanks to my beta readers and reviewers!

Much thanks and love to my children, Caitlyn Elizabeth and Joshua Alexander, for supporting my dream for many years and giving me time to write.

And most of all to my Lord Jesus, who makes all things possible and directs my paths.

Author's Note

Laguna Vista isn't a real town, but it's based on the area of Orange County that I lived in for twelve years. It's a beautiful location with the ocean to the west and foothills and mountains to the east and the austere-but-beautiful desert within driving distance.

Holcomb Valley and the Palm Springs tram to Mount San Jacinto are real places that I've have visited and enjoyed. You can see pictures from my trips there on my Pinterest board at Pinterest: Author Jennifer Crosswhite

The military has become active in diagnosing and treating TBI in service members. The Defense and Veterans Brain Injury Center (DVBIC) TBI Recovery Support Program Network helps service members locate a center for coordinated treatment for them, their family members, and caregivers. DVBIC.org

I wanted to explore how doing the right thing can come with a high cost. And how we navigate our futures when everything we've dreamed about comes crumbling down. Scott and Melissa wrestle with understanding and accepting God's unfathomable journey for their lives and trusting Him with the outcome.

I hope you will take away from reading *Special Assignment* that you can trust God with your future, no matter how incomprehensible it may appear to you and be encouraged with how uniquely God has crafted your life.

About the Author

My favorite thing is discovering how much there is to love about America the Beautiful and the great outdoors. I'm an Amazon bestselling author, a mom to two navigating the young adult years while battling my daughter's juvenile arthritis, exploring the delights of my son's autism, and keeping gluten free.

A California native who's spent significant time in the Midwest, I'm thrilled to be back in the Golden State. Follow me on social media to see all my adventures and how I get inspired for my books!

www.JLCrosswhite.com
    Twitter: @jenlcross
    Facebook: Author Jennifer Crosswhite

Instagram: jencrosswhite
Pinterest: Author Jennifer Crosswhite

facebook.com/authorjennifercrosswhite
twitter.com/jenlcross
instagram.com/jencrosswhite
pinterest.com/jtiszai

Sneak Peek of Off the Map: In the Shadow book 1

The lights in the spacious atrium dimmed, and a spotlight shone on the marble floor. Allie Ellis turned in her chair at the round banquet table to watch the bride, her friend Cait, get swept up in the arms of her new groom, Grayson, for their first dance. The band leader announced the bride and groom, and the band played "It Had to Be You."

Steve Collins—he'd always gone by his last name—was her date for the wedding. His gaze was steady on her but unreadable. She'd been half in love with him since their high school days, but was he just an idealized fantasy she'd created? Would getting to know him shatter the dream man she'd created in her mind? Could high school dreams even survive into adulthood?

The band leader invited everyone to the dance floor. Their table cleared. It had been full of their friends—all couples. Her sister Melissa with Scott, Kyle and Heather, and Joe and Sarah. She glanced at Collins. Would he expect her to dance to such an obviously couples' song when she wasn't sure if they were anything but friends?

He grinned at her and held out his hand. "Shall we? I have to warn you, I'm not a great dancer, but I can sway to the beat."

But Allie's heeled sandal caught in the floor-length tablecloth, and she whacked her knee on the table leg as she pivoted. Graceful.

"Are you okay?"

She nodded, hoping he hadn't seen her clumsiness and that her smile looked warmer and more confident than it felt as she placed her hand in his warm one. Was hers too cold or too sweaty? Why did being around him make her feel like she was back in high school?

His large, warm fingers enveloped hers, and tingles swirled along her arm. This was the first time he'd ever held her hand. But it was just out of courtesy. Wasn't it?

She rose, being careful not to tangle herself in the tablecloth, and let him lead her toward the rapidly filling dance floor. She turned sideways to avoid an older lady in a sequined jacket pushing out her chair in front of Allie. But that caused her heel to catch on the leg of another chair. She tugged on Collins's hand to slow his progress and steady herself.

He stopped and turned.

Just as Sequined Jacket spun into Allie with a full cocktail glass.

As the icy, sticky liquid splashed down the front of her organza bodice, she gasped and pulled out of Collins's grasp.

No, no, no, no, no! This could not be happening. She'd wanted this night to be perfect. And now her dress was definitely not.

Sequined Jacket looked up, just now recognizing what she had done. "Oh dear. I'm so sorry. Let me help you." She snatched up a cloth napkin from the table and handed it to Allie, but the polyester did little to sop up the wetness. "I'm so sorry. Oh your poor dress. And it was so pretty on you."

Was being the operative word. Allie sighed and looked at Collins. "Let me head to the ladies' room and see if I can't do something with this." She wove her way through the chairs and tables, scooting around the edge of the perfectly romantic atrium. She'd used her real estate connections as a corporate relocation specialist to secure it for Cait. Wedding venues were at a premium, but this was a luxury office space with a lush tropical-and-marble atrium that soared five stories. With fairy lights added to the existing lighting scheme, it was a beautiful place for a wedding. Their friend Sarah Brockman was the architect who designed it, and between the two of them, they convinced the building's owner to let them rent it. It had become a magical space for Cait's wedding.

As she left the atrium, footsteps followed her. She turned.

Collins was behind her.

"Oh, you don't have to wait for me. Go enjoy the wedding."

He shoved his hands in his pockets, a sheepish grin crossing his face. "I'd rather wait for you."

She got it. He didn't know the bride and groom. And everyone was on the dance floor.

He closed the gap between them, resting his hand lightly on her lower back as they continued down the hallway to the restrooms.

The sounds of the band faded, and the squeak of the restroom door seemed particularly loud as she pushed it open into the marble-lined ladies' room and made her way to the sink. The mirror reflected the wet red splotch that covered her pale-pink dress. She snatched a handful of paper towels and dampened them, dabbing at the front. It was so pretty. The pale pink organza swirled just above her knees, flattering her generous curves, and the hue brightened her nothing-special coloring.

Collins had certainly seemed appreciative when he'd picked her up, his eyes lighting up and his voice had deepened as he said, "You look beautiful" as he helped her into his large truck. But the ride had felt awkward. Had she made a mistake by inviting him? He seemed the perfect plus-one since he knew everyone at their table, even though he wasn't friends with Cait and Grayson. Neither was she, really, but she'd helped pull off the location, so she'd been invited.

She and Collins had reconnected last November, but then

he'd left on an assignment to help as a detective for the police department in Holcomb Springs, a small resort town in the San Bernardino mountains about two hours from here. So they'd been texting and talking on the phone for the past four months. But friends did that too. She was hoping tonight would give her a better insight into the man he'd become from the boy she once knew.

But bringing him to a wedding... Didn't that imply something about their relationship? Did they have a relationship beyond old friends? That nervousness and uncertainty had made her clumsy. Well, she couldn't blame the ruined dress on her clumsiness. That landed squarely on the sequined shoulders of the older lady. But Allie was the one who would reek of alcohol all night.

She peered in the mirror. Despite her best efforts, the slightly less-red spot still dominated her dress. With nothing further to do, she tossed the paper towels in the trash. *Get a grip, Allie. Enjoy the evening. No one's even going to notice you, anyway.*

With a final fluff of her hair, she turned and pushed out the bathroom door.

Collins stood outside, gazing at his surroundings. His wavy hair was beginning to escape whatever product he had used to confine it. It made her want to play with his curls. She squeezed her hand shut.

He smiled at her. "This is some space, isn't it? Sarah's really good at what she does."

"Yes, she is. I'm glad we could use it for Cait and Grayson's wedding." She held her dress out. "I couldn't do too much with it. Maybe the cleaners will be able to fix it."

"I hope so. It's a pretty dress." Collins's gaze turned intense and he cocked his head. "Do you hear that?"

"The music?"

"Yes, but that song." He reached for her hand and pulled her a few steps down the hall. "Remember it?"

It sounded familiar, an alt-rock ballad from their high school years. "Oh, that's Lifehouse."

"Yep. It's 'You and Me.' We should go dance to it since I didn't get to take you to prom."

A thousand thoughts collided in Allie's head. "Oh, but my dress. It's still wet and… stained." *Brilliant, Allie.* State the obvious. And, he wanted to take her to prom?

He swung her around in front of him, sliding his hand along her waist. "We could dance here. The twinkle lights almost look like stars." He grinned.

She put her hand on his broad, football-player shoulder and began swaying to the music, laughing. "Wasn't that the theme of one of our proms, An Evening Under the Stars?"

"Something like that. All I know is that you went with Chris Mendoza before I could ask you."

She groaned. "He cornered me in the hall. I couldn't turn him down. I wish I'd known…you'd wanted to take me. I would have rather gone with you." Her voice softened, and she looked away. Had she said too much? She and Melissa had found a dress for her at a thrift shop and remade it a bit so she could go. Chris had paid for the tickets and bought her a wrist corsage that his mother had picked out.

Collins tugged her a little closer, apparently not concerned that her wet dress could touch his cobalt-blue dress shirt or navy tie. "We can make up for lost time."

She didn't know what to say to that, so she didn't say anything, just enjoyed the warmth of being in his arms as the music and memories swirled around them. She had been thinking of him as a wedding date, but now he'd taken her down memory lane to high school. And rewritten the history she thought she knew.

He'd wanted to take her to prom? She'd always thought that her crush on him was one way, and she'd worked to hide it so as not to ruin their friendship or make things awkward. But perhaps their feelings were mutual. If she'd gone to prom with him… a different life spooled out in front of her. She shook the thoughts away. Her imagination was running away with her. *Enjoy the moment.*

The scent of him, clean like soap with a hint of something spicy, drew her closer. She forgot about her dress and let the music swirl around them.

Footsteps sounded on the marble floor, growing closer. Probably someone looking for the restrooms. She glanced up. Melissa.

She was frowning and biting her lip.

Uh oh. That look always meant trouble. Great.

Allie stepped out of Collins's arms and saw the confusion in his gaze. But Melissa wouldn't share her concern unless it was important.

Collins pressed his hand against the small of her back, maintaining their connection. She didn't pull away. But it was all she could do to concentrate on Melissa and not the feel of his hand.

Melissa glanced at Allie's dress. "Oh, no! What happened?"

She shrugged. "An older lady bumped into me with her cocktail. The cleaners can probably get it out. I'll be fine. What's up?"

Melissa shoved her cell phone into Allie's hand. "Both Daniel and Brittney are bailing on us."

She studied the screen. "The Great American Road Trip? You can't be serious." No wonder Melissa looked upset. They'd planned this trip for years and finally were able to agree on dates and get it on the calendar last Thanksgiving. Planning future trips around an old map kept them occupied as kids during some difficult times. This trip was supposed to make those dreams a reality finally.

"Why did he text you right now? Didn't he know we were at the wedding and that Scott was down from Washington?" Allie handed the phone back to Melissa.

Melissa shrugged. "He never pays attention to our social lives."

Allie touched Melissa's arm. "Let's not think about it now.

Go back in and enjoy the reception. We can figure something out tomorrow."

Melissa opened her mouth, but Scott stepped up and slipped his arm around her waist. "I know you, Melissa. Just let it go for now. Allie's right."

As Scott led Melissa back toward the wedding, Allie turned to Collins, shaking her head. "We had been planning a sibling road trip, something we'd dreamed about for years. But it looks like Daniel and Brittney can't make it. So that just leaves Melissa, Matthew, and me. Well, and Scott. He was going to go with us." She let out a sigh. "I know Melissa will turn it over in her brain, trying to think of solutions instead of enjoying the evening. Speaking of which, we should get back in there." She brushed her hand down the front of her dress. "Nobody's going to be looking at me anyway."

Collins frowned. "Why do you have to cancel the trip? Why can't the rest of you go? Maybe you can all try to go another time, but it doesn't mean the rest of you should miss out."

"Daniel has the trailer. None of the rest of us has one or anything to pull it with. And I don't want to sleep in a tent. The amount of gear we'd have to buy..." She shook her head. "Let's go back inside. I think they're going to cut the cake."

Collins reached for her hand, intertwining their fingers.

She tried to act casual, like it didn't mean anything, like she didn't feel as if her feet would float off the ground as he navigated them back to their table. But in that moment, she was suspended between two realities, two dreams that had been a part of her life for far too long: Collins and the Great American Road Trip. Maybe childhood dreams were never meant to see the light of day.

She focused on the feel of her hand in his. Because if they couldn't pull off the sibling road trip, would it mean her dreams of a future with Collins would disappear like a misty dream as well?

Order here: www.jlcrosswhite.com/rl/1713893

Books by JL Crosswhite

Sign up for my latest updates at www.JLCrosswhite.com and be the first to know when my next series is releasing.

Romantic Suspense

The Hometown Heroes Series

Promise Me

Cait can't catch a break. What she witnessed could cost her job and her beloved farmhouse. Will Greyson help her or only make things worse?

Protective Custody

She's a key witness in a crime shaking the roots of the town's power brokers. He's protecting a woman he'll risk everything for. Doing the right thing may cost her everything. Including her life.

Flash Point

She's a directionally-challenged architect who stumbled on a crime that could destroy her life's work. He's a firefighter protecting his hometown… and the woman he loves.

Special Assignment

A brain-injured Navy pilot must work with the woman in charge of the program he blames for his injury. As they both grasp to save their careers, will their growing attraction hinder them as they attempt solve the mystery of who's really at fault before someone else dies?

In the Shadow Series

Off the Map

For her, it's a road trip adventure. For him, it's his best shot to win her back. But for the stalker after her, it's revenge.

Out of Range

It's her chance to prove she's good enough. It's his chance to prove he's more than just a fun guy. Is it their time to find love, or is her secret admirer his deadly competition?

Over Her Head

On a church singles' camping trip that no one wants to be on, a weekend away to renew and refresh becomes anything but. A group of friends trying to find their footing do a good deed and get much more than they bargained for.

Writing as Jennifer Crosswhite

Contemporary Romance

The Inn at Cherry Blossom Lane

Can the summer magic of Lake Michigan bring first loves back together? Or will the secret they discover threaten everything they love?

Historical Romance

The Route Home Series

Be Mine

A woman searching for independence. A man searching for education. Can a simple thank you note turn into something more?

Coming Home

He was why she left. Now she's falling for him. Can a woman who turned her back on her hometown come home to find justice for her brother without falling in love with his best friend?

The Road Home

He is a stagecoach driver just trying to do his job. She is returning to her suitor only to find he has died. When a stack of stolen money shows up in her bag, she thinks the past she has desperately tried to hide has come back to haunt her.

Finally Home

The son of a wealthy banker poses as a lumberjack to carve out his own identity. But in a stagecoach robbery gone wrong, he meets the soon-to-be schoolteacher with a vivid imagination, a gift for making things grow, and an obsession with dime novels. As the town is threatened by a past enemy, can he help without revealing who he is? And will she love him when she learns the truth?

Made in the USA
Columbia, SC
29 June 2021